The Day After Never

Blood Honor

Russell Blake

Books@RussellBlake.com

ISBN: 978-1530850648

Published by

Reprobatio Limited

Author's Note

The Day After Never series portrays a future where civilization has broken down after a confluence of remarkable events – a deadly global pandemic and the resultant collapse of the monetary system. While it would be reassuring to say neither could happen, reality is that pandemics occur with some regularity every five to six generations, and the global monetary system is interconnected to a degree where the demise of one lynchpin player could cause a systemic collapse – one where faith is lost in paper money and the world suddenly finds itself without a mechanism to trade. Fiat currencies historically fail with some regularity, and it's interesting to note that reserve currencies typically last thirty to forty years before a new standard supplants them. This was true when the dollar replaced the British pound in 1944, it was true when the gold-backed dollar collapsed following Nixon's closure of the gold window in 1971– 1973 (replaced by the petrodollar), and it nearly happened again in 2008 – but for global money printing by all the world's central banks at historically unseen levels.

The world envisioned in this scenario isn't pretty, and *The Day After Never* series mines the dark side of human nature that surfaces when order collapses. My experience, having lived through a massive hurricane that shut down power, water, roads, hospitals, and the rule of law for two weeks in Mexico, is that when systems catastrophically fail, those entrusted with providing emergency services stay home to protect their own, while predators, sensing opportunity and weakness, become emboldened and come out in force. The frightening part is that it only takes a small number of lawless miscreants to dominate the majority in those circumstances. What that says about us as a species isn't pretty. But it's been the case throughout history, and it's only recently that a notion took hold that the world is a benign place and our better natures will prevail.

This being a work of fiction, I've taken some liberties with accuracy, particularly with a small town in New Mexico and with pretty much everything about Pecos, Texas, which I'm sure is a lovely place to visit and live – only not so much in this apocalyptic future. Likewise, I've imagined a reality that may seem farfetched, but only to those who haven't lived through a Hurricane Katrina in New Orleans or an Odile in Baja, Mexico. Anyone who has might find this reality far more plausible than they'd like, which for me, at least, makes it an interesting read.

Thanks for giving *The Day After Never* series a shot, and I hope you enjoy this first installment, *Blood Honor*.

Russell Blake
2016

Chapter 1

Lucas squinted through a pair of binoculars at a horizon distorted by the heat of a broiling West Texas sun and scanned the barren landscape. Greenish-brown scrub blemished the hillsides like tumors. A big bay stallion shifted beneath him with a shake of its head, and he leaned slowly forward and patted its neck for reassurance.

"Easy, Tango. I know it's been a long one," he murmured.

The horse stilled and Lucas returned to his task, his mouth a thin line in a face dusted with two days' growth. The straight brim of a brown beaver felt cowboy hat shaded steel gray eyes and skin bronzed from a life outdoors.

A hot wind blew from the mountains to his left, carrying with it the scent of rain. A band of plum-colored clouds pulsed with flashes of lightning where the peaks met the sky – still a ways off, he calculated, at least four or five hours, which increased the chances that the storm might spend itself before reaching him.

Not that he'd mind a night in the rain. He had his tent and his bedroll, and his saddlebags were loaded with sufficient gear to stand him for weeks. He couldn't predict how long it might take to track the herd of feral horses he was pursuing, and on expeditions like this, he traveled well-prepared for anything nature or man could throw at him.

Lucas's attention fixed on a distant spire of brown dust. He lowered the spyglasses and glanced at the heavens. It would be dark in a few more hours. He eyed the old mechanical pilot's watch on his wrist, not because he had much use for time anymore, but to help with reckoning. The dust was maybe five miles off, and he didn't want to blow out his horse on the trek – Lucas would need the animal's speed to lasso his targets, and that was the priority.

He nodded to himself. At a moderate pace, he could make it to the dust by twilight.

Lucas adjusted the M4A1 assault rifle strapped across his back and felt automatically for the stock of his Remington 700 Police DM .308-caliber rifle in its scabbard by his right knee.

Not that he would need them.

Assuming the dust was the herd.

There wasn't much to forage in the arid gulches, all the homes having long ago been abandoned and stripped of anything of value, but that didn't stop looting parties from Mexico from making their way north. The situation south of what had once been the border was as bad or worse than it was here, and based on what he'd seen firsthand, life was cheap to the border scavengers. They lived hardscrabble from anything they could steal, and would kill a man just as soon as look at him – gringo or Mexican, didn't much matter.

That was one of the reasons Lucas avoided the deserted highways that spanned the area. Other than the pavement being hard on Tango's hooves, there were the depressing hulks of rusting vehicles dotting the road, left where they'd run dry. Even now, five years after the day everyone had said would never come, the highway was a threat, and there were still scum who lay in wait to ambush travelers – often desperate families trundling carts loaded with their possessions, heading toward somewhere they'd heard might hold better prospects for a life. Fuel had long ago degraded and was unusable, even diesel, leaving survivors to cobble together whatever they could for transportation – bicycles, animals, it didn't matter as long as it enabled them to keep moving.

"Fool's errand," he spat, and stopped at the dry sound of his voice. Talking to his horse was one thing; holding conversations with himself was a warning sign – one of many he was alert to. The fear that he might be cracking up was constant since things had come unraveled.

Lucas made a clicking sound from the corner of his mouth and Tango plodded onward, the horse's footing unsure on the loose shale. The soft sough of the wind was the only sound besides Tango's clomping and an occasional snort. Lucas's senses told him he was alone, but he remained alert. His clothes blended with the backdrop, and he hoped his worn jeans, tan shirt, and plate carrier in desert camouflage made him a difficult target. Unlike in the movies, it was harder than hell to tag a moving figure from any distance, especially with a brisk wind.

He grunted as they moved over a particularly difficult section, and he urged Tango forward, Lucas's lower back protesting the jolting ride. What he wouldn't have given for an ATV, or even a dirt bike, much less a four-wheel drive vehicle like his old truck. He'd loved that big Chevy; the truck, like his M4, had been a perk of his service as one of the youngest Texas Rangers in the history of the force, operating with the E Division out of El Paso. But the vehicle, like the organization, hadn't lasted, and it had been a sad day when he'd left it for dead in the high desert.

The sun was a red ember sinking into the line of clouds when the reports of rifles reached him from the distance. The distinctive chatter of automatic weapons rattled in bursts across the landscape, barely louder than muffled firecrackers, but unmistakable. Tango drew up short, and Lucas's eyes narrowed as he soothed the horse.

"Looks like the dust wasn't the herd," he whispered.

The shooting stopped after several minutes. He guessed that he was still at least a mile away. Lucas scanned the horizon again with the binoculars but saw nothing. Whatever had occurred had taken place out of sight, over a far crest.

His instinct was to investigate – if there was a band of gunmen in the area, he needed to know sooner than later and would cut short his search for wild horses until they cleared out. He intended to use the animals for barter – the ranch was running low on stock items he could trade at a nearby outpost – but he had to be alive to do so, and he wouldn't be able to cover his tracks adequately while droving unruly mustangs.

"Come on, Tango. Time to earn your feedbag." Lucas guided the horse to his left, opting for a circuitous path to avoid detection.

Purple and salmon streaked the sky as he dismounted near the crest and tied Tango to a scraggly mesquite tree. He withdrew the Remington 700 rifle and patted the four spare thirty-round magazines of 5.56mm full-metal-jacketed rounds for the M4 in his ATS Aegis V2 plate carrier vest, reassured by the weight of his pride and joy, a Kimber 1911 Tactical Custom II .45 semiautomatic pistol on his hip. Lucas checked the safety and the flash suppressor on the M4, and then his gaze rose to the ebony forms of buzzards wheeling overhead.

Lucas removed his hat as he crept toward the rise and froze behind a cover of dense brush. Bodies lay strewn around the base of a dry gulch. Lucas could tell at a glance that the group near the center had been ambushed from above – it was obvious from their position that the defenders had died staving off the attack.

He regarded the area through his binoculars for several minutes, taking his time to study the bodies: four men wearing army-surplus camouflage shirts and pants, two with plate carriers over their shirts, clutching the distinctive shapes of their AR-15s or M16s. Two of their horses had been gunned down and were already bloating nearby, with a crude travois fashioned from a pair of crossed poles collapsed behind one of them. Nearby, thick crimson globules trailed up the arroyo, probably from horses that had been wounded, but not so badly they couldn't put distance between themselves and the battleground.

Five assailants ringed the area, their blood streaked against the hard rocks where they'd fallen as they'd closed in. In his mind's eye Lucas could visualize the battle, which he knew from the shooting had been short and fierce. Judging by the tracks, the smaller group had been traveling northwest along the gulch toward a small lake, where they'd probably planned to spend the night. The attackers had chosen an advantageous spot and, with the sun to their backs, opened fire. But they'd been overconfident and moved in too quickly, suffering heavy casualties in their haste.

Lucas squinted at the steep rock face of the opposite wall of the ravine, dotted with cave openings, wary of any possibility of ambush. Movement from near one of the fallen men in camo drew his attention, and he watched as a vulture withdrew its bloody beak from where it had been feasting. The big bird cocked its head in his direction and sized him up, and then flapped its ebony wings and returned to its meal, having decided Lucas posed no immediate threat from the crest.

It was unlikely that any of the attackers remained, or the buzzards would have been more cautious. Besides, there was no reason for anyone to stick around – assuming there had been any survivors. He didn't see any horses, so theirs had likely run off as well. More for Lucas to capture, he reasoned pragmatically. Better domesticated animals than wild ones. Easier to sell.

Lucas had seen plenty of death since the collapse. Unmoved, he returned to Tango and remounted. The days of reckoning, of law and order, of consequences, were over, leaving in their wake a brutal alternative of predator and prey. When he'd been a Ranger, he would have made it his life's mission to hunt down any surviving attackers and drag them to justice, but now no such concept existed, other than that issuing from the barrel of a gun.

He slid his boots into the stirrups, gave Tango a soft slap against his neck with the reins, the M4 clutched in his right hand, and the horse began making his way down the slope toward the grisly scene. Lucas continued to survey the surroundings, sweeping the scene with his rifle barrel.

The vulture hopped away and lifted into the air to join its companions in their overhead vigil as Lucas approached. Satisfied he was unobserved, he dismounted and whispered in Tango's ear. "Stay."

Tango blinked at him with mahogany eyes and stood, waiting.

Lucas took in the scene, sickened by the senseless loss of life, and moved to the first of the defenders' corpses and rolled it over. Three wounds stitched across the man's chest, the final one having torn away half his shoulder. His sightless eyes stared into eternity with a look of surprise that Lucas knew well, and he laid the man back down and moved to the next, repeating the process of verifying they were dead. It didn't take long, the pools of blood beneath them all the evidence he needed. All had the rawboned look of men whose diets had dramatically changed when society ended, their consumption of processed crap replaced by whatever they could hunt or grow. He noted that they had reasonably cropped hair and decent gear, which he gathered quickly and placed in a pile, concentrating on the weapons and ammunition, finding little else of barter value he could easily ride with.

Next he moved to the dead horses and checked their saddlebags, which held plastic containers of rice, pots, more ammunition, compasses, dried venison and other durable food, and the usual assortment of paltry belongings that counted for treasures nowadays. He emptied the bags and did a quick inventory, and then replaced the items he couldn't carry – space and weight would be at a premium, and the value of a good buck knife or an AR-15 and several hundred rounds of 5.56mm were far higher than anything else he'd found.

When he reached the first of the dead attackers, his nose wrinkled in distaste. The man's head was grimy and buzzing with flies; the front of his skull had been vaporized by a round, leaving only his black, oily hair trimmed into a Mohawk on top and a filthy, unkempt beard below.

"Raider," Lucas muttered. The Mohawk was the calling card of one of the gangs that roamed the region, terrorizing anyone they came across. They were undisciplined amateurs, but still as dangerous as scorpions and utterly ruthless. Most were career criminals who had taken to the road when the grid had shut down, creating a tribe of cutthroats who lived by robbery and murder rather than the sweat of their brow. The collapse had brought out both the best and the worst in humanity; unfortunately, the worst had largely prevailed, their willingness to employ savagery against the meek giving them the edge.

Lucas had seen the Raiders' handiwork more than a few times in the undefended homes that had once populated the region. Like a plague of locusts, they destroyed everything they came across, killing all but the young females, whom they pressed into slavery – a fate worse than death, he understood from the rumors. He gave them a wide berth, and they left the town he lived near alone, preferring easier pickings than its heavily armed residents. Like the Raiders, Lucas had a reputation that preceded him, and they avoided the ranch where he lived with his grandfather just as he shunned their stronghold at all costs.

Three of the other dead were also Raiders, one indicator being their weapon of choice, the Kalashnikov AK-47s, whose 7.62mm ammunition was easily obtained from trading with bandits from Mexico, which had been flooded with the guns during the war on drugs. Called the *Cuerno de Chivo* in Spanish – the goat's horn, so monikered after their distinctively curved thirty-round magazines – most were fully automatic and, while not as accurate as Lucas's M4, possessed a prodigious punch at ranges up to three hundred yards. Lucas gathered the assault rifles, two of which were the AKM variant with folding wire stocks, and tossed them near the rest of the weapons.

A gurgle from a figure he'd yet to search stopped him in his tracks, and he swung around in a crouch, M4 at the ready. The man, his Mohawk bleached canary yellow, was dressed identically to the other Raiders in filthy black jeans and a sweat-stained shirt. Lucas jogged toward him, ready to open fire, but the man seemed oblivious. Blood from a head wound was crusted across his forehead and eyelids. Lucas relieved him of the Glock in his waistband and toed the AK away, and then knelt beside him cautiously.

The man's eyes fluttered open and he stared vacantly at Lucas. He tried to speak, but all that emanated from his mouth was a gush of blood; and then his head rolled to the side and he moaned, the death rattle drawn out for a good five seconds.

Lucas went through his things and removed a folding buck knife from the man's back pocket. It was of high quality and would command a reasonable trade. The Glock and the two spare magazines would also be prized for barter, he knew, although he personally had little use for a 9mm weapon. Lucas's philosophy had always been that the trade-off of temporary deafness that accompanied firing his Kimber was more than compensated for by its raw stopping power.

Once all the weapons were accounted for, he did a quick inventory and then carried the ones with the highest trade value over to Tango. Lucas loaded his saddlebags to the bursting point with guns and ammunition, disappointed but unsurprised that he had to leave two of the AK-47s and several pounds of ammo behind.

The boom of distant thunder echoed off the gulch walls, and Lucas turned in the direction of the approaching storm – and froze when he spied another figure near a boulder outcropping, chest heaving and obviously alive. He hadn't spotted the figure earlier, so whoever it was had been well concealed. He sprang into motion, sprinting in a zigzag toward the downed shooter, M4 trained on the figure as he ran.

When he reached the outcropping, he stopped short, mouth open in disbelief.

It was a woman.

Unconscious and gasping, an AR-15 dropped nearby.

But alive, her chest laboring with each ragged breath, her shirt and pants stained dark with blood.

Chapter 2

Lucas slowly lowered his weapon as he neared the woman and took in her condition. She'd been hit in the thigh and the upper chest, her cheap body armor affording inadequate protection against rifle rounds. He crouched by her side and eyed her pale face: her features twisted with agony even in unconsciousness.

He frisked her and found a snub-nose .38 revolver at the small of her back. He tossed the gun aside and glanced up at the sky, concerned that he was losing the light, and then returned his attention to the woman and eased her out of the vest. His fingers came away slick with blood, and he quickly ferreted in his flak vest for a small LED flashlight that used rechargeable batteries.

Lucas twisted the penlight on and trained the beam on the woman's wounds. The leg didn't look too bad, but the upper chest wound did – judging by her pallor, she'd lost considerable blood and was in danger of going into shock, assuming she wasn't already there. More blood oozed from the entry wound, and Lucas made a quick decision. He would have to risk the flashlight drawing any bad guys lingering in the area, or the woman would die.

He retraced his steps to Tango and retrieved his first aid kit from a pouch dangling from his saddle. The horse seemed to intuit his agitation and whinnied softly.

"Don't worry, big guy. We'll be out of here soon enough," Lucas murmured, and made his way back to the woman.

After flicking on the flashlight again, he extracted a plastic bottle and unscrewed the top. The heady aroma of high-octane alcohol caused his nostrils to flare. Triple-distilled by his grandfather from corn he grew on his ranch, the white lightning in the bottle came in at 160 proof. Besides being a hotly sought-after barter item, it made an ideal disinfectant, although his grandpa frowned at the idea, mocking it as a waste of good liquor.

Lucas lifted a plastic sheet from inside the case and laid out the kit. After inspecting the chest wound again, he sterilized a pair of long-handled forceps. When he was satisfied he wouldn't cause any infection from the instrument, he first examined the thigh wound, noting that the entry and exit were clean. She'd been lucky on that one, but not so on the chest. The round had missed her lung, but there was no exit, and he was hardly prepared to perform surgery by flashlight in the great wide open.

He probed the entry, trying to see if he could feel the slug, but after several minutes of fruitless effort, gave up. The best he would be able to do was sterilize the wound with the alcohol and rig a pressure bandage. If she survived the night, he'd try for the nearest trading post, where someone more qualified could help. Lucas was no stranger to blood and had tended to a few wounds since the collapse, but nothing this severe, and even though he'd read an army manual on emergency first aid, he was out of his depth.

The blood loss was probably more dangerous than the chances of the bullet moving and causing any further damage. Judging by the flow, it hadn't hit any major arteries, but he couldn't be sure. He watched for any telltale arterial spurting and, when he only saw a faint pulse of red, reached into the kit for the syringe of morphine that he'd liberated from a medical clinic after the collapse. He'd never had to use the drug before and hoped for the woman's sake that even though it was well past the expiration date, the caramel liquid would still pack a wallop.

Lucas poured some more alcohol on her arm and emptied three-quarters of the syringe into her, and then immersed the needle in the alcohol, using the bottle top as a receptacle. After thirty seconds of disinfection, he capped the syringe and replaced it in the kit.

The woman's breathing eased and became more regular. Lucas removed his hat and held his ear to her chest in an effort to determine whether her lungs were congested, but couldn't make out much. Her chest sounded clear, but he was winging it at this point – if she were drowning in her own blood, there was nothing he could do for her but offer a prayer and the rest of the morphine.

Lucas sat back and reached for the alcohol, resisting the urge to take a swig to steady his hand. He splashed some on the leg wound, rinsing the drying blood away, and she barely stirred. Before attending to her chest, he opened up one of the sealed packages of bandages and affixed two to her thigh, wrapping them with gauze to hold them in place after generously dabbing them with expired antibacterial ointment.

Better than nothing, he reasoned and then moved to her traumatized chest. This time the alcohol produced a pained moan and a squirm, but the woman didn't open her eyes. He slathered the wound with ointment, leaving some of the alcohol in the cavity for good measure, and then improvised a pressure bandage to quell the bleeding.

Five minutes later he was repacking the kit, enshrouded in darkness and anxious to extinguish the bright beam of the flashlight before it drew any danger. He strode back to Tango and replaced the kit in the pouch, and then switched off the flashlight and slid it back into his pocket.

Lucas stood by his steed as his eyes adjusted. Over the far hills flashes of lightning forked from the thunderheads, followed by the occasional shuddering boom. He counted between the next large flash and the arriving explosion, and figured the storm was still at least fifteen miles away, maybe more.

Guilt ate at him as he looked around in the darkness at the dead. If he'd had more time and there had been no wounded woman, he would have covered the corpses with rocks or excavated shallow graves with his collapsible camp shovel. But with the storm on its way and the woman in dire straits, the best he could manage was a few words of prayer while standing over each body.

"May God have mercy on your souls," he finished, wondering at the fickleness of the universe that these men, Raiders and travelers alike, had been spared death through the greatest catastrophe to have befallen mankind since biblical times only to die in a rutted gulley with no name. He supposed that it had ever been so, but at times like these his faith was tested by the seeming randomness of it all.

The wind moaned like an old woman, jarring him from the moment, and he led Tango to where the woman rested in narcotic slumber. He debated giving her some canteen water, but decided against it, not knowing whether it would hasten any congestion or, worse, choke her. Instead, he found the dead horse with the travois and detached the pair of long poles from its back, relieved that neither had broken when the poor beast had dropped. The crude sled, a sling suspended between two poles used by Native Americans, had been adopted by enterprising survivors who traveled by horse, mule, or cow, which enabled them to carry far more than they could on their animal's back, even across rough terrain that would have proved impossible for a cart.

Lucas lashed the contrivance in front of the saddle horn, and the crossed poles spread wide behind Tango. He hadn't thought to check the sling on his first pass, but was gratified to find plastic jugs of water and several baskets of half-rotten apples and oranges. He debated how much of the cargo to haul and settled for two jugs of water, one basket of fruit, and the remainder of the weapons he couldn't fit in his bags, reasoning that if he had to ask Tango to haul the woman's weight, a few more pounds of hardware wouldn't hurt.

When he was done, he inspected his work. It would easily support the woman, and if he took it slow, wouldn't pose too much of a challenge for the big stallion. He scooped her up, surprised by how light she was. It had been so long since he'd had a woman in his arms, he'd almost forgotten…

He shook off the thought and placed her in the cradle, securing her with a length of rope so she wouldn't fall out. He didn't plan to go far at night – traveling after dark was asking to be ambushed, and he typically avoided it.

Lucas swung up into the saddle in a fluid motion and snicked at

Tango. The stallion pulled forward, and Lucas was relieved to see that the horse wasn't visibly straining at the extra load.

They followed the ravine until a dip in the terrain enabled Lucas to guide Tango back onto the ridge. He took a break at the top and swept the horizon with his binoculars. Other than the line of roiling clouds to the west, there was nothing to see. He reckoned by the sound of the thunder that the storm was hovering over the mountains, where it would hopefully stay, blowing itself out and sparing him a muddy slog the next morning.

After another stretch he found a spot where he'd made camp before, with good lines of fire and only two ways into the clearing at the base of a jutting rock outcropping. He unharnessed Tango and removed the saddle, taking care to pat the horse appreciatively before setting him loose to graze. Four and a half years old, Tango had been raised by Lucas, and the horse was as attached to him as it was possible for an animal to be. Lucas had no fear that Tango would wander far, preferring to stay close in the clearing, where there was plentiful grass this time of year.

Lucas checked on the woman and then set out his trip lines fifty yards from his position. He painstakingly strung plastic-coated wire eighteen inches off the ground between two trees that framed the main approach any intruder would likely take, and then repeated the process on the rear passage between two boulders, tying the wire to a pair of stout saplings to produce the same result.

He padded back to where the woman lay on the sling, opened one of the water containers, and after sniffing it, held it up to Tango, who was contentedly munching at the long grass a few yards away.

"Want some water, buddy?" he whispered, and Tango moved toward him as though understanding. The horse drank the entire thing, and Lucas reminded himself that Tango needed at least ten gallons a day, preferably more when he was exerting himself.

Lucas unfurled his bedroll, draped it over the woman, and sat beside her. He listened to her breathing, interrupted only by the occasional hoot from an owl and the rumble of thunder. Lucas brushed a lock of light brown hair off her forehead and studied her face in the faint moonlight streaming through scattered clouds.

"What are you doing out here, huh?" he muttered, the question more to himself than anything. "Good way to get yourself killed."

He decided to risk a small fire – given the clearing's isolation and placement within a rocky area, it should be safe, and he'd done so before when he'd camped there in the past; in fact, his old fire pit was only footsteps away. After gathering some dried kindling and moving the small rocks of the fire pit closer, he doused the wood with his grandfather's secret recipe and lit it with a disposable butane lighter – one of three he owned, and a highly prized trading item.

The fire blazed to life, and he watched the flames dance as the wood crackled. He chewed slowly on some of the jerky he and his grandfather made at the ranch, lost in thought, mesmerized by the orange tongues licking at the night air.

Lucas blinked away his fatigue and glanced over at Tango, who had returned to his grazing, unconcerned by his master's one-sided discussion. Lucas shrugged in silent apology and sat back against the hard rock, his M4A1 in his lap with its Exelis NE-PVS-14 night vision scope in place and Kimber holstered at his hip, his lids heavy after the adrenaline from the day had burned off. He allowed himself the small luxury of a few seconds of shut-eye, just to relieve the burning itch. A vision of his late wife, Kerry, drifted into his mind, and he gave a sigh of quiet misery. Lucas held the image of her face as long as he could, and then it evaporated, fading like morning mist, her smiling eyes the last to go.

Was that why he was taking the risk of trying to rescue the woman? Guilt over having failed to save his wife, the love of his life? At having chosen his job over her?

"That's not true," he whispered, but the words sounded hollow.

He'd been in the field in those early days of the collapse, trying to maintain order in an increasingly difficult environment. As the flu had spread, many law enforcement officials hadn't reported to work. The National Guard was supposed to be deployed, although Lucas had serious doubts that many of them would report for duty either. Kerry had promised to stay at home with the doors locked and the shades drawn, but something – what, he'd never know – had compelled her to leave the safety of the house.

When they'd found the body, it had taken all of Lucas's resolve not to eat his Kimber and join her in the afterlife. He'd never discovered who had abused her in unspeakable ways before snuffing out her life, and in the degrading spiral of the following days he'd been forced to give up and concentrate on survival.

"You couldn't have done anything," he whispered, rubbing a tired hand across his face. "Nobody could."

Which was true, yet felt like a lie. He should have been home, protecting her from evil instead of out on the job. He should have done…something.

Of course, that would have required Lucas to have been a different man than the one he was – a man who would abandon his duty at the first sign of trouble, who would refuse to protect those he was chartered with guarding, who'd reject his sworn duty just in case his willful wife might have thought he'd overstated the growing danger.

That was never an option.

But she'd paid the price.

His mind wandered, replaying in agonizing slow motion the inexorable grind into chaos as civilization had broken down. The population had been woefully unprepared for the reality of a food chain with only three days of supply, dependent as they were on the state for protection, for gas, for clean water, and electricity. Their faith proved misplaced as the bodies piled up and food riots swept the nation, followed by total anarchy. He still remembered that last time he'd seen a television program – an anxious newscaster, beads of sweat on his face, assured viewers that all would be well and urged them not to panic, to remain inside as martial law was imposed, his promise that it would never come to the apocalyptic scenario spreading via social media a transparent lie.

The word *never* was burned into Lucas's mind, its certitude so false, so patently wrong.

That had been only hours before the Web had shut down;

whether by the government or vandals, it made no difference. He woke the following day to his empty home, his wife dead less than a week, the television dark, the power gone, gunfire reverberating in the near distance, his comfortable routine of job and mission and duty forever over now that the day after never had arrived.

Lucas sighed again, wondering why he was torturing himself with toxic memories. It had been an eternity since those days. Now he was just another survivor trying to make the best of a living hell. How or why it had unfolded was ultimately unimportant. That it had was all that mattered.

He opened his eyes and stared at the glow from the tangerine moon on the tall grass and then back at the fire, which had diminished by half. His eyes drifted back to the woman, his mind racing, wondering what her story was, where she had come from, where she was going, and why she had been in the middle of nowhere with four heavily armed militiamen, traversing a region well known to be as dangerous as a striped snake in even the best of circumstances.

Chapter 3

Lucas started awake with a whispered curse. He swept the area and his eyes settled on the nearby ring of stones – the fire was nothing but smoldering remnants, the fuel exhausted, coils of smoke twisting from the charred ash all that remained of the blaze.

He'd drifted off, tormented by his past, but something had broken through the haze of sleep. Tango snorted again from nearby, as clear a warning as Lucas needed, and he was already forcing himself to his feet when he heard an oath and the twang of the trip line he'd strung across the main approach.

He didn't wait to see who the speaker was. Operating on automatic pilot, he moved quickly but quietly through the gap at the rear of the clearing, avoiding the trip wire there, and made his way toward the rock outcropping, where he'd have a decent view of the area from the cover of the stones.

Moments later he was at the top, staring down at three figures creeping through the grass toward Tango. The woman lay comatose on the sling blanket a few yards from the horse. Lucas considered his options – he could probably take all three, but if he missed one, they'd be firing toward Tango and the woman, and there was no way of guaranteeing kill shots in the gloom.

No, he'd have to try to circle around and flank them while they were making for the outcropping. He watched their movements for several seconds; they were goons, he concluded, no training to their approach, just slow steps into what could have been a trap.

That made them idiots.

No less dangerous, but a potential advantage for him.

He edged away from the gap and retraced his steps down the outcropping, and then hurried around the periphery of the boulders that encircled the clearing. He saw the silhouettes of three horses near a grove of trees a hundred yards downhill and reassessed his earlier impression – the bandits couldn't have been that dumb if they'd spotted his camp and taken the precaution of leaving their mounts behind.

Lucas arrived at the trip wire and stepped over it. The men were thirty yards in front of him, motioning at each other with hand signals, unaware of his presence behind them. He knelt down and steadied the M4 against a tree trunk and felt for the fire selector switch to confirm that it was in three-round burst mode.

The breeze shifted, denting the tops of the tall grass near him and carrying the stench of sour perspiration and decay from the gunmen in front of him. Typical for the scavengers who roamed the badlands, whose interest in bathing and personal hygiene was minimal. Lucas grimaced at the odor and sighted on the first figure through the night vision scope, the greenish image bright as day thanks to its rechargeable CR123A battery. The gunman was carrying what looked like a double-barreled shotgun, confirming Lucas's impression that these were border rats who'd probably seen his fire and been drawn by the glowing invitation – opportunists looking for an easy takedown.

Which, if he had anything to say about it, would be the last mistake they'd ever make.

His finger tightened on the trigger and the rifle barked a three-round burst that slammed into the shotgun-carrying man, spinning him around before he dropped into the grass.

Lucas was already sighting on the second man, who twisted and fired in his direction, missing by a wide margin. Lucas cut him down with another well-directed burst, and the man's weapon flew from his grip as he tumbled forward.

Lucas peered through the scope, searching for the third man, and swore to himself.

Nothing.

He'd disappeared into the grass and was apparently savvy enough not to fire blindly.

Which left Lucas with a difficult choice: wait for the man to show himself and hope that he was faster, or take evasive action and move to higher ground, where because of the perspective from above, the grass would provide less shelter for the gunman.

It didn't take him long to decide. Lucas backed away from the tree and crept into the shadows, retracing his steps to the rear of the clearing and the jutting outcropping of rocks.

When he arrived, a part of him hoped that the scavenger had cut and run after seeing that his companions were finished. The man couldn't have any idea how many were defending the camp, and now alone, with the element of surprise gone, he had no advantage.

Lucas removed his hat and set it beside him, and then peeked over the rocks, through the gap. As he'd expected, the grass offered no cover from above, and he could clearly make out the dead assailants.

But not the third man.

A whinny from down the hill confirmed Lucas's suspicion. The third man had retreated, unsure of where the shooting had come from, and had made for the horses.

Lucas waited for several minutes and, when he saw no further movement, jogged in a low crouch down the trail to the trees.

The horses were gone.

He nodded to himself. Dead men wouldn't need rides, and everything they owned was probably in their saddlebags, so the third man had just gotten significantly more prosperous by virtue of his companions' possessions and the trade value of the horses.

Lucas made for Tango, still on alert. He paused at each of the corpses, holding his breath, and shook his head at the poor condition of their weapons and the filthy rags they wore. That humanity had been reduced to this level saddened him, but he didn't feel any remorse. It was a kill-or-be-killed situation, as were most these days, and he couldn't afford to hesitate or second-guess himself. The ugly new world had little use for mercy, and a part of him wondered whether he'd made the wrong decision in allowing the scavenger to escape.

Tango was waiting for Lucas, visibly shaken by the gunfire but standing his ground. The woman was still unconscious, oblivious to the drama playing out around her. Lucas wasted no time in retrieving his precious trip wires, refastening the travois, and saddling Tango, and in minutes was riding away from the clearing, the surrounding hills luminescent in the starlight.

The last of the storm, its forward motion and energy exhausted by the terrain, flashed trees of lightning over the mountains. Lucas truly hated traveling at night, but didn't want to chance the scavenger returning with friends. The campsite was blown, useless now for his purposes, and from this point on he'd skirt it whenever he was down this way. The buzzards would take care of the downed men, and within a day at most nothing would remain but bones picked clean by scavengers – coyotes, vultures, and finally, insects. Nothing went to waste in this no-man's land, even human excrement like those who hunted other men rather than putting in an honest day's work.

"Got a long way to go," Lucas whispered to Tango, patting his neck, his fatigue banished by the effort to stay alive.

Chapter 4

Lucas sighted the trading post as dawn broke. The compound wasn't much to look at: two buildings and a covered outdoor area built on a rise near the Texas–New Mexico border. Its proximity to the Red Bluff Reservoir and the Pecos River made it an ideal location for trade, with Carlsbad and Loving to the north in New Mexico, and Pecos, Texas, to the south.

Lucas lived on a ranch that occupied fifty acres near Loving, having abandoned his home in El Paso after his wife's death. The ranch was a hard day's ride from the outpost under the best of conditions. But his grandfather's white lightning, as well as the occasional wild horses Lucas captured, required an outlet, and the trading post was the last vestige of civilization until Pecos, which had degraded into a prison-gang stronghold where depravity was the order of the day.

Lucas twisted to look at the woman. Her face was blanched with pallor from shock, a stark contrast to the tanned skin on her forearms. That she'd made it this far was a minor miracle, but one that was out of his hands, his bag of tricks now empty. His hope was that Duke, the scoundrel who operated the trading post, would be able to attend to her chest. He had the reputation as a jack-of-all-trades and had been in the service before setting up shop, so might have more experience with bullet wounds than Lucas.

It took another hour to make it to the trading post, and as he neared, Lucas noted with approval the occasional rocks on either side painted red, yellow, and finally, white. They had been placed at hundred-yard intervals to make establishing range easier if the trading post was attacked. It had been several times in the past, by roving gangs who'd mistaken it for easy pickings, unaware that Duke's retinue of helpers were also all ex-military, battle-hardened and ruthless as scorpions. Lately, however, it had enjoyed relative peace, its reputation as a place not to be trifled with firmly established, as were the stories of its wealth of forbidden items that could be had at the right price.

Ever since the collapse, barter was the way goods were exchanged. Duke took five to ten percent of the value for facilitating a trade between two parties in a safe location; he was also the buyer of last resort if there were no takers for a traveler's offering, and would exchange either goods or gold and silver for the wares. He kept an inventory of weapons that would have made a Marine battalion envious, tanks of purified water, food brought by locals from their gardens…in short, anything of value that was in demand.

Which, of course, made him a target. Lucas smiled to himself as he neared the compound's iron gates, steel plates welded into place to prevent anyone shooting through them, and gave a wave to the man lounging in the shade behind some sandbags: Clem, one of Duke's men, who was on guard duty.

"How's it going?" Lucas called out.

"Pretty good, Lucas," Clem replied, returning the wave.

"Thanks for not shooting me to pieces."

"No problem. Had you on the scope from a half mile away," Clem said, tapping an old telescope mounted on a tripod.

Lucas noted the distinctive muzzle of a Barrett .50-caliber sniper rifle poking from the bags and had no doubt that if Clem had sensed any danger, Lucas could have been dropped from that distance, easily – the idea being to take out any threat before it got into range. There were too many armories that had been looted, and National Guard weapons that had been abandoned and scavenged, floating around, to allow anyone unidentified to get too close. Add into the mix that

RPGs and grenades purchased from Mexican cartels were not unknown, nor were automatic weapons of every variety, so it was prudent to err on the side of caution.

Clem motioned at the travois. "What you got there?"

"Woman. Hurt. Duke around?" Lucas asked.

"Of course. Probably grumpy as hell, though. Up late last night."

Duke enjoyed a drink now and again. More like again and again, Lucas knew, based on the trader's bottomless appetite for Lucas's grandfather's elixir. "She needs help."

"How bad's she hurt?" Clem asked.

"Bad enough."

The right gate slid open, and Clem nodded at Lucas as he rode in. "Go ahead and tie your horse over by the water trough," he said.

"I'll need some feed, too," Lucas replied.

"Everything's for sale."

"That's what I figured." He paused, drawing Tango up short. "Could use a hand getting her into the main building."

"The boys are inside. They'll help. I've got to stay on duty. Rules is rules."

Lucas tied Tango to a post and the horse drank greedily from the water as Lucas took the stairs to the cinder-block building and knocked on the steel door, noting a gleaming bank of solar panels to his left, arranged behind a short protective wall in the courtyard to benefit from the sun's arc.

The door swung wide and one of Duke's men looked him up and down. "Yeah?"

"Duke awake?"

"Might be. Who's asking?"

Lucas's eyes narrowed and he held the man's stare. "You're new, aren't you?"

"That's right. So?"

"Tell him Lucas is here. Got a wounded woman needs some help."

The door slammed behind the man, and two minutes later Duke appeared, his eyes bleary and red, underlined by puffy bags. His haystack hair and florid complexion told the story of his life at a glance.

One corner of Lucas's mouth pulled upward at the sight. "Got hit by the lightning stick, did we?" Lucas asked.

"Nonsense. I was just meditating," Duke said, his sandpaper voice gruff. "What's up? Doug here says you have a damsel in distress?"

Lucas eyed him skeptically. "You up to it?"

"Ever ready. That's my middle name." Duke looked past Lucas at the travois and then turned his head and yelled into the interior of the building, "Doug! Aaron! Help get this woman into the dining room. Come on. Double time!"

The man who'd answered the door and a short black man shaped like a fireplug, whom Lucas recognized as Aaron, shouldered past them to where the woman lay. "Careful, gents," Lucas warned, and watched with Duke as they carried her into the building.

Duke shrugged to Lucas. "Might as well come in. I expect you've got some booty to trade for this?"

"Of course."

"Then *mi casa*, and all that crap."

Lucas followed Duke to the dining room, where Aaron and Doug had placed the woman on the massive rectangular wooden table. Duke snapped his fingers at Doug. "Get me my magnifying glass and one of the portable LED lamps," he ordered.

Doug, his arms emblazoned with tribal and military tattoos, nodded and hurried away without a word.

Lucas cleared his throat. "New boy?"

Duke nodded, never taking his eyes off the woman. "Solomon got himself killed."

"Shame. I liked him. How?"

"Snake bite." Duke shook his head. "Kid wasn't the brightest."

Doug returned with a work lamp on a stand and a large magnifying glass attached to an olive green hinged arm. Duke took the glass from him and clamped it to the table, and then pointed at an extension cord in the corner. Doug plugged in the lamp, and the dining room flooded with cold white light.

Lucas blinked. "Batteries still holding a charge, I see."

"During the day we run these outlets directly from the panels. Consumes almost nothing."

"Smart. Mine are doing okay."

"Should be able to eke another couple or three years out of the batteries, I'd expect," Duke offered. "By then the grid will be back up."

Both men chuckled at the notion.

"Been hearing about that for the last, what, five years?" Lucas said.

"Never been closer. I hear the feds have got D.C. online. Or maybe part of it."

Lucas's eyebrows rose. "Verified?"

"A little bird told another little bird, who whispered something to a guy I know, who told me."

One of the common themes of survivor hopes was that someone was going to impose order, that the government would get the country operating again. Which ignored that the government had been composed of people, not superheroes, most of whom didn't do the actual work – and that the worker bees who knew how to keep power plants operating, how to repair turbines, how to keep thieves from stealing the copper out of power lines, who could be convinced to drive trucks or trains laden with necessities in spite of a contagious killer flu and civil unrest that made war zones look inviting, had shown their unwillingness to show up and work for free instead of staying home and protecting their families.

As with most black swan events, so named because they were unpredictable singularities, the combination of the super flu – regardless of whether brought to the U.S. by refugees, illegal immigrants, or returning servicemen – and an economic meltdown had never been envisioned. There were simply no scenarios for it, and when it happened, civilization had unraveled far faster than anyone would have believed.

Yet not a week went by that someone didn't hear that some area had been brought back to life and that the men in black suits were working furiously to restore the nation's systems.

Lucas had long ago recognized the futility of hoping that anything would ever normalize again, at least during his lifetime. Self-sufficiency was the new normal. Radio reports from around the world had shown that no country had remained unscathed – Europe was in ruins, Russia was a graveyard, Asia and the Middle East disaster zones. China had made a fumbled attempt to invade Japan in the early days of the collapse, but had been repulsed by the U.S. threat of nukes. Within weeks it hadn't mattered – everyone was either dying or too sick to work. Famine had raged across India and Pakistan, China's mortality rate rose to nearly sixty percent due to lack of adequate medical facilities, and soon it was impossible for anyone to keep up with disposing of all the bodies, much less maintaining infrastructure and order.

So the notion that the wonks in Washington had somehow gotten their act together and been able to organize was a pipe dream, and Lucas just rolled his eyes when he heard the speculations. Those beholden to the idea that the same bureaucrats who'd been unable to see this disastrous confluence of events coming had somehow managed to demonstrate anything but incompetence once all the support systems had given way were not long for this world.

Better to suck it up and do what had to be done to stay alive than to believe fairy tales. If anything, the collapse had shown just how unprepared the vast majority were to deal with harsh reality, and how dependent what passed for civilization was on the nanny state coming to the rescue.

When it failed to do so, as it had for many weeks during prior regional natural disasters – like the hurricane that had wiped out New Orleans – the only surprise to Lucas had been the number of people caught completely off guard.

Duke adjusted the lamp to shine on the woman and turned his attention to the wound. He studied the bandage and then called out to Aaron. "Bring the surgery kit. Alcohol. Gauze. Soldering iron."

"Be right back," Aaron said, and went into one of the back rooms.

"What's her story?" Duke asked as they waited.

Lucas shrugged. "Beats me. I found her in the desert, along with some dead friends."

"Kind of a looker, ain't she?"

Lucas grunted noncommittally. "Business been good?"

"Can't complain."

Duke had set up the trading post once the worst of the chaos had subsided, and it had thrived ever since. Duke's terms were simple: he was relatively honest, and he didn't ask or tell where items came from. His discretion was prized, although he reserved the right to refuse anything he didn't want.

A shortwave radio crackled softly in a corner and went silent. Lucas tilted his head toward it. "Anything new going on in the world?"

Duke laughed, the sound a harsh bark. "Black helos. The Russians are coming. The grid will be back online any day. A nuke plant in California melted down and we're all doomed. Take your pick."

"So same old."

"Yep." Duke collected gossip like a fishwife and spent his off hours monitoring the airwaves, exchanging rumors with other survivors around the country. It was because of his hobby, in fact, that he'd been one of the first to recognize the true danger as the collapse had unfolded. The media had lied early and often, the Internet had been increasingly censored in the interests of national security, and straight answers had been few and far between. But Duke had collected reports from all over the nation from other like-minded, self-sufficient folks who'd seen disaster coming years in advance and taken appropriate steps to defend themselves.

When the first casualties of the new super flu had begun appearing in Asia and the Middle East, he'd heard accounts from returning servicemen who were in his network, and the stories differed materially from those online or in the news. Unlike prior flu pandemics, this one had a longer infectious cycle with extremely mild, almost undetectable symptoms, enabling the virus to spread like wildfire before anyone realized the extent. By the time the domestic media and the CDC had been willing to admit that the case-fatality ratio of the airborne, highly infectious bug was approaching forty percent, the damage had been done: sixty percent of those infected ultimately survived, but even the survivors were bedridden for ten days to two weeks in the second stage of the disease, and transmission levels were near ninety-six percent, with only a fraction escaping unscathed due to natural immunity.

Speculation had been rampant in the early days that the flu was a conspiracy, lab-generated, an attack on the U.S., part of a larger depopulation scheme, a takeover of the world by some shadowy group, while cooler heads had pointed out that every hundred years or so a bug came along and wiped out a significant portion of the population. The prior lethal pandemic had been the Spanish flu, which had effectively ended World War One, both sides being too sick to fight, and which, in a time before plane travel, had decimated the population with an estimated ten to twenty percent mortality rate.

But as bad as the super flu had been, it was the collapse of the financial system and the breakdown of law all over the world that had tipped the scales. Unlike in 1918, the globe's financial system was deeply intertwined due to the unregulated derivatives market, with mega-banks in the U.S. holding tens of trillions of paper from European and Asian banks, and vice versa – meaning that if one in the queue collapsed, it would take the rest with it. With the major industrialized nations incapacitated from the flu, derivative instruments in the hundreds of trillions of dollars had come due, and in a daisy chain, every economy and bank on the planet froze up as they were exposed as being insolvent. Once confidence was shaken, the next pedestal of modern finance to collapse was sovereign debt, and the American T-bill became unsellable overnight. The central banks tried turning on the money presses to counter the effect, but that had only resulted in a loss of faith in paper currency, and hyper-inflation that had made Zimbabwe look like a poster child for fiscal conservancy.

When the banks didn't open, credit cards stopped working, and nobody wanted to accept the government's paper currency, then nothing could function, not even the military – nobody would work for worthless paper IOUs backed by the nonexistent faith and credit of a bankrupt regime. When a gallon of gas went from $3 a gallon to $30 to $300 in only two weeks, faith in fiat currency and the government's continued ability to operate in perpetual debt collapsed – and faith was all the system had been running on for generations.

Americans had quickly discovered that their prosperity was a fragile construct that could collapse in a matter of days, and watched in horror as their wealth was revealed to be a mirage, as was every other economy in the world where the same cartel of interdependent, privately owned banks had convinced the population that paper IOUs were a good exchange for their labor and land. When riots swept the cities, starting on the west and east coasts and working inland, the authorities had been unable to cope, and what had previously only been seen in brief flare-ups in Baltimore, Los Angeles, and New Orleans quickly went nationwide as the desperate turned on each other with the realization that survival was now a zero-sum game.

Lucas was jarred from his reverie by Aaron's arrival with the surgery kit.

"Here you go, boss man," Aaron said with a smile, and set the kit down beside Duke.

Duke opened the oversized plastic tackle box and extracted a bottle of white lightning and a dizzying array of gleaming surgical instruments. He placed a tray near the woman's head and filled it halfway with alcohol, and after a long look at the bottle, chugged two swallows and burped.

Lucas regarded him with a neutral expression. "Sure you're okay?"

"We'll soon find out." Duke's expression darkened. "Aaron, I need more gauze than this. And the soldering iron."

Aaron nodded. "Be right back."

Duke busied himself placing scalpels, forceps, clamps, spanners, and a variety of other instruments in the alcohol, and then turned to Lucas. "Let's go wash our hands. Can you assist?"

"Tell me what to do and I'll try," Lucas said.

"First, let's wash all the grime off. Then, go put on a clean shirt.

29

Don't need her getting infected from road dust."

"I don't have an extra handy."

"Don't worry; I do. I'll put it on your tab." Duke gave him a hard stare. "Hope you've got some real goods to trade, or you'll be delivering white lightning for free for the duration."

"I've got a half dozen ack-ack guns. Maybe a thousand rounds. Some handguns. Don't sweat it."

"What kind of rifles?"

"AR-15s and AKs."

"Shape?"

"Better than your liver."

Duke's face cracked in a pained smile. "Man after my own heart, Lucas."

Lucas matched his expression. "No accounting for taste."

Chapter 5

An hour and a half later, Duke set down the soldering iron and wiped sweat from his brow. After inspecting his work, he turned to Doug.

"Open some windows. Smells like a Texas barbecue in here."

The pungent odor of burnt flesh had filled the room as he'd cauterized the wounds, the round finally removed in three fragments. He'd injected the woman with another shot of morphine before operating and had used local anesthetic in the tissue around the chest wound as an additional measure.

Duke and Lucas walked together to the door and stepped out into the morning sunshine.

"What do you think?" Lucas asked.

Duke inspected his nails and then met Lucas's gaze. "Fifty-fifty. She's lost a ton of blood. Next thing, we need to do a transfusion."

"How do you know what blood type she is?"

"Doesn't matter. Aaron's O negative. Universal donor."

Lucas nodded. "That's a lucky break. How much?"

"Probably a pint or two. I'll get a line going to start a bag in a second."

"No, I mean how much for him to do it?"

Duke named a price in ammo, and Lucas whistled. "There goes my retirement."

"Unless you've got gold or silver. In that case, quarter ounce of gold should do the trick. Silver, fifty ounces."

"You still collecting, huh?"

"Damn right I am." Duke had once explained to Lucas that the reason he was stockpiling precious metals was because whenever trade with other nations was reestablished, the likelihood of trading partners accepting anything but gold was zero after the fiat currency nightmare. Even now, with the continent a wasteland, gold and silver were prized for the same reason – they had been money for thousands of years and would likely continue to be in demand as such for the foreseeable future. Lucas had twenty gold coins he'd ferreted away for emergencies that he'd carried with him since the collapse, but he'd part with just about anything else before resorting to using any of it.

"Between the operation and the blood, you've pretty much wiped out half my stash of guns and ammo."

"Best things in life may be free, but here, no tickee, no laundry."

Lucas shrugged. "It is what it is."

"I'll have Doug check out the weapons and ammo while I'm draining Aaron dry."

"Send him out. I want to check on Tango."

Duke studied Lucas's face. "You look like you've been rode hard and put away wet, partner. Maybe take a nap."

"I'll sleep when I'm dead."

"That's the spirit. If you change your mind, there's a hammock over there in the shade. No charge." Duke hesitated. "How much do you know about her?"

"She never said a word."

Duke nodded. "You notice the tattoo on her upper arm?"

"What, the Egyptian-looking eye? What about it?"

Duke eyed a droplet of dried blood on his boot and scowled. "Probably nothing."

"Spit it out, Duke."

"Let's see if she makes it."

"You have something to say, best to say it," Lucas said.

Duke shook his head and turned to go inside. "None of my business, buddy."

Lucas gave Duke an annoyed look and moved to Tango to unpack the saddlebags and the travois. Doug joined him a few minutes later, and they went through the rifles first. The younger man examined the Kalashnikovs with a practiced eye and nodded as he set each aside.

"They're beat but seem serviceable. We'll test fire them later."

"Probably Mexican," Lucas observed.

"Now let's look at the AR-15s."

The assault rifles had all been modified to full auto and, based on the work, by someone with skills. The AR-15 was the civilian version of the M16 rifle, sold as single-fire only, but with a full-auto sear, disconnector, and bolt carrier, they could be converted with considerable machine-shop time by cutting out the lower receiver to accommodate the full-auto sear.

Doug smiled as he finished inspecting the last rifle. "Nice work. Where did you say you got these?"

"In the desert."

"Duke will be happy. They look pretty clean compared to the AKs."

"So's the ammo."

Half an hour later, Doug had counted the rounds and separated out the lots he wanted. He'd grown friendlier as he'd worked and, as with many of the people Lucas had met after the collapse, had been quite open about the circumstances leading up to his working at the trading post.

"I was stationed in Houston. We were supposed to ship out for the sand bowl, but by the time our lot got called, everything was going haywire already. Most guys on the base were sick or dying, and the few officers left standing wound up immobilized by conflicting orders from Washington. Ultimately, we stayed put, and later my group was sent on riot patrol in Dallas and then funeral duty. Man, talk about ugly." Doug swallowed hard. "Anyway, you know how it went down after that. Eventually no food, no money, and one day, no chain of command."

It was a common story: soldiers in their late teens and early twenties ordered to fire on their fellow citizens by officers who were themselves conflicted. Soon the contested zones were open warfare areas among heavily armed gangs of criminals, civilians trying to protect themselves, and the authorities. Once power went down and food and potable water became nonexistent, the military mission stopped even trying to maintain order and degraded into an effort at self-defense as the streets clogged with the rotting bodies of the dead. What the flu had failed to destroy, starvation, thirst, and desperation had their way with, and within weeks the cities were ghost towns, the vast majority of the citizenry dead.

"You never saw combat?" Lucas asked.

Doug looked away. "Plenty. All of it in Texas. Some of the older officers said Iraq was Disneyland compared to Dallas at the end."

Lucas yawned and rubbed the back of his neck. "Tell Duke I'll be in the hammock."

"Roger that."

It was midafternoon when Duke nudged Lucas awake. The temperature was cool, the air crisp. Luke's eyes were slits when he looked at Duke.

"News?" Lucas asked.

"Gave her a shot of antibiotic – expired, of course – but she's still in pretty rough shape. She needs a full course, Lucas. The wounds are already getting infected."

"You have any more?"

Duke shook his head. "Nothing I'd use on her."

"So?"

"I can send Clem up to Loving. I talked to the doc up there on the radio. He's got some that's still pretty good."

"I can just take her myself."

"Clem can ride a lot faster than you dragging teepee poles on that barn-sore mule, Lucas."

"Hey. Tango's a trooper."

"Just saying. He looks tired as you do."

Lucas considered the offer. "You're probably right. How much?"

"Another five hundred rounds."

"What!? You're a thief, Duke."

"Strictly business, Lucas. This isn't a nonprofit."

Lucas got out of the hammock and spit to the side. "Remind me never to play cards with you."

"Easy come, right?" Duke said with a smile.

Lucas grew serious. "Think she'll make it?"

"She's looking a little better since the transfusion. In the old days, we might have been able to use some plasma. That would have increased her odds."

"Has she come to?"

"Negative. She's on the edge, Lucas. It could go either way."

"Well, hell. Might as well go back to being broke again. Take the rest of my ammo, you swindler."

"I'll throw in a meal."

Lucas nodded. "Tell Clem to stay off the road. Lot of bandits lately."

"You tell him. He'll be up and around again soon."

Lucas shook his head. "I want to get back to what I was doing – chasing a herd of mustangs. Can't do anything loafing around here."

"You're leaving?"

"I'll check back in when I've got the horses. Doesn't look like she's going anywhere."

"You got that right."

Lucas held the trader's stare. "Duke? I'm leaving her under your protection. Means you're responsible she comes to no harm."

Duke nodded. "10-4, good buddy. Nobody'll lay a hand on her. You have my word."

"Get her whatever she needs. On my tab."

"Sure thing, Lucas."

Lucas walked in silence back to the main building with Duke, hoping that when he returned to the trading post he wouldn't owe Duke for a coffin.

Clem appeared a few minutes later, Kalashnikov in hand, plate carrier cinched snugly to his torso, well rested after four hours of sleep following his shift, and ready to leave. Duke warned him about staying off the highway, and Clem nodded as he mounted up. He saluted Duke and Lucas as he departed, and they watched as he sped away on a sleek chestnut mare, kicking up a faint trail of dust behind him.

Duke elbowed Lucas. "Must be hungry by now. Probably smart to fill your belly while you can."

Lucas checked the time. He'd slept longer than he'd intended – it would be dark again in a few more hours. "I could eat."

"Let's chow down before you hit it."

"How long do you think it will take Clem to get back?"

"They agreed to swap a new horse, so figure, what, six hours each way at a fast trot, maybe a little more."

"Think that'll be soon enough?"

"It's going to have to be."

Lucas sniffed the air as they neared the doorway. "What's cooking?"

"Fricassee of rat," Duke said with a grin.

"Been a while since I had fricassee."

"You'll never forget this one."

The meal was actually fresh fish from the reservoir, accompanied by corn and potatoes. Preparation took an hour, and when the meal was ready, the men ate until they couldn't swallow another mouthful. Doug carried a plate out to Travis, another of Duke's entourage who was working guard duty, while Lucas stood beside the woman, who had been moved to a dilapidated sofa they'd covered with a clean sheet.

Duke joined him and felt her forehead. "I'll be right back," he said, and ducked into his bedroom. When he returned, he was holding a glass thermometer. He pulled back the sheet, exposing her bandaged chest, and slid it beneath her underarm. "She's lucky the bullet didn't ricochet and do more damage. Missed her lung by half an inch, no more. Weird that it didn't exit, though. Shoulder blade must have stopped it."

Lucas hadn't told him about the woman's body armor.

Duke removed the thermometer and shook his head. "She's burning up. Not good."

"Anything else you can do?"

"Not really."

Lucas strode to the door and swung it open. Duke followed him out and stood by his side as he saddled up, making small talk. When Lucas was finished, he patted Tango's flank absently and adjusted his hat.

"Not very busy today, huh?" Lucas asked.

"You missed a couple of traders from down Pecos way, while you were sleeping."

"Yeah? What did they get?"

"Swapped me the corn we ate and some other odds and ends for a peashooter. Wanted a varmint rifle, .22 long, for hunting."

"They say anything about how it is down there?"

Duke's expression darkened. "Not good."

"Where were they from?"

"Didn't get specific."

"Ah."

Rifle shots rang out in the distance, faint but clear in the crisp air, and both men froze.

Chapter 6

"You hear that?" Duke whispered.

"Yep."

"Sound like it came from the north, didn't it?"

Lucas nodded, his face grim. "Up the highway."

They exchanged a glance. "You thinking what I'm thinking?" Duke asked.

Another nod from Lucas. "He took the road. You told him not to."

"Let me try his radio. He's got a two-way. He should still be in range."

They returned to the building, and Duke retrieved a handset from a row by the shortwave radio and powered it on. The trader spoke rapidly, depressing the transmit button as he did, and then released it, listening.

Nothing but white noise.

Duke tried again with the same result and shook his head as he replaced the radio in the base. "You know as much as I do."

Another shot reached them, this one even fainter. Lucas glowered at the open door and made for it. "Time to ride."

"You going after him?"

"Don't see any choice."

"I'd send a man, but…"

"I know."

Duke's hired hands earned their keep defending the trading post;

38

Clem's absence had already weakened their ability to do so. Duke couldn't spare anyone further, especially with evening approaching. "He knew the risk."

"Might have been some other poor soul."

"Quite a coincidence if it was."

Neither man believed in coincidence.

Lucas retrieved his M4 from his saddlebag, checked the magazine, and swung up into the saddle. "Time's a-wasting."

"Watch your back."

Lucas rode through the gate, his eyes blazing, both at the idea that Clem could have been foolish enough to ignore his warning and at the ramifications for the woman's survival if he had. Duke's men were tough, but perhaps they'd spent too much time behind the walls of the compound. All it took to lose your life out in the open was one poor decision. He hoped Clem had been smarter than that, but a coil of anxiety twisted tight in his stomach, warning him not to expect much.

He tracked Clem's horse to a trail that skirted the river and followed it at a trot. Normally he'd have let Tango set the pace, but he didn't have the luxury of letting up until he'd confirmed what had happened. Half an hour north, his worst suspicions were confirmed – the hoofprints veered left toward the highway a half mile away.

Rather than making the same mistake Clem had, Lucas slowed and picked his way along the river, using a game trail wide enough for Tango to navigate without any problem. At a tributary fork, he was forced to use a two-lane road that led to a bridge over the wide canyon, and the hair on the back of his arms stood up as he galloped across it, no cover anywhere if a sniper wanted to take a crack at him. He varied Tango's speed, listening for any telltales, but heard nothing other than the wind and the rush of water below as the river roared past.

Once across, Lucas weighed his options and slowed to allow Tango to catch his breath. As he did so, he spotted dust from the vicinity of the highway. He retrieved his binoculars from his saddlebag and draped the strap around his neck as he gazed through them. Definitely a dust cloud, and from more than one rider, by its size.

He continued north along another trail and, when he estimated that he was well clear of the riders, directed Tango toward the highway, his M4 at the ready. Fifteen minutes later he reached the road and stopped near some bushes to dismount.

The tracks in the dust that coated the road were fresh and looked like at least a dozen riders. That they were riding down the middle of the highway told Lucas that they weren't concerned about detection – they were the most dangerous thing on the road.

He looked north and raised the glasses to his eyes. The highway was largely flat, with only a few skeletal vehicle chassis rusting where they'd stalled on the shoulder. It never failed to amaze him how survivors inevitably pulled to the side as their cars ran out of fuel, hope springing eternal that they'd be able to find more and return, he supposed – a hope that never came to pass. His grandfather had tinkered with the idea of refining his corn alcohol into fuel that could safely power a car, but he'd dismissed the idea as time had passed, based on Lucas's admonition that an operating vehicle would be an open invitation to be shot apart, the engine noise providing ample signal in a landscape devoid of sound. Lucas was sure that plenty, surely the military, had managed the feat; but to him, in God's country, the concept of presenting a target to the plentiful predators was suicide.

He returned to Tango, remounted, and guided him off the road, along a trail that ran parallel, crossing farmland that had gone unplanted or watered for half a decade, any fences blown down by the tornadoes that infrequently roared across the land. He stopped after what he reckoned was a quarter mile and eyed the highway again, and this time saw the distinctive form of a body on the far shoulder.

Lucas road hard and was off Tango in a flash when he reached Clem's fallen form. He leaned forward and rolled the man onto his back, ignoring the flies that had already begun swarming around his head. A bullet hole, small caliber judging by the entry wound in his temple and lack of an exit hole, was crusted with coagulated blood, and Clem's open eyes were vacant. Lucas took in the mangled fingers and broken arm – clear evidence of torture. He noted the two wounds in Clem's abdomen that his flak vest had partially stopped before the ceramic plate had shattered; those would have been the rifle shots they'd first heard, the final shot the coup de grace after a hurried interrogation. There was no doubt that Clem had told his killers whatever they wanted to know. Anyone would have.

He'd seen every manner of atrocity over his years as a lawman; then, as a survivor, found the handiwork of the outlaw gangs worse than anything he'd imagined prior to the collapse. Even so, why torture a rider before killing him? It wasn't as though he'd been carrying anything but his gun, which was missing, as was his horse, both no doubt stolen by the shooters.

He dragged Clem off the shoulder and into the brush, more than aware that it would be dark soon, and considered his next step. The soil was soft – it wouldn't take him long to dig a shallow grave and bury the dead man, sparing him the indignity of being picked apart by the carrion birds. Besides which, Tango was breathing hard and needed a chance to get his wind, so Lucas pulled his collapsible camp shovel from a saddlebag and began digging, his mind working furiously.

He could keep riding north for another three to four hours, the final stretch in the dark, get the medicine for the woman, and leave Tango in town while he rode back to the trading post – again, at night. Alternatively, he could ride back to the outpost and give Duke the bad news, foregoing the meds, which might well be the woman's death sentence. Neither choice was a good one.

He stood back, sweat streaming down his face, and examined the trench he'd created.

"It'll have to do," he muttered, and after setting the shovel down, dragged Clem's body to the depression and rolled it in. Lucas refilled the grave with dirt and stepped away, looking around. He spied a decent-sized rock and carried it to the mound, lay it at the head of the grave, and stood with hat in hand as he said a prayer.

If he was hoping for divine guidance on which path to choose, it came in the form of automatic rifle fire from the south, as distant as the shots that had brought down Clem.

Lucas nodded. Of course. That was why they'd tortured Clem – to learn what he knew about Duke's defenses.

The riders were attacking the trading post.

The deep staccato bark of Duke's big .50 caliber machine gun made Lucas's decision for him. The battle was joined.

And Lucas wasn't one to run from a fight.

He leapt onto Tango's back and pointed the horse south, his decision made. He would help his friends and worry about the problem of the woman later. If the trading post were breached, she'd be worse than dead anyway, so the imperative was to stop that from happening.

Lucas was under no illusion that doing so would be easy or without risk.

But there was no alternative.

He just hoped he could make it in time.

Chapter 7

The gloaming darkened the sky as Lucas rounded the final bend on the trail to the trading post. He'd avoided the highway, retracing his route down the secondary road and the track along the river as gunfire echoed from Duke's compound. The shooting was still going on, but with less intensity, the attackers probably conserving their ammunition until they could make a push after dark. They'd apparently underestimated the extent of the trading post's defenses, and he was sure that Duke and his men were making them pay dearly for the mistake.

Lucas had taken his return easy and allowed Tango to set a comfortable pace, resisting the impulse to spur him to a gallop, unsure how much more travel the brave horse would have to be capable of before the night was over. Tango was ordinarily able to cover a solid forty or more miles a day after a night's rest, but he hadn't had that luxury, and Lucas was aware that he'd keep pushing to please his master until he dropped from exhaustion.

The gunfire was deafening now that Lucas was near. He tied Tango to a tree away from the fight and moved stealthily toward the trading post. By the time he'd covered the final quarter mile on foot and was close enough to see muzzle flashes, it was completely dark, which would work in his favor, given his night vision scope.

The attackers, unaware of his arrival, would believe the threat to be entirely in front of them. Any shooting from their flank or behind would be assumed to be coming from one of their number. If Lucas was lucky, he might be able to take most of them out before they realized what was happening, depending on how they were positioned.

He had four spare magazines in his flak vest and one in each back pocket of his jeans, giving him 210 rounds, including the magazine in his rifle. Assuming he was careful with his fire, it would be more than enough, although it was always better to expect the worst.

Lucas surveyed the field around the trading post and spotted three shooters to his right, maybe a hundred yards away. Beyond them, he saw two more gunmen firing intermittently. He raised the M4 to peer through the NV scope and saw a shooter to his left and what might have been two more – he couldn't be sure, given the tall grass.

Nothing much seemed to be happening – nobody was moving, the assault force having learned the hard way that they had walked into a killing field. Lucas hoped that Duke's men had neutralized a fair number of the attackers.

He crept toward the first shooter on his left and, when he was sixty yards away, put a three-round burst into the man's torso. Lucas waited for incoming fire, but none answered his salvo, vindicating his strategy – at least for now.

Lucas repeated his maneuver, continuing left, and realized that what he'd thought was another shooter were in fact two, side by side. That would make things tougher for him, but not impossible. He switched the M4's fire selector switch to three-round burst mode and sidled closer, biding his time as occasional salvos rattled from the attackers' guns, answered in kind from the trading post.

Lucas dog-crawled another ten yards and took aim at the pair in front of him. He was about to fire when four high-wattage spotlights on the trading post roof blinked to life, illuminating the field with a blinding glare. He ducked down in the grass as bullets whizzed around him from the compound, and realized belatedly that Duke and his men thought he was one of the attackers.

The gunmen to his right opened fire at the lamps, and one by one they blinked out, but not before he heard an anguished scream from his left. One of the pair had been hit – how badly remained to be seen. Lucas closed his eyes in an effort to regain his night vision as quickly as possible and, when he could make out the silhouette of the trading post again, took careful aim through the PVS-14 night vision scope.

One of the group on his right called out, and a man clambered to his feet. Lucas fired a burst and then another, and the man went down hard. His companion returned fire at Lucas, and he sprayed the area with the remainder of his magazine, the downed man impossible to make out in the grass. Better to be sure he was out of the fight than discover from a bullet to the back that he had only been wounded.

Lucas ejected the spent magazine and slapped another into place, and then the soil around him fountained as rounds pounded into the earth. Lucas rolled, his pulse thudding in his ears, trying to ascertain whether the latest salvo was from the trading post or the attackers. Another burst shredded the dirt to his right and he had his answer – the attackers were onto him.

A long rattle issued from the sandbags by the gate. The three men who had shot at Lucas spread out as bullets tore the grass near them to shreds. One grunted as several rounds found him, and then Lucas joined in with his M4, creating a lethal crossfire with his rifle, its fresh magazine empty in a matter of seconds.

He slapped home another magazine and caught motion from the corner of his eye. The pair that had been two hundred yards away to his right were on the move, rushing the trading post, confused by the shooting that was coming from Lucas on their left. He loosed burst after burst, but his shots went wide, the men moving too erratically. He watched as they neared the compound wall and gasped when one hurled a grenade over it before taking cover against the outside of the wall.

The blast from the grenade's detonation flared orange from the trading post grounds, and Lucas forced his breathing slower and zeroed in on the visible shooter. Lucas would have to drop him – from inside the compound he was out of Duke's line of sight, having made it close enough that the wall shielded him from exposure. If the man had more grenades, he could continue to lob them from his position at the base of the wall, inflicting maximum damage without firing another shot.

Lucas exhaled as he squeezed the trigger. His first rounds were low, and he raised his aim slightly and stitched the man to the wall with his second and third bursts.

Which left one more shooter.

Who'd bugged out and was nowhere to be seen.

Lucas waited for the man to show himself. A minute went by with no more shooting. Another passed, and he swore under his breath. He couldn't very well lie in the grass until morning, but if he called out to the trading post, he would give himself away.

Discretion being the better part of survival, he waited. And waited.

After ten minutes, he dared a glance at the glowing hands of his watch and rolled onto his back. He cupped his hands, tilted his head, and called out at the top of his lungs.

"Duke! It's Lucas. Don't shoot."

A voice answered – Duke's.

"See any hostiles?"

"Negative, but assume they're out here."

A long pause. "What do you want me to do?"

"Push that big wooden cart of yours out for cover. I'd be much obliged."

"You serious?"

"I took down four of them for you. Least you can do."

Several minutes later the gate opened, and a cart laden with crates and sacks creaked out of the compound, pulled by a mule that looked as unenthusiastic as any beast Lucas had seen. Behind it followed Aaron with an AK, a spare magazine combat taped to the one in the weapon for a quick change. Lucas crawled toward the cart as it rolled forward and, when the mule was thirty yards away, drove himself to his feet and sprinted toward the cart as Aaron swept the field with his muzzle. When Lucas reached him, he pressed against the rear of the cart and glanced around.

"There was one left that I could see. Looks like he took off," Lucas said in a loud whisper, more than aware they were all half-deaf from the gunfire.

"We can get some more lights up and confirm that," Aaron said.

Lucas eyed him. "Any casualties?"

"Travis bought it. Doug's wounded, but he'll live."

Lucas nodded. "Let's get behind the walls and turn some lamps on."

"Works for me."

The mule required little coaxing to return to the outpost, and they kept the cart between them and the field until they were through the gates, just in case their lone shooter was still out there. Duke heaved the iron barrier shut and bolted it, and then returned to his position behind the sandbags.

"Clem?" Duke asked.

Lucas shook his head.

Duke frowned. "Damn. He was a good man."

"Aaron said Doug's wounded?"

"Yeah. Leg. I rigged a tourniquet. It'll hold till we mop up."

Aaron motioned to the smoking crater created by the grenade. "I'll go get a couple more bulbs for the field lights."

Duke nodded. "We'll hold the fort."

When Aaron was gone, Lucas joined Duke behind the bags and looked out over the darkened field. "Any idea who they are?"

"No. They came straight at us. We mowed down a half dozen of them before they fell back and dug in. Then they waited for nightfall. Which is what they should have done all along."

"Strange, isn't it?"

"I've known stranger."

Five minutes later the lights went on again, illuminating the field to the three-hundred-yard markers. Nothing stirred. Aaron rejoined them and wiped his face with a trembling hand. Duke grunted and stood. "You boys keep watch. I've got to patch Doug up."

He walked to the main building and disappeared inside, leaving Aaron and Lucas alone. Lucas looked over to his right at the grenade tosser's corpse sprawled by the wall, and his jaw clenched. They must have been desperate, or high, to try to take on Duke's group.

"How's the girl?" Lucas asked.

"Out of it. But you could light a smoke on her. She's that hot."

Lucas nodded. At least she was still alive.

Aaron eyed Lucas. "Clem?"

"Didn't make it."

Aaron nodded. "Figured as much. When your number's up..."

"Yup. Rest in peace."

Chapter 8

The interior of the trading post main building was bathed in the dim glow from two LED lamps. Doug lay on the table, biting a strip of leather as Duke finished his ministrations.

"This will hurt," Duke said, and Doug looked away as Duke seared his leg wound with the soldering iron, the sound like a steak frying on a too-hot grill. Doug's scream was muffled by the leather strap and faded to a moan as Duke set the instrument aside and carefully bandaged the damaged flesh.

Duke stepped away and regarded Doug. "Sorry about only using lidocaine, but I need you sharp in case there's more fighting to do."

Doug grunted. "Burn's worse than the bite."

"You can have some morphine come sunup. Till then, we're all on duty. Can you walk?"

"Should be able to."

"I'll help you out to the sandbags."

Nearby, Lucas stood over the woman, noting the sheen of sweat on her face. When Duke returned from helping Doug, the trader sat down on a hardwood chair nearby and took a swig from a plastic water bottle. Lucas turned to him.

"She's not going to make it, is she?"

"The truth? No," Duke growled. "Not without antibiotics. Danger is sepsis, and her fever tells me she's going in the wrong direction."

"I was afraid of that."

Duke nodded. "What about you?"

"Looks like I can either chase horses or risk it all to get her to Loving before she dies."

"You thinking about taking her?" Duke asked, his tone skeptical.

"Be faster than a round trip, don't you think?"

"Yep. But traveling at night... And your horse has been through a lot." Duke hesitated. "You don't look so spring fresh yourself."

"We'll be fine."

Duke fixed Lucas with a probing stare. "What is it about the woman that's got you sticking your neck out, Lucas? This ain't like you. No offense."

Lucas's voice was soft when he answered, "None taken." But he offered no elaboration, and Duke didn't ask again.

Duke gave the woman another injection of morphine and helped Lucas carry her outside to the travois. Lucas rigged the contrivance as Tango waited patiently, and then they set her onto the sling between the two poles. Lucas patted his empty magazines and held one up.

"Used up a lot of ammo," he said.

Duke nodded. "Fair's fair. Fill 'em up. Cost of doing business."

Lucas wasted no time reloading and, when he was finished, shook hands with Duke.

"See you soon. With mustangs," Lucas said.

"Best of luck."

Lucas offered a curt nod. "You too."

Once on the trail north, Tango settled into a plodding walk that would get them to Loving by morning. Lucas kept a sharp eye out, sticking to the back roads and trails, wary of ambush. He'd been involved in two firefights in a matter of hours, which, even post-collapse, was a record for him. He went out of his way to avoid conflict, keeping to himself on his grandfather's ranch, avoiding contact with his fellow man to the extent he could.

Duke's question burned in his ears. Why was he risking his neck for the woman? Ordinarily he'd have continued south the following morning in search of the herd, and if she survived, super – if not, it was just the way things worked out. Reality was hard, and it took no prisoners. Lucas was as compassionate as was practical, but was in no particular hurry to shorten his life, especially with his grandfather relying on him. The old man was hard as saddle leather, but he wasn't a spring chicken. When he'd invited Lucas to move north to the ranch in New Mexico when the troubles had started, Lucas had refused; but once Kerry passed and his job had gone the way of the dodo, he'd had no other kin, and he'd packed everything he could carry in his truck and braved the drive.

That had been before fuel became unavailable, and he knew he'd been more lucky than smart to leave El Paso when he had. While the old man was self-sufficient due to his lifestyle on the ranch, Lucas hadn't done much more than assemble a bug-out bag with essentials, stash some gold, ammo, and weapons, and stored a few basic food stores and water containers in case of calamity. Still, that had been more than most, as he'd quickly discovered when El Paso disintegrated into riots. Rival gangs had taken the opportunity to settle scores and run amok, and the police and National Guard had been overwhelmed within a short period – it turned out that there were a lot more bad guys than good, and the delicate social contract wherein the vast majority behaved well quickly turned ugly and became anything goes.

A part of him realized that the flu and financial collapse had been catalysts and that the dark side of human nature had always been lurking just below the surface, for all the pretensions that it had been eradicated in modern times. Any moral superiority he'd felt had dissolved when he'd seen the wolf packs of murderers in action – including those who'd snuffed out his wife's life without a thought.

Lucas had prayed for a forgiving nature, but it had eluded him, so he'd settled for being a loner who tried to do no harm. By staying detached from humanity, sticking to his knitting, and taking each day as it came, he'd remained sane in a world gone mad.

So why this, why now? Why risk it all for a woman he didn't know?

Was it really as simple as a shot at redemption? Was he projecting his guilt at being unable to save his wife, some infantile part of him believing that the endless nightmares of Kerry's final hours might stop if he could save this one? She looked little more than a girl, once her face had been cleaned off – early twenties or so. Was he doing it because he hoped for gratitude, to be repaid...however? A good-looking woman in the wilderness, owing him her life...

He shook off the thought. No, it was more than guilt or lust. Something about her, her situation, had struck a chord. He wasn't big on the concept of a deterministic universe, never had been. Lucas had free will. Things were not written, they were earned, carved out of nothingness and made manifest through sweat and intestinal fortitude.

He twisted his head to the side and spit road dust into the brush. That line of reasoning was useless. There was no such thing as destiny. People who believed they were preordained for anything inevitably used it as an excuse to do harm or delude themselves. It was a comforting weakness, but a liability he couldn't afford.

"Enough of this," he whispered. He couldn't allow his mind to wander. He needed to stay sharp and focused, or his destiny would be to wind up dead in a ditch, like poor Clem.

The monotonous clip-clop of Tango's hooves on the loose dirt marked the passage of hours as the moon rose in the night sky, the stars a glimmering tapestry that stretched into infinity. Lucas paused for five minutes every so often to water Tango and stretch his legs, checking at each stop to verify the woman was still breathing. At the second break, he poured a trickle of water into her mouth and she swallowed reflexively, but other than that, she remained dead to the world, an enigma with long hair and an angelic face, precariously perched at the edge of the abyss with only Lucas between her and oblivion.

Chapter 9

Pink and orange glowed in the predawn sky as Lucas arrived at the outskirts of Loving. What remained of the townspeople had organized themselves into a loose militia responsible for guarding the perimeter, and everyone had pitched in to create defenses that encircled the town. At last count there were ninety-seven residents, the population down from a pre-collapse high of 1500, reduced by the flu, starvation, other diseases, and raids by criminal groups before a coherent civil defense had been mounted.

For the last few years, life had settled into a routine, with twenty of the adult residents on guard through the night, working six-hour shifts, and five keeping watch during the day, when visibility was such that they could easily see approaching strangers coming. Lucas knew most of the residents by name because of the farmers' market on Saturdays, when the collective gathered and traded among themselves. The survivors were a hardy bunch who'd faced down adversity and clawed an existence from lousy circumstances, much as their ancestors had when they'd crossed the Great Plains in search of opportunity. Most were involved in farming or hunting and fishing, with a few creating value with specialized skills – two handymen, the local doctor who also resolved disputes and acted as veterinarian, a school teacher for the twenty children, a minister who tended cattle, and a sheriff and his part-time deputy responsible for the town's defenses.

Theirs was a simple, agrarian life, most living without power, their water brought from the river and sterilized over a fire. The community had grown tight-knit, and neighbors helped each other, watched each other's kids, and lent a hand when someone was sick. While imperfect as any society, despite its differences this one had managed to find a way to function, probably because even before the collapse most of the population was self-sufficient by virtue of the rural location.

"Morning, Lucas," a tall Hispanic man called from behind the thick wall that guarded the entry to the town.

"Morning, Manuel," Lucas allowed. "I'm here to see the doc. He's expecting me."

"Sure thing," Manuel said, and pushed open the heavy wrought-iron gate the residents had erected across the main street as part of their fortification. That and the wall, some sections nothing more than tall barricades built from debris and ruined houses and cars, others from homemade adobe, had paid for itself many times over. "You know the way?"

"I remember."

A rooster crowed nearby as the town awakened, and the sun's early rays warmed Lucas as he rode down the dusty street toward an empty water tower in the distance. The doctor's house was near the church off the main square, and as Lucas rode through the area, he gave an occasional tip of his hat to residents emerging from their homes to start their workday in the fields near the river. Horses stood by makeshift barns, and he recognized a few of them, having bartered many of the animals from his successful forays in the foothills. A brindle-coated dog loped along beside him for a block, hoping for a scrap, but gave up when none was offered.

Lucas stopped at a simple single-story house, a rudimentary affair devoid of the slightest charm, whose paint had faded from a vivid green to something resembling vomit in the few places it hadn't peeled away. He dismounted and stretched his arms over his head, and then approached the front porch and knocked on the door.

When it opened, a man in his late sixties regarded Lucas over scratched steel-rimmed spectacles beneath a crown of thin white hair

54

worn longish in the back with a few wisps combed over a pink scalp.

"Lucas!" the man said, his voice gravelly. "Wasn't expecting you. Is...Hal all right?"

"Course, Eric. No stopping him."

"What can I do for you?"

"Got a wounded woman needs tending."

"Wounded? Ah. The antibiotics Duke asked about." The doctor looked past Lucas at the travois. "Bring her in. Here, I'll give you a hand."

Lucas waved him off. "I can carry her. Doesn't weigh hardly anything."

"Suit yourself. Let me get the exam table cleared."

Lucas carried the woman inside to the first bedroom on the right, which was set up as the doctor's examination room. Morning light streamed through the window as Lucas laid her on the cracked vinyl table. The doctor leaned over the woman and felt her forehead with a frown. "She's burning up. What did they give her?"

"Morphine and a shot of some kind of expired antibiotic. That's all I know."

"Let me see if I can raise Duke on the radio. I don't want to give her just anything."

Lucas nodded and waited as the doctor moved to the living room desk. He had one of four shortwave radios in town and enough solar panels to provide minimal power during the day. When the doctor returned, he looked like he'd gargled vinegar.

"Well?"

"Let me give her a shot and clean her wounds. Duke worked on her?"

"Yes."

"I'll check to make sure she's not hemorrhaging or necrotic. Best if you wait out in the living room to avoid any more contamination."

"Lot of road dust on her."

"So I see."

Lucas took a seat in an overstuffed easy chair whose surface was thick with cat hair. The doctor had moved to Loving after the collapse; his nearby retirement ranch was too difficult to defend for one man and of no use to him when there was a town that needed health care. He'd sold his private practice in Taos two years before the collapse and bought a small piece of land to live out his days in bucolic tranquility, but reality had intruded, and now he was the sole caregiver for not only the town but visitors from the surrounding compounds, who traveled hours, and in some cases days, to be seen.

A furry form scurried from a dark corner to the kitchen. Lucas sniffed the air and rose to attend to Tango.

After watering the stallion, Lucas negotiated a half bale of hay for a couple of rounds of 9mm ammo he'd held onto for pocket change and fed him. As he watched Tango munch on his breakfast, a tall, reed-thin figure approached.

"Lucas. Is that you?" the man asked, his tone sonorous.

"Yes, minister."

"What brings you to town? Everything's well, I hope?"

"Yes. Found a traveler in need, so I brought them to the doc."

The minister smiled. "A good deed."

"Let's hope it goes unpunished."

Both chuckled. The minister, a Baptist, tended to a more moderate stance, one of the bones of contention among the townsfolk, some of whom believed that the collapse was due to sinfulness and loss of faith. Everyone had an opinion, Lucas supposed and found considerable value in keeping his to himself.

"Haven't seen you for a while," the minister said, the reproach in his voice clear.

"Been in the field a lot."

"Well, you're missed at Sunday worship."

The minister continued on his way, and Lucas was turning to go back inside when a voice called out from across the street.

"Lucas!"

Lucas sighed softly and rolled his eyes, and then slowly pivoted to face the speaker crossing the street. A pair of revolvers hung at his side in hip holsters, slung low like an old west gunfighter. The sheriff, Carl Green, was irritating, if harmless, and Lucas was short on patience given the paltry sleep he'd gotten over the last forty-eight hours. Carl bore him a small grudge, having been the town's second choice for lawman after Lucas had politely declined, and Lucas could tell that it still ate at the man, even after years had gone by.

"Carl," Lucas acknowledged.

"Miriam told me you had someone in that rig? Brought them to the doctor, did you?"

Miriam was the town gossip, whose house looked out onto the main street near the entrance gate.

Lucas nodded. "That's right."

"What's the deal?"

"Found her in the hills. Shot up. Raiders," Lucas said.

"What was she doing there?"

"Beats me. Ask her." Lucas paused. "If she lives."

"Rough, is she?"

"Shot twice."

"Was she alone?" Carl asked.

Lucas shook his head and gave the sheriff a brief account. When he finished, Carl's eyes were wide, although he quickly masked his expression. "Interesting. So you don't know anything about her?"

"Nope. Just what I told you."

"Well, I'll stop in to check on her later. Whereabouts did you find her again?"

"About fifteen miles southeast of Duke's place."

"Not much out there."

"Just banditos and crazies," Lucas agreed.

When the sheriff had departed, Lucas walked back into the doctor's house and almost ran headlong into him in the doorway.

"Well?" Lucas asked.

"I did what I could. Duke's not half bad at triage, actually. It's the blood loss and the infection that's the danger now. The wounds will heal. Shouldn't be any lasting damage she can't live with. I shot her full of antibiotic. In the old days I would have run it in an IV drip, but…" He didn't have to finish the sentence, frustration evident in his tone. Everyone was doing the best they could given the circumstances, but Lucas could see that the doc was annoyed at the limitations, which were growing worse as time passed and all the meds were past their expiration dates. "How about you, young man? Any complaints?"

"No," Lucas said. "What do I owe you?"

"For the antibiotics, fifty rounds of 5.56mm was what Duke and I agreed to. For the visit? Maybe a jar of your granddad's devil juice?"

Lucas nodded. "Deal. In any hurry?"

"Nah. I know you're good for it."

"I've got the rounds. I'll bring the white lightning next trip."

Lucas and the doctor counted out the rounds from Lucas's saddlebag, and they shook hands at the conclusion.

"Where you headed now?" the doctor asked.

"To the ranch. I need some rest."

The doctor studied Lucas's face, now with four days of growth, and nodded. "You could use it."

"I'm afraid to look in a mirror."

Lucas followed him to the patient exam bedroom and regarded the woman a final time. When he was done, the doctor walked with him onto the porch. Lucas hesitated and looked down the street before speaking in a hushed voice. "You're an educated man. What do you make of her tattoo?"

"The eye? Oh, that sort of thing was popular in the old days. It's the Eye of Providence – the all-seeing eye of God. It's been used by many groups. The Masons, for instance. Or the Mormon temple in Salt Lake."

Something about the doctor's tone gave Lucas pause. "What else?"

"Well, it's really just folklore. But it was also the symbol of the Illuminati. In that context, it was the eye of Satan. On the old paper dollar, the symbol over the pyramid was a classic example of the eye of the devil watching over the masses."

Lucas's eyes narrowed. "You believe that?"

"Like with most icons, the original meanings get lost with time. The eye was originally Egyptian, I believe: the Eye of Horus. Reality is that there are few common symbols that haven't been appropriated by various groups, whether good…or bad."

Lucas's face could have been carved from granite as he rode out of town, the empty travois trailing behind him, every step of the four-and-a-half-mile trek from town to his grandfather's ranch labored. He wasn't sure what to make of the doctor's explanation of the tattoo, but as the morning sun beat down on him, Tango snorting occasionally with fatigue, Lucas's mind was anything but at peace.

Chapter 10

Lucas guided Tango down the final yards of the uneven dirt road that led to the ranch, and stopped at a ten-foot-high iron gate, which was padlocked shut. A sign beside it advised visitors that if they could read it, they were at risk of being shot. A delighted bark sounded from inside the dirt walls that encircled the ranch, made higher by the six-foot-deep sheer trench he'd dug outside the wall to make scaling it harder.

A chocolate Labrador bounded toward him and barked again, and Lucas lowered himself from the saddle and approached the lock.

"Hey, Bear," he said, and reached through the gate to give the big dog a scratch behind his ears as his tail furiously fanned the air. Lucas leaned forward and pulled a lanyard from inside his shirt and slid the key into the industrial lock, noting that it was still adequately lubricated and opened with a sharp snick. He unbolted the gate and led Tango through, Bear barking nonstop to announce the arrival of his owner. Massively muscled for his breed and with a head the size of his namesake, Bear's fierce appearance belied his gentle nature, and in reality he was a butterball.

Lucas locked the gate behind him and loosened Tango's girth. His grandfather stepped from the shade, dressed in his ubiquitous jeans and jean shirt, a ten-gallon Stetson making his head seem small in comparison. Once over six feet, he'd shrunk since Lucas had moved in, and although still vital enough to work sunup to sundown around the ranch, he was clearly in the twilight of his years. The old man's ramrod posture was a sharp contrast to the doctor's stoop; even though his grandfather was fifteen years older than the physician, he had the demeanor of a much younger man.

"That was quick," his grandfather said.

"Morning, Hal," Lucas replied. The old man insisted Lucas address him by his first name. "Ran into some trouble, so going to sleep it off before I head back out."

"Trouble? You hurt?" Hal asked.

"No. I'm fine." Lucas gave him a quick rundown of his adventure as he unsaddled Tango and led him into the barn. When the horse was in the cool interior of his stall, drinking from a water trough supplied by the ranch's well, Lucas removed his weapons and set them aside for cleaning.

"Been quiet here," Hal said when Lucas had finished his account.

"Beats the alternative."

"Glad to see you made it in one piece, boy."

Lucas swallowed hard. That was as close to affection as the old man got. "Me too."

Even though they were awkward in each other's presence, Hal was the closest living person Lucas had, and the old man had raised him like a father when his own had met an untimely end. Also a Texas Ranger, Lucas's dad had been bigger than life, a rawboned man who laughed loudly and whose spirit filled a room. When he'd been gunned down in the line of duty when Lucas was nine, Hal had stepped into the gap and acted as surrogate. Only as he got older did Lucas realize that his mother's extended absences from Hal's original West Texas ranch had less to do with job opportunities in the city and more to do with numbing her chronic disappointment in life with alcohol and drugs. Lacking any other model, Lucas had followed Hal's lead, and he saw much of himself in the older man as he approached middle age himself.

"Place looks pretty tidy," Lucas observed. "Ruby been by?"

Hal snorted. "None of your business, that. And in any case, she's hardly the domestic type. I'm perfectly capable of looking after myself."

Lucas looked as though he was about to pose another question, but Hal deflected him. "How much ammo you burn?" his grandfather asked, adjusting his belt.

"Net even. Duke reimbursed me."

"Good."

Growing up on a rural Texas ranch, Lucas had learned respect for nature as well as weapons from Hal, who'd been a Marine for two tours before working on an oil wildcatting crew. Over the years Hal had saved enough to buy a ranch north of El Paso, and he'd used the wide-open spaces to teach young Lucas how to ride and shoot in the best tradition of a lost Western way of life. Hal's only complaint, voiced every birthday, was that he'd been born a century too late and had missed out on all the fun – the birth of the state, the frontier, cattle drives, gunfights at the OK Corral. Partially a joke, there was some truth to the regret, and when Hal had been offered a sizeable chunk of money for his spread by a speculator, he'd jumped at it, bought the more manageable current ranch outside of Loving, and never looked back.

"Getting too crowded around here, anyway," Hal had announced when he'd phoned Lucas to break the news of his move from Texas to New Mexico. "Can't hear yourself think with all the development. Not like it used to be."

"Nothing is," Lucas had agreed, busy with his own life in El Paso. "Need help moving?"

"Nah. I'll sort it out."

That had been thirteen years ago, and Hal had adapted to his new surroundings like he'd been there all his life. He'd bought fifty head of reasonable cattle and built himself a three-bedroom ranch house with a barn big enough to store a dirigible, and had gone to work like he still had miles of runway left.

Lucas snapped back to the present and realized he'd missed the last thing Hal had said. "What?"

"Bear's been mooning around like a lost puppy since you left. I swear that fleabag's got a few screws loose."

Bear, hearing his name, leapt from where he was lying in the corner beside some hay bales and came running over like a charging bull. The big dog nearly knocked him over as he pushed through Lucas's legs like when he had as a puppy, apparently unaware that he was now over ninety pounds of canine muscle.

"He's a good boy. Aren't you?" Lucas said, patting Bear's flank and giving him another ear rub. When he straightened, he yawned and collected his guns and the crossbow he kept in his saddlebag. "I'm going to clean and stow these and then hit the sack. I feel like someone beat me with a board."

"Getting soft from all this easy living. That's your problem."

Lucas managed a wry grin. "Guess so."

"I'll be out here doing all the work, then," Hal said.

"Same as ever. I'm gonna take a bubble bath and do my nails."

Lucas carted his weapons into the house and set them on the round dining room table before hanging his hat on one of three hooks by the door, beside which stood an upright gun safe that contained a small arsenal, Lucas's weapons on the right, Hal's on the left. Lucas opened it, inventoried the two Browning shotguns, a sack with a half dozen grenades he'd bartered from Duke, and a half dozen handguns, all .45s, and then removed a universal cleaning kit and carried it to the table, leaving the safe door open. Hal favored lever-action Winchesters, a pump-action riot shotgun with a pistol grip, and a converted AR-15, the latter a concession to Lucas, who'd pointed out that having common ammunition for their automatic assault rifles would be important for efficiency's sake in any kind of ranch-defense scenario.

Like Lucas, the only handgun Hal had any use for was the 1911 model .45, and he had two, one of which was on his hip at all times.

Lucas hummed as he broke down the M4A1 with practiced hands and cleaned it thoroughly, his eyes occasionally wandering to the safe. Neatly stacked military ammunition cans occupied the center, mostly 5.56mm jacketed rounds. Cartons of twelve-gauge double-aught shotgun shells completed the cache, along with a box of .22 long rifle for the hunting rifle Hal kept in his bedroom for rabbits and smaller critters.

Lucas looked over at the framed photographs that lined the bookcase's middle shelf and stopped at the photo of his father in his Ranger uniform, so alive he seemed like he could jump from the frame at any moment. Lucas had inherited his chiseled facial features and gray eyes, and both were over six feet, but there the resemblance ended, far as Lucas could see. Whereas his father had been a bull, Lucas was leaner, though still muscular. That he was now two years older than his father had been when he'd died occurred to him every time he looked at the picture, and he quickly turned away.

Finished with his task, he slipped the Remington 700 into the safe and carried his M4 into the bedroom. He stripped and gave himself a gravity-fed shower, the water cold and refreshing, and then pulled on clean underwear and crawled into bed. Bear was already snoring softly on the floor beside him, and after placing the Kimber on the night table next to the bed, his M4 leaned against the wall beside it, Lucas was asleep less than a minute after his head hit the pillow.

Chapter 11

Hal's voice cut through the silence of the bedroom like a bullhorn. "Lucas! Wake up, boy!"

Lucas bolted upright, already reaching for his Kimber before his eyes were completely open.

"Easy. No need for iron," Hal said from the doorway.

Lucas looked around the room and, after ascertaining no threat, lowered his weapon. Hazy sunlight filtered through the open window, the breeze cooling the house during the heat of the day.

"What's wrong, Grand...Hal?" Lucas corrected, rubbing his eyes.

"Visitor."

"What? Who?"

"That Deputy Alan fellow. Get some clothes on and come out. He's in the living room."

"What does he want?"

"Wouldn't say."

Lucas coughed and threw off the sheet as Hal turned and trundled back into the living room, pulling the door closed behind him. Lucas emerged two minutes later and eyed Carl's deputy, a towheaded young man with thick features and sky blue eyes and a faded yellow Caterpillar baseball cap pulled low over his brow.

"Afternoon, Lucas. Sorry to bother you," Alan said.

Lucas nodded wordlessly, not bothering to conceal his annoyance.

Alan soldiered on, staring at his shoes. "Sheriff wants to see you in town."

"Yeah? Why?" Lucas growled.

"That woman you brought this morning? She came to. Fever broke."

Lucas's expression didn't change. "And?"

"Sheriff said to get you. That's all I know, Lucas. I swear."

"Been too long since I got more than a few hours' sleep, Alan."

"More than a few. Been sleeping for six," Hal corrected.

"Feels like two," Lucas said, and then sighed. "Don't want to ride after dark, Alan. Takes an hour each way. Won't have much time to talk."

"I appreciate it," Alan said, looking relieved that Lucas had agreed.

Lucas gathered his things and donned his hat. Bear accompanied him to the barn, where he saddled up a liver chestnut yearling with a white blaze that Lucas rode sometimes – Tango had pulled more than his weight and needed the rest. Alan was waiting for him by the front gate beside his mount, a buckskin mare. Bear gave the men a farewell bark as they rode onto the dirt road, and Hal closed and locked the gate behind them.

Neither man spoke on the way into Loving. Alan was a decent enough man; he'd been only a teenager when he'd lost his parents to the flu, and after recovering, he'd put his back into helping create a viable environment, working long hours on guard duty and building the barricade wall. He'd eventually married a survivor girl who'd given birth to a little boy last year, which made Alan part of the hope they all had for the future, to varying degrees. The deputy role was an honorary one, which was why Lucas didn't bust Alan's chops for waking him – all the man could expect for his service was appreciation and an occasional gift.

A blood-red sun hung low in the western sky, and Lucas's and Alan's shadows were long as they rode into town. Curious residents watched them trot by, and Alan guided them to the police station by the main square. Sheriff Carl stood outside, hands on his hips, watching as they tied their mounts to a streetlamp that did duty as a hitching post.

"You wanted to talk?" Lucas said without preamble as he neared.

"Appreciate you coming in. Water?"

Lucas shook his head. "No, thanks."

"Let's take a walk over to the doc's. We can talk on the way."

"Riding's faster."

"We're not that far."

Lucas decided not to fight any pointless battles and acquiesced. "Watch the shop?" Carl said to Alan, who nodded and sat on a plastic chair outside the main door. Lucas adjusted his M4 strap and looked to the sheriff with a raised eyebrow.

Carl set the pace as they negotiated the dusty street. "You mentioned that the men who attacked the woman's party were scavengers?" he began.

"Raiders. They had Mohawks," Lucas corrected.

"Right. Kind of off their turf, weren't they?"

"Probably slim pickings in their area. They must be running out of people to rob."

"That's what it looked like to you?"

Lucas threw him a look. "What else would it be?"

"I don't know. I wasn't there."

"Neither was I. I just brought the girl to the doc."

"Lot of chatter on the radio today about the attack on Duke's," Carl said, changing the subject.

"It was bad," Lucas said, his words clipped.

"They Raiders too?"

"Didn't get a close look at many of them, but the ones that I saw didn't have Mohawks."

"So you don't think they're related?"

Lucas frowned. "Why would they be?"

They turned onto the doctor's street. "I don't know. I'm just trying to put things together, Lucas. Figure out whether we're looking at the start of something that could endanger us."

Lucas shrugged. "You need to get out more. There's a lot of ugly on the other side of the wall."

"You said it looked like they tortured Clem?"

Lucas nodded. "He was messed up."

"Why?"

They were interrupted by the sound of a woman screaming from inside the doctor's house. Lucas and the sheriff exchanged a glance and then ran for the front door. The doctor appeared at the threshold, his expression troubled, but brightened when he saw the pair of them.

"What is it, Doc?" Carl asked, huffing slightly.

"She's awake, but she's not making a lot of sense," the doctor said.

Another cry sounded from inside, and the doctor stepped aside. "Might as well see if you can calm her down. I couldn't."

Lucas drew a deep breath and followed the sheriff into the gloomy interior. A cat shot across the floor like black lightning and scurried out the window at the sight of their boots, the space suddenly too crowded for its liking. The house was furnished simply, the only exception an upright piano occupying a place of honor in the living room. Carl approached the examination room, beckoned to Lucas, and then entered.

When Lucas followed the sheriff in, the woman was sitting up, the back of the exam table raised to support her, and her eyes were wide, as though terrified. She looked from Carl to Lucas and then back to Carl, stopping at the badge pinned to his shirt.

Carl shifted from foot to foot. "Ma'am, my name's Carl Green; I'm the sheriff. You're safe, but you've been hurt. Wounded, so please take it easy. You were shot in the leg and shoulder." He paused, giving his words time to register. The woman looked at him uncomprehendingly. After a moment he continued, gesturing at Lucas. "This man rescued you. He brought you here. His name's Lucas Shaw."

Lucas nodded to her. Her blue eyes shifted to his, holding his stare without blinking. When she spoke, her voice was thick, and she had to clear it and try again after an unintelligible start.

"You...you saved me?" she asked.

"Yes."

She closed her eyes. "Water..."

The doctor nodded and returned momentarily with a one-liter plastic bottle. He handed it to Lucas, who walked to the woman's side and held it out to her. She sensed his presence and opened her eyes, and then took the bottle and drank, gulping without pausing for breath.

"Easy there. It's not a race," the doctor cautioned.

She drained the bottle and handed it back to Lucas. "Where am I?"

Carl answered. "Loving, New Mexico. Little ways north of the Texas border."

"How far from where we were attacked?" she asked in alarm.

"Maybe…twenty-five miles as the crow flies," Lucas said.

"Oh no…" She looked into Lucas's eyes. "What about the others?"

He shook his head and looked away. "They didn't make it."

"None of them?"

"I'm sorry."

She didn't seem to hear them, her eyes wild again. "I've got to get out of here."

"You're not going anywhere for a while," the doctor said. "You just about died. It's a miracle you didn't."

She shook her head and clutched at the sheet the doctor had draped over her. "No. You don't understand."

Carl threw a look over his shoulder at the doctor, now out of his depth. Lucas stayed by her side, and when he spoke, his voice was soft. Calm.

"What is it?"

"She's still there. I told her to hide, to wait till I came back." The woman closed her eyes. "How long since you found me?"

Lucas calculated quickly. "Two days." He waited until she opened her eyes again and then inclined forward. "Who's still there? I didn't see anyone."

"Because she's hiding." The woman swallowed hard and seemed to deflate. She struggled for breath and winced, and then shook her head. "I left her with a canteen and some dried venison. But she'll be out of water by now. She's got to be terrified. Alone…she's only five."

"Who?" Carl whispered.

When the woman spoke, her voice contained all the misery of the world. "Eve." She hesitated and turned toward the wall. "My niece."

Chapter 12

Carl moved closer to the prone woman. "Let's start at the beginning. What's your name?"

"Sierra. Sierra McKinley."

"Where are you from?"

"Originally? Chicago. But we moved to Dallas when I was fourteen."

"What were you doing in the foothills?"

Sierra sighed. "Traveling."

"From where to where?"

"What does it matter? Isn't everywhere pretty much the same these days?"

That stopped Carl. Lucas stepped into the awkward breach. "Why don't you tell us what happened in your own words? Take your time."

"Didn't you hear me? My niece is still out there."

Lucas nodded. "We heard you. Tell us what happened."

Sierra pursed her lips and seemed to think for a beat. "We were making our way from Dallas. Eve, myself, and four men who were our guards. It was late afternoon, and we had stayed off the roads, which we thought would be enough, but it wasn't. Somehow we attracted the wrong kind of attention. One of the guards spotted dust approaching and had me find a cave to hide Eve." She blinked away a tear. "They were on us so fast. It was blinding. One minute we were alone, and the next we were under attack. It...it didn't last long. They were unorganized, but there were more of them, and we were caught in the open."

"Did you get them all?" Lucas asked.

"I think so. It all…it gets foggy after I was hit."

"That's not unexpected," the doctor said.

Lucas nodded again. "Why did you have guards?"

Her eyes narrowed. "Not guards like I was a prisoner. Guards to keep us safe."

Lucas's expression remained neutral. "Who were they, and how did you find them?"

Sierra seemed to tune out. Lucas waited until she was back with them. "Does it matter?" she asked.

"To me it does."

She nodded. "Fine. They helped us escape from a hellhole near Dallas. Eve and me."

"Escape?" Carl demanded.

"That's right."

"Escape from what?" Lucas asked.

"We were being held by…have you ever heard of the Crew?"

Lucas nodded. "Prison gang."

"They pretty much run Houston – most of Texas, now, actually, by the sound of it," the doctor said. "I hear reports on the radio every so often. Really crazy stuff."

Sierra grimaced. "You have no idea. But I'm surprised you heard anything. They make it clear that you're under their control. If you broadcast anything about them, they hunt you down and kill you. End of story. They're brutal."

"Why were they holding you?" Carl asked.

"Because they wanted to. They do whatever they feel like. I caught their eye." She didn't have to finish the thought. Stories of atrocities were legion. The Mexican cartels had come over the border in places like El Paso and, between them and their gang affiliates in the city, had turned the cities into death camps. The same scenario had played out in many areas, and no place had gone unscathed. Houston had a particularly dark reputation since the collapse.

"What's Dallas like now?" Carl asked, and Lucas gave him a sidelong glance.

Sierra's gloom deepened. "It's a nightmare. There's power, but only for them. They set up some kind of steam turbine, and they've been systematically tearing down anything that they can burn to fuel it. The survivors are mostly used as slave labor to demolish houses so they can keep the turbine going round the clock. There's a constant cloud of polluted smoke hanging over what's left of the city – which is a ghost town. I mean, you can't imagine how bad it got after the grid went down. Dead bodies everywhere. Disease, no water, gangs, killings on every block. When the Crew showed up, they introduced a kind of order, but it quickly degraded into slavery and mass murder of anyone who opposed them. And there were plenty, at least at first. But a few isolated people with a stash of guns and food, trying to survive the best they can, are no match for a prison gang made up of former military, hit men, gang enforcers, all armed to the teeth with the latest weaponry…"

"Why didn't you leave?" Carl asked.

"And go where? To what? I had my clothes, but nothing else. I don't know how it was here, but in Dallas, food ran out after a week. I stretched what I had for another week, used up my bleach purifying water, but what was I supposed to do? By the time I realized things were never going to return to normal, it was too late. So I just holed up." She looked away again. "I did what I had to do to survive."

"You say that the Crew has the latest weaponry. How?"

"Rumor was they overran an army depot. So they've got anything you can imagine and then some. I've seen AT-4s used on resisters. Trust me, it's not pretty watching an entire family blown to pieces for refusing to do their bidding."

Lucas cut in. "What's the story on your tattoo?"

"The eye? That's how they brand their property. It's to send the message that they see everything and will find you if you defy them."

Carl cut in. "So these guys that helped you escape. Who were they?"

"Good Samaritans."

Lucas's tone hardened. "Pretty well armed for Samaritans. And why guard you? From what?"

"From the world. From the Crew if they came after us."

Lucas wasn't satisfied with the answer. "But why? What was their motivation?"

"I…look, my niece is shivering in a cave out in the middle of nowhere. Can we put aside all the questions about the dead and talk about that? You have to go get her. Please. She's all alone, and she's running out of time."

Carl looked to Lucas. "You think you could find the spot again?"

"I'll draw you a map. I'm not ready to do that ride again. I haven't slept more than a handful of hours in the last couple of days, and my horse is more exhausted than I am. Sorry. It would be suicide to press it."

Sierra shook her head. "You have to go."

Lucas returned her stare. "I saved your life because I was there. I'm not there anymore. Carl here wants to play hero, that's fine, but leave me out of it. Desert's filled with dead heroes."

"She's only five."

"She's a long ways away, across dangerous terrain where I've been in all-out gun battles over the last twenty-four hours." Lucas's tone softened. "Look. I understand you care about your niece, and I feel bad for you, but I did my part. I'm not going to risk my life for anybody."

Sierra looked at him oddly. "Sounds like you did for me. For which, thank you."

Lucas waved her off. "Like I said, I was there. If I'd known what I was getting into, maybe I wouldn't have."

For the first time, a trace of a smile flittered across Sierra's face before it grew serious. "Somehow I doubt that."

"Think whatever you want." Lucas turned to Carl. "You going looking for her?"

"I kind of have to, Lucas."

"No, you don't. Town chose you to protect it, not to go off on suicide runs."

"I'll put it to a vote, but I suspect I know how it'll turn out. A defenseless child abandoned in a cave…" Carl shook his head and eyed Lucas grimly. "Takes a hard man to turn his back on that."

"Or a man who's used up his nine lives and is out of gas." Lucas stepped away from the bed. "Carl, I'll draw you a map. Shouldn't be impossible to find the spot. I'll wish you all the luck in the world, but there's no way in hell I'm riding on the trail all night with no sleep. That's tempting fate, and I don't feel lucky."

Carl's expression hardened. "Suit yourself. A map would be much appreciated."

"Doc, you think you can rustle up a pencil and paper?" Lucas asked. He tried a final time with Sierra. "I'm deeply sorry about your niece, and if anyone can get her back, it's the sheriff here."

Sierra didn't respond, just gave him a look of pained disgust.

Lucas followed the doctor into the living room and sat at the dining table while he rummaged around for a pencil and paper. The doctor returned with a stub and a notepad. "If it's any consolation, Lucas, I completely agree with you about not going. You're in no kind of shape to do anything but harm to yourself."

Lucas busied himself with a sketch of the landmarks he used for orientation. When he was done, he pushed his chair back. Carl emerged from Sierra's room at the sound.

"What do you make of her story?" Carl asked quietly.

"Part of it doesn't add up, but I'm so tired I can barely think."

"And the kid?"

"If you want to wait till morning, I was planning to ride down that way anyway. But I need sleep, Carl. I'm running on fumes. I'd just slow you down."

"No problem. Alan and I will go. Got the map?"

Lucas handed it to him. "Night riding's a good way to get yourself killed before you can help anyone, you know. I've done enough to know better."

"We'll be heavily armed. Plate carriers. Whole nine yards."

"NV gear?" Lucas asked.

Carl looked uncertain. "You mean night vision? I wish."

"That makes you hamburger for anyone that has it."

Carl eyed Lucas's M4. "You're the only one I've ever seen in these parts with one."

"Duke has a second-generation monocle. Uses a rechargeable battery like mine."

Carl frowned. "I wouldn't do business with that bandit."

"That wasn't what I was suggesting. I'm just pointing out they're available. Don't assume anything about what any hostiles might or might not have."

"We have to do something, Lucas."

Lucas rubbed a tired hand across his beard stubble, fatigue darkening the area below his eyes. "You want that on your headstone?"

"You were a lawman once, Lucas. I'm surprised at your attitude."

"That was a different life, Carl. No such job anymore," Lucas said, a rebuff to Carl's insinuation. Carl was a good man, but he'd been a National Guard reservist before the collapse, not a cop – he'd actually worked at a nearby shipping company and had volunteered to keep the peace when it had become obvious that things were going to stay bad for the duration, and Lucas had said no to the job.

"There's still common decency."

Lucas nodded and made for the door. "That there is. But you have to be alive to have it. I aim to stay that way a little longer." He paused at the threshold. "If you're in a rush to get to the pearly gates, that's your business. Don't try to drag me into it."

Carl watched Lucas leave and shook his head in silent disapproval, the doctor by his side. The cat poked its head up to look through the window at them before disappearing again, its late afternoon nap postponed until the house was quieter.

Chapter 13

Darkness had fallen by the time Lucas made it back to the ranch. He unlocked the gate to Bear's joyous barking and walked the horse to the barn. Hal sat on the porch, watching him, his lever-action Winchester propped up against the house beside him. When Lucas made his way to the house, the older man took a sip from a half-filled glass.

"I fed and watered Tango," Hal said by way of greeting.

"Thanks, Hal. He deserves some pampering."

"How'd it go?"

"She'll make it."

"I've seen you happier."

Lucas shook his head. "Damn fools plan to ride tonight." He gave Hal a rundown on his meeting with the woman. When Lucas was finished, Hal didn't say anything, just took another appreciative sip of his drink.

Lucas sniffed. "White lightning?"

"You got a problem, Lucas?"

Lucas took the wood chair next to Hal and turned it slightly so he could face his grandfather. He set his weapons beside him, and Bear pushed his head into Lucas's lap. Lucas scratched him to tail wagging and a low growl of pleasure. After several moments, Lucas patted the dog's head and eyed Hal, who appeared to be enjoying the evening without a care in the world.

"You think I did the right thing? I keep thinking about that old

Indian saying about saving a life creating an obligation. I don't want that. Slate's clean, far as I'm concerned."

"Man's got to do what his conscience tells him. You're right about it being a lousy idea to ride at night, especially when you're worn out."

"What would you have done?"

Hal laughed. "Nobody's asking old men to ride off into the sunset, boy. Glad I don't have to make that decision."

"Which means you would go."

"It means never walk in another man's shoes. You did what was right for you. End it there." Hal set the glass down. "How old you say the little girl was again?"

"Five."

Hal sat wordlessly for a few moments as the last of twilight faded behind the hills. "That's a tough one, sure enough."

"I almost said yes. But it's a fool's errand."

"Got to live with your choices."

"I know this is the right one."

Hal eyed him. "Don't sound sure."

"I'm going to clean up."

"Got rabbit stew on the stove."

"Battery bank charged up?"

"So far, so good."

"You know that won't last forever," Lucas said, rising and collecting his weapons. The solar batteries were eight years old. If they got another two out of them, they'd be lucky. After that, they'd be running dark at night and on rainy days, the solar panels only providing electricity real time during daylight.

Hal toasted Lucas. "Neither will I."

"Don't talk that way. You'll live to a hundred."

"Never had much interest in doing so."

"Nobody's asking."

Lucas entered the house and switched on one of the LED lamps, and then stowed his Remington 700 in the gun safe and toted his M4 to his room. All of the window shutters were closed to avoid any light leaking from the house – a sensible, routine step Hal took every night. They'd never been attacked, but there was always a first time; and by now, living with the expectation of imminent danger was second nature. Hal's time in the Marines had served him well for the current challenges, and the old man had never forgotten the harsh lessons combat had taught.

Lucas learned quickly, coached as he'd been by Hal as a teen, and the pair worked efficiently together, Lucas deferring to his grandfather in tactical matters involving the ranch's defense. Fortunately, they usually saw eye to eye and were as prepared as anyone to repulse threats. Preparation being the key – even as a youngster, Hal had drilled self-sufficiency and the importance of readying one's self for the worst through Lucas's head, and the discipline instilled in him as a boy had served him well as an adult.

Not that anyone could have been fully prepared for the super flu and collapse of civilization. Lucas had been fortunate to have Hal's ranch to bug out to when it all crumbled. If not, he probably would have survived, as Duke had, but it wouldn't have been as comfortable. With power, well water, and a garden, they were well set, and the cattle and horses were icing.

Sierra's description of Dallas returned to him as he moved to the kitchen, taking in the mouth-watering aroma of stew. He couldn't imagine an existence in one of the cities. The few travelers that made it as far as Loving invariably described a living nightmare, where the most vicious ruled over the less aggressive like feudal warlords. Sierra's accusing eyes floated through his memory and he shook off the vision, busying himself with preparing the meal for Hal and himself. Bear would finish anything they didn't, and truth be told, ate as well as any of them – certainly better than most of the unfortunates who weren't members of tight-knit communities like the town.

Occasional stories of California had chilled him from groups migrating east. Los Angeles, with its population density and lack of resources, had quickly turned into a war zone, with the population caught in the crossfire as warring factions battled it out, killing anything in their path. San Francisco had fared little better, the story the same in every instance: the lion's share of the population had believed that their government would protect them. The discovery of their error had proved terminal.

He tried not to think of a little girl lost in the wilds, strange night sounds all around as her water ran dry, her stomach growling from hunger, every moment possibly her last – tried but failed, as the image insisted on dominating his thoughts.

Why was he fixating on this? It was unlike him. He evaluated situations, made a determination based on all criteria, and then took action and moved on. Second-guessing and mulling over doubts was a sure recipe for failure, he knew from harsh experience, so why was he doing it now?

"You okay?" Hal asked from the doorway.

"I'm fine."

"You look like somebody pissed in your Wheaties."

"No such thing anymore."

Hal shrugged. "Hope you've got an appetite, or that freeloader will get it all," he said, glancing at Bear lounging on the floor, drooling in anticipation of the meal to come. Hal closed the front door and bolted it, and then moved to a bank of blinking controls and checked them. They had prepared for a night attack by booby-trapping the grounds immediately outside of the perimeter, between the main wall trench and a shallower one fifteen feet beyond it to keep animals from wandering into one of the traps or the trip wires. Lucas had improved on the system over the years, trading moonshine for the motion detectors and wire that used little power and added an additional sense of security to a perilous situation. Trip alarms in the house provided just one more safeguard. In spite of all the precautions, he and Hal kept shifts at night, five hours apiece, and took a few hours during the heat of the day for naps. They'd grown conditioned to the routine and neither questioned it, although Lucas secretly wondered how much longer Hal would remain active enough to pull the long hours. He required less sleep than Lucas, but the years couldn't be denied, and Lucas knew better than to expect him to be a fully functional partner indefinitely.

"Bear deserves anything he can get," Lucas chided. The dog spent nights outdoors, another early warning system should anyone be foolhardy enough to want to take on the ranch.

"He eats more than both of us combined."

"He's a growing boy."

Lucas had adopted the dog as a puppy on one of his trips to Loving four years earlier and had never regretted it. Like Tango, the dog had provided company and silent, nonjudgmental understanding as he'd grieved for his wife. Though the pain had softened over the years, it was still with him and likely always would be. He'd come to accept that and didn't fight it. The truth was that in the darkest hours of night, he missed her, for all his tough exterior and seeming coldheartedness.

"You sort your situation out?" Hal asked as he sat at the dining table.

Lucas set a steaming plate in front of him before serving himself. "You want some water?" he asked, sidestepping the question.

"Sticking to lightning. But only one tonight. I'll leave you to sleep. I got plenty of rest the last couple days without you around to keep me up."

"Suit yourself," Lucas said, carrying over a heaping plate and sitting down opposite Hal. They bowed their heads as Hal said grace and then dug in, the only sound their chomping and the clinking of spoons against plates.

"I'm thinking 'bout heading into town day after tomorrow for the market," Hal said. "Could use some of Miss Pam's fresh bread and corn tortillas."

"They are good," Lucas agreed between mouthfuls.

"When you heading back into the hills for the horses?"

"Probably tomorrow."

"No rush," Hal agreed. "How is it out there?"

"Never changes. My ears are still ringing from the shootout at Duke's, though."

"That'll stay with you a day or three."

"Yup."

They continued eating, and as Lucas scooped up the last of his portion, he sat back abruptly and dropped the spoon with a clatter. "Crap."

Hal didn't comment, just looked up, his expression wooden. "Be careful."

Lucas pushed back from the table, slopped more stew onto his plate, and set it on the floor for Bear. He moved to Hal's shortwave radio and powered it up, and then transmitted a call for the doctor on the channel the radio operators in town monitored. A moment later the doctor's voice answered after a burst of static. Lucas asked about Carl.

"He and Alan rode out about twenty minutes ago," the doctor said.

"Which way?"

"Staying off the highway. Keeping to the road to the east."

"Thanks, Doc. How's she doing?"

"She's sleeping. Not out of the woods yet, but she's scrappy. You saw for yourself."

Hal watched Lucas and, when he switched the radio off, rose and moved to the pantry, where they kept their food in resealable containers. The refrigerator was a high-efficiency model that consumed almost no power, but they didn't keep much in the way of perishables, preferring to hunt every two or three days and store what they dressed for immediate consumption.

"You're going to want more jerky. Some of these rolls should be okay for another day," Hal said.

"I'll get my guns and body armor."

Hal nodded. "I'd pack for a couple of days. You'll want a lot of water. She'll be dehydrated."

Lucas eyed him. "You okay with this?"

Hal shrugged. "Not my call."

Lucas went to prepare his kit. Much as he wanted to ignore the little girl's plight, leaving it to the do-gooders who would probably get themselves killed bumbling around in the desert, he just couldn't.

Maybe it was his experience losing his wife, or just the way he'd been raised, but he ultimately had no more choice in the matter than a compass had to point due north.

Carl's and Alan's horses tromped along the shoulder of the secondary road at a moderate pace, the route south clearly visible in the moonlight. Both wore plate carriers stuffed with extra magazines and clutched AR-15s. The lawmen also sported 9mm Berettas in hip holsters and toted twelve-gauge shotguns in their saddle scabbards.

Carl slowed as they rounded a gentle bend and cocked his head, his Stetson perched at an angle. After several seconds, he leaned toward the younger deputy and whispered, "You hear that?"

Alan shook his head.

"My ears are probably playing tricks on me," Carl said in hushed tones, eyes roving over the brush.

"Maybe not," Alan said a moment later, and pointed ahead, where a rider waited motionless in the center of the road, astride an impressively large stallion.

Carl spurred his horse forward until he drew even with Lucas. The sheriff looked him up and down, and then cleared his throat and tried not to grin. "Lovely night for a ride."

Lucas spun Tango around wordlessly and let Carl and Alan take the lead, already nodding off in the saddle as the three of them headed south.

Chapter 14

Dawn was still several hours away when they turned off the secondary road and cut toward the foothills where Lucas had rescued the woman. Duke's trading post lay six miles due south, but by riding in a more westerly direction, they could bypass his place and cut three hours off their trip. They were taking it easy on their horses, stopping regularly to rest and water them, and hadn't seen anything but coyotes and the occasional night bird.

A ranch house stood to their right. Its roof had burned away, leaving only the cinder-block walls. Lucas sniffed the air before turning to Carl, his tone grim. "The other day there were people settled there. I gave them a wide berth, but saw a couple and their kid through my glasses. Had a roof then, too."

Carl nodded. "They never learn. Probably the cartel out of Pecos got them."

"God rest their souls," Alan said, and all three men nodded.

Travelers would spy a promising dwelling lying vacant and take it over in the hopes of finding peace, only to be butchered by one of the armed criminal groups that viewed the area from the river south of Loving as their hunting ground. The group in Pecos, the nearest large town, was a Hispanic gang that called itself the Loco Cartel, especially savage in its raids. It left Duke alone, since his outpost served as a useful venue where its minions could trade their ill-gotten wares, but anyone else was fair game, and it demanded stiff tithes for protection, mainly from itself.

Lucas didn't know anything about the settlers, but suspected they'd either bypassed Pecos and were unaware of the danger they faced from the cartel or were simply out of energy and had decided to take their chances squatting for a while before moving on. Either way, they'd learned firsthand that there was no place too remote for the cartel to extort, and if they hadn't had anything to pay, the males had probably been killed and the woman enslaved and carted away – assuming they'd taken her alive. They probably had, as live females held barter value in the criminal underworld of the cities, whereas corpses were worthless.

The men skirted the ruined home, and the horses whinnied softly as they passed, as though sensing the death in the atmosphere. Nobody spoke; the scene was unremarkable, just as similar scenes played out on a daily basis in battlegrounds all over the world, whether in the Middle East or Ukraine or Africa, the end result always more crops for the grim reaper's scythe.

Lucas had snatched some sleep in hour-long increments as the horses plodded along, and was more rested than he had a right to be by the time veins of crimson marbled the eastern sky. He stopped to check his compass and, after taking his bearings, pointed at the hills.

"Maybe five more hours' ride," he said, scanning the surroundings, and then raised his binoculars to his eyes and did a slow inspection of the horizon.

"See anything?" Alan asked.

"Nothing to see."

"That's good, right?" Alan persisted.

"Every day you draw breath is," Lucas answered, and dropped the spyglasses back against his chest. He dismounted, removed the night vision scope from his M4, and packed it into its hard case before dropping it into one of the saddlebags, and then removed one of the five-gallon water jugs and set about watering Tango. The other men did the same and after twenty minutes were back in the saddle, pressing forward to where, hopefully, the little girl was still alive.

"People are fools trying to settle out here alone," Carl said, obviously still thinking about the destroyed ranch house. "You'd think they'd have learned by now."

"Everyone hopes that it's getting better," Lucas said with a shrug. "Price to find out you're wrong is pretty steep."

"So you don't think it will ever improve?" Alan asked. "It has to. It can't just stay…like this."

"Oh, eventually it might. But if you know your history, the world's always been a dangerous place. People forgot that, but it's true. One of my ancestors died at the Alamo, fighting Mexicans. More Americans died in the Civil War than in any other. The U.S. has been at constant war in one place or another since WWII, but because none of them were fought on our soil, they were out of sight and mind. But if you lived in one of those countries, it was like this all the time, for the most part, I'd imagine. Warring groups taking what they wanted, killing indiscriminately, battling for turf, destroying rather than building. Some areas stayed like that for decades, even with no killer flu or global collapse. So do I think it will improve? Sure. Eventually. But eventually can be a long, long time, and my bet is that we won't have learned anything when it does."

"What do you mean?" Alan asked.

"We're a selfish, brutal, venal species. Whenever there's a disaster, we see that time and time again. Nothing's changed. We're still made of the same stuff we were when the Mongols were sweeping across Asia, or the barbarians were ravaging Europe, or our ancestors were slaughtering the Indians, or we were bombing Vietnam and its neighbors into the Stone Age." Lucas spat to the side. "Think about what happened here. The power went off and a lot of us got sick and died. That's it. But what really happened was that the darkness that's always lurking just out of sight spotted weakness, and darkness always looks for any way to defeat light. Been that way since original sin."

"Pretty pessimistic philosophy," Carl observed.

"You seen anything to convince you I got it wrong?" Lucas asked.

"We aren't that way in Loving. You and your grandpa aren't. There's plenty of good in the world. Not everyone's bad."

"Not saying everyone's bad. I'm saying we're damaged goods, and any day we can show our mean side. Only way to keep it in check is to acknowledge it's true and be on the lookout for it in ourselves."

"The ones that burned that house down or attacked the woman are scum, Lucas. We both know that. Don't lump everyone in with them. You do yourself a disservice."

"They're flesh and blood, too. Sure, they're evil, but that same evil's in all of us. You see that working in law enforcement." Lucas didn't say *real* law enforcement; he didn't have to. "You arrest a teenage girl with a face like a saint for cooking her baby in the oven because she couldn't handle it crying, you'll see what I mean. You interrogate a young man who killed his parents for a lousy ten grand life insurance policy, you see how petty evil can be, how it looks pretty much like you or me. Clean up after a mass shooting, where a guy who was polite and went to church on Sundays decides to wipe the earth of a dozen of his fellows, and tell me about how good we are at heart." Lucas paused. "We're seeing how we truly are with this collapse. That's all. The bad are winning. Darkness is winning. That's what this is, nothing less. We built an artificial reality where everything seemed safe, but it was a lie. World's never been safe, and it never will be. Just bad guys trying to dominate good ones. Old as the devil."

Alan and Carl exchanged a look. "That was an inspiring sermon," Carl said.

Lucas squinted at the rising sun. "He asked."

"Yet you're helping us. We're all risking our lives to find a child," Alan said.

"That's the light, Deputy. That's our hope for a better tomorrow. Like I said, we're capable of extraordinary goodness. No question."

"Then things could get better."

"Oh, I expect, assuming the reactors don't melt down. Anything's possible. But if you think a bunch of faceless cheats in Washington are going to wave a magic wand, you're nuts. They're probably all dead. And if they aren't, they've got to convince people like you and me to do the work, because they'll never get their hands dirty. No, they'll set up their admiralty courts and pass laws and rules the rest of us have to follow, and find ways to screw us out of the fruits of our labor, but they won't risk their own skins. That's not how it works. Not how it's ever worked." Lucas spat again.

Carl looked at Lucas for a long time. "Hard to believe you were ever a Ranger."

Lucas pulled his reins tight and Tango stopped. Lucas stared daggers through Carl, and when he spoke, his tone could have cut glass. "Carl, you're a decent enough sort, but you ever say anything like that again, you'll be eating through a straw the rest of your life."

Carl didn't speak. Lucas snicked out of the corner of his mouth and Tango started walking again.

When Carl looked over at Alan, the younger man averted his eyes and busied himself with inspecting the blisters forming on his hands from the reins.

Chapter 15

The temperature rose as the morning sun ascended, and by the time the procession was near the gulch where Lucas had rescued the woman, all three men were sweating. Alan fiddled with his plate carrier, trying to adjust it so it was more comfortable.

"I hate this thing. It's heavy and bulky," he complained.

"It's like a seatbelt. You're happy for it when you need it," Carl said, and looked to Lucas. "Yours looks more comfortable."

"None of them are, but this one's better than most. Each plate's seven and a half pounds. The level IV composite plates will stop an armor-piercing round."

"Ever have to test that theory?"

"Whole point's avoiding that."

Lucas held a finger to his lips and stopped, and Carl and Alan followed his lead, quizzical expressions on their faces. Lucas peered through his binoculars and then leaned toward them.

"Someone's there. I see smoke."

"That's not good," Alan said.

Lucas didn't bother responding, preferring to dismount and walk Tango forward. Carl did the same, Alan bringing up the rear, and they made their way on foot, leading the horses until Lucas pointed to a shady spot beneath the spread of a tree. Lucas tied Tango's reins to a branch and whispered to the others.

"Let's see what we got down there. Keep out of sight, and watch for sentries."

They set off toward the ridge that overlooked the gully, and ten minutes later were looking down at the site of the battle. Skeletons picked clean by buzzards and insects were stacked in a pile near the boulders where Lucas had rescued Sierra, and more than a dozen Raiders, their Mohawks as distinctive as war paint even at a distance, were sorting through the dead men's belongings near a cooking fire – the source of the smoke Lucas had spotted from afar.

Lucas studied the Raiders for a moment and then shifted his focus to the caves that peppered the sides of the canyon. Carl and Alan waited patiently until he pulled himself back from the crest and turned to them.

"Too many to take on."

"We have the element of surprise. We could ambush them and neutralize them all before they knew what hit them," Carl said.

"Maybe. Maybe not. All you need are a few to escape the first salvo and take cover behind those rocks, and then we're at a stalemate – they could hold out for hours, and the numbers aren't in our favor. Especially if there are more out there."

Alan shook his head. "If we each take four or five, we could do it."

Lucas regarded the younger man. "You been in many firefights?"

A flush of color rose in Alan's cheeks. "I'm just saying we could take them."

"It's rarely like what you think," Lucas advised. "A smart man avoids confrontation, doesn't look for it. Besides, the more shooting, the more likely we draw other unfriendlies. I'd rather not chance it."

"Then what do you suggest?" Carl asked.

"We need a diversion."

"With no shooting? How do you see that working?"

Lucas thought for a moment. "You ever fired a crossbow?"

Carl nodded. "Sure. For hunting. Half the town uses the same three bows."

"If we could get right on top of them, we could hit one with a bolt, and that would draw the rest of them after us."

Carl nodded slowly. "And then what?"

"We lead them on a chase, get them out of the area. Look for, and hopefully find, the girl – and then rendezvous at a prearranged point later."

"I take it you've got a crossbow?"

"In my saddlebag. I use it in the field for game."

"Alan and I will lead them away. You hunt for the girl," Carl said.

"We need more of a plan than that," Lucas said.

Carl studied Lucas's face. "How well you know this area?"

"Well enough."

"Where would you lead them to lose them?"

"There's a bunch of ravines a mile or so north. What I'd do is have Alan wait there for you to lead them to him, and then pick them off as they ride by. They won't be able to take cover easily on horseback. Your rifles auto or single-shot?"

"Auto," Alan said.

"Got plenty of ammo?"

"Enough."

"They'll have a hell of a time finding their way back up out of the gulch there, so you'll have a good head start on them. Make sure you go slow enough so you don't lose them," Lucas said.

"Don't want to get back shot."

Lucas nodded. "Let's go pick a spot."

An hour later they were back at the trees, talking in low tones. Alan shook hands with Lucas and Carl, and rode off. Carl accompanied Lucas to the rise, and then Lucas continued along the crest, out of sight of the party below. Carl would shoot one or two of the Raiders with the crossbow and then leave a dust trail for them to chase. Hopefully, seeing their companions fall, they would all take off after him, leaving the gully for Lucas to search.

It was far from a perfect plan, but few ever were. Both Carl and Alan knew that they had the more dangerous part of the job, but neither complained, preferring to focus on their mission. Lucas had warned them that when it all happened, it would go faster than they expected, so to be prepared and calm. Now it was out of his hands.

He peeked over the crest and eyed the Raiders. They were loud and boisterous, untroubled by their surroundings, at the top of the food chain out here in their element. Nobody would be stupid enough to attack an armed party of their ilk, so they had no reason to fear a threat.

That was about to change.

Chapter 16

The Raiders were chortling as they amused themselves playing soccer with one of the corpses' skulls. The men were disappointed that most of the weapons were gone, but there was sufficient booty to keep them happy, and after packing up later they would go in search of greener pastures. After the attack, a surviving member of the original ambush party had ridden back to their stronghold and reported back on the carnage, and led them to the site the prior day so they could collect what they could before the scene was picked completely clean by opportunists.

"Goooooooalllll!!!" one of the Raiders screamed in triumph as the skull skittered between his adversary's legs, and then let out a whoop, arms extended overhead in victory. The exclamation was cut off when the feathered shaft of a quarrel materialized in the center of the Raider's chest. He sputtered and grabbed the shaft before slowly sinking to his knees, a trickle of blood drooling from the corner of his mouth.

The other Raiders stood transfixed, failing to process the unexpected assault for several critical seconds. By the time they sprang into action, another had dropped, a bolt sticking from between his shoulder blades. The Raider leader howled in outrage and pointed at the top of the ridge, where a cloud of dust hung in the air like a taunt.

"Mount up!" he yelled, and the men rushed to their horses, unprepared for the sudden requirement that they give chase. None of the horses were saddled, and by the time they were galloping off toward the narrow trail that led up the side of the ravine two hundred yards away, precious minutes had slipped away.

Carl drove his horse hard, aware that the greater his lead, the likelier he would be to escape with his life. After further discussion, he and Lucas had agreed that if he could lead them far enough away from the gulch, he might not have to resort to a gun battle, and if they continued to hunt for him long enough, Lucas would have a decent shot at finding the girl.

Carl's horse was fatigued after the long night's forced march, but strained gamely as he urged it to greater speed. The desert soil was perfect for leaving a dust trail for the Raiders to follow, but he wanted to stay out of range – not that it was likely they'd be able to hit him on horseback, firing from the saddle. Even with automatic weapons that would be nearly impossible, but nevertheless he rode as fast as his horse would gallop, leaning forward like a jockey to increase his speed.

The Raiders' only advantage would be that their horses were fresh, but that lead would diminish as they tired from clambering up the steep gully and giving hard chase. After five minutes he dared a look behind him and saw that his pursuers were just now on the flat, easily a half mile behind him.

He hoped that would be a sufficient head start. Lucas had advised him that it was a fifty-fifty proposition that they would eventually tire of the hunt and slow as their horses faltered. Carl's goal was to lead them higher, into the mountains, where he could lose them among the twisting tributary ravines that fed the dry main washes. He'd leave clear tracks for them until he was on the rocky gravel further up the grade, where his hoofprints would vanish.

For now, he just needed to buy Lucas an hour. If he couldn't locate the girl and get clear within that timeframe, she wasn't destined to be found, and their adventure would have been for nothing. Which meant his horse only had to be able to extend the burst of effort for another twenty minutes, tops, and then he could slow and be more selective about his route.

Carl's jaw clenched in determination as he bounced with each stride, and he avoided the temptation to veer into the brush, where he could lose his pursuers with relative ease. As the elevation increased, so too did the surrounding vegetation, but he followed the trail that led to the canyon where Alan was waiting with a pile of full magazines, weapon at the ready.

Another glance over his shoulder and he eased up on his steed. The Raiders weren't gaining on him, so he still had a five-minute lead. That translated into a margin of safety he was comfortable with, and there was no point in killing his horse to gain a few more yards. Now it would be an endurance match, and his ace in the hole was that his mount was in better physical condition than those of the Raiders, who tended to be as slovenly and uncaring tending to their animals as they were with themselves.

Minutes ticked by and he checked behind him periodically, happy that the plan was working. He had no way of knowing whether all the men had scrambled when he'd attacked, but that was Lucas's problem, and Carl couldn't affect that part of the operation no matter what he did.

The surrounding hills rose around him as he entered the area they'd chosen for the ambush. To his right, up two hundred yards, Alan was positioned behind a boulder outcropping well above the gully. Straight ahead was the continuation of a larger canyon that led higher into the Guadalupe Mountains, carved by millennia of flash floods from rain runoff. Now it was a question of how lucky he felt, and how many of the Raiders would choose the wider canyon rather than the smaller branch.

He was leaning toward continuing up the canyon when his horse misstepped on the difficult terrain and tumbled forward. Carl barely had time to register what had happened, and then he was falling, the ground rushing up at him before he could react.

Behind Carl, the Raider leader was riding hard, yelling furiously for his men to speed up. A Kalashnikov AK-47 was clutched in his right hand and the reins in the other while his brain worked furiously to try to figure out who would dare to attack his men. Not the Pecos cartel – the Raiders and the cartel cooperated with each other: the cartel stuck to the roads and left the barren wastes to his group.

Could this be the beginning of an encroachment? A change in the cartel's strategy? Were they finally out of options in Pecos and the roads that led from north to south, which they controlled completely, and whose travelers they routinely plundered?

That made no sense. The cartel members were city thugs. While they did own horses, they'd only bothered learning to ride when their fuel supply had run out after a year and a half. The Locos were definitely hard, but they weren't Raiders, who had early grasped the inevitable dearth of fuel and built their model on silent mobility over rough terrain. Most of them had been more than familiar with horses from their lives before the collapse, so it had been natural for them to form allegiances with like-minded criminals and pool their resources, creating a rural outpost where they numbered over eighty strong – a respectable force in an area nobody valued, but one that saw sufficient travelers desperate to escape the constant violence in El Paso and Ciudad Juarez to sustain them.

The pounding of hooves all around him and an occasional shout of encouragement or rage spurred him on, and he grinned when he saw that they were gaining on the rider. They would skin him alive and drag him behind their horses all the way back to the camp. Nobody attacked the Raiders and lived.

When the rider's horse buckled and went down, the leader screamed in triumph, and his men joined in with a ragged ululating that echoed up the canyon.

"He's down! Come on, boys! Playtime! Try not to kill him – I've got plans for our new friend!" the leader yelled, and fingered his rifle's trigger guard in anticipation.

The man would die a thousand deaths before they finally sent him to hell.

He would see to that.

Chapter 17

Dust drifted from the base of the gulch, past where Lucas hid behind a strip of juniper bushes wavering in the light wind. When the sound of hoofbeats had diminished to a faint pounding in the distance, he poked his head over the rise and took in the empty wash.

Descending into the gully was easier on foot than on his prior attempt on horseback, and he hurriedly navigated the steep bank to the gravel below. Above him on the opposite side were the caves, and after another glance down the ravine, he ascended until he was near the closest opening. He listened, his head cocked. Hearing nothing, he moved to the entrance, cupped his hands around his mouth, and called into it.

"Eve? Are you in here? Your aunt Sierra sent me."

Lucas's ears strained for any hint of movement inside, and after a long pause, he called out again. "Eve. Eve. It's safe. If you're in here, yell. The bad men are gone."

He waited.

Nothing.

Painfully aware of the clock ticking, he scrambled to the next aperture and repeated his overture.

"Eve. If you're here, call out. Aunt Sierra sent me."

He heard something – a faint movement in the inky interior.

"Eve? Is that you?"

Lucas froze at the sight of a pair of orbs weaving side to side three feet from his face. A rattle sounded, signaling the snake was preparing to strike, and Lucas slowly backed away, hopeful that the rattler would slither off rather than going on the offensive.

If Eve had been in that cave, she was beyond Lucas's ability to help now.

Lucas edged to another opening and called for her, only to be met by the same stony silence. He checked his watch: seven minutes had gone by.

He tried again and was struck by the futility of his task. If she had been in one of the caves, after three days there was no guarantee she was still there. It had been a fool's errand, as he'd feared. The girl was five. She'd probably hidden for a couple of hours and then gone in search of her aunt, scared to be alone. Which meant she could be anywhere, including dead from exposure or snake bite or dehydration, or any of a hundred other causes, none of them pretty. What had he been thinking, getting his hopes up? He knew better.

Still, he was there, so he yelled for her again, his voice echoing off the cave walls. It sounded like this opening led into a larger space, judging by the reverberation. He slipped his flashlight from the plate holder pocket and switched it on. The beam shone into the depths of the passage and stopped at a bend in the entry. Roots hung down from the ceiling of hard-packed dirt still a million years from its transformation into stone.

He thought about Sierra's description of the cave where she'd hidden Eve. She'd said it had been above the rock outcropping where he'd found her.

Lucas cast his eyes over the area again, trying to remember which outcropping that had been, and realized that he'd been facing west, not east, when he'd spotted Sierra. Which meant that he was on the wrong side of the gulch.

He cursed under his breath and dropped back to the wash bed, verifying that the jumble of stones he was looking at were the correct ones. The problem was that there were a number of rock formations, none particularly memorable, on both sides of the gulch, where over the years the softer earth around them had been eroded by periodic flash floods.

Lucas scrutinized the bank and saw a small gap in the cut. He forced himself up until he was even with the hole and called into it. "Eve? Your aunt sent me. Eve, if you're in here, say something."

He listened and thought he heard something deep in the earth, but he wasn't sure. It could have been the wind – and the fact that his ears were still ringing slightly from gunfire-induced tinnitus didn't help.

"Eve? Eve!"

He turned his head and heard the sound again. It wasn't his imagination.

"Eve!"

This time, he was rewarded with a tortured sob of terror from the farthest reaches of the passage. He directed his penlight into the chamber and saw nothing but more dirt. But he knew what he'd heard. "Eve, it's okay. The bad men are gone. Your aunt Sierra is very worried about you. Are you hurt?"

A flood of crying answered his query from what sounded like a larger cavern beyond the turn in the entry passage, judging by the echo. "Say something, Eve. I've got water. Food. A horse. I'm here to take you to Aunt Sierra."

More crying, and then the sound of a pair of horses approaching from the east drifted down the gully. Lucas swore and dragged himself into the opening, flashlight between his teeth, but it was too narrow for him to negotiate. His plate holder and M4 scraped and stopped him from getting any farther in, and the hoofbeats grew louder. Lucas's arms strained and his boots fought for purchase, but it was no good.

He shrugged out of the gap and made for a larger opening ten yards to his right. He dragged himself into the opening just as the riders arrived below, and he hurriedly pulled his legs all the way in, praying that he'd been fast enough that the Raiders hadn't seen him.

Lucas inclined his head and forced himself to quiet his breathing. He waited a few moments and then dog-crawled further into the earth, wincing as his rifle barrel scraped against the low ceiling. The sound was amplified by his surroundings, and he hoped that it was an auditory illusion. But even if they didn't hear him, he understood that he was now in a worst-case position: trapped, with the Raiders outside, and no way to escape.

Chapter 18

Carl landed hard, having barely gotten clear of the stirrups in time to avoid shattering his leg as the horse went down. He hit the chunky shale and his left arm went instantly numb. Several ribs snapped from the impact, broken by his elbow in spite of the plate holder, and they sent a white-hot lance of pain through his body. He struggled for breath as he lay staring at the sky, and then rolled with a groan toward the horse, which was fighting to its feet, stunned but uninjured. The mare then bolted up the canyon, leaving Carl to his fate with the Raiders bearing down on him.

The sheriff forced himself to his feet and grimaced as he blinked away blood from a gash in his forehead where a shard of rock had slashed him. He tried to wipe it away with his left arm, but the appendage wouldn't obey. Possibly broken or nerve damaged, he thought as he tested his weight. His ankle and knee throbbed, and when he looked down, his pants were torn and his shin was puckered and white from where multiple rocks had punctured it. He watched as blood welled from the lacerations as if in slow motion, and then the pounding of the approaching Raiders drew his attention.

He eyed the ravine where Alan was waiting and did a quick estimation of how long it would take him to hobble to relative safety. The riders were nearing fast, but if he was lucky, he'd be able to make it to cover. Carl retrieved his AR-15, his left arm hanging uselessly at his side, and concentrated on managing the uneven terrain, ignoring the shrieks of pain from his leg with every unsteady step.

He was nearly at the bend when he chanced a glance behind him. The Raiders were a vision from a medieval past, their faces distorted with bloodlust as they steered their horses into the canyon mouth. Carl knew that his survival was now measured in minutes as the dust cloud approached, and drove himself faster, blood streaming freely from his mangled leg, his boot wet from it pooling in the sole.

He estimated that he had another fifty yards of distance before he was in reasonable range for Alan to cover him, and realized with a sinking heart that he wouldn't have time to make it all the way. Hopefully the younger man was ready for what was to come – their carefully crafted plan was unraveling and would turn into a chaotic gun battle within moments.

He made it to the turn just as the first shots rang out from behind him, but the Raiders were still out of accurate range, and their shots went wild. He continued with determined effort, ignoring the agony that accompanied every step, and once out of sight of the horde bearing down on him, he increased his pace to a stumbling jog, aware that he was leaking his lifeblood onto the rocks as he searched for a good place to take cover. If he could find some place ideal, the gunmen would be wide open as they rode into the crossfire – and maybe, just maybe, he'd live to see another day.

Feeling was gradually returning to his arm, but the news his body sent wasn't good. While the bones didn't feel broken, he'd torn ligaments, and the appendage would be of limited use. He tried to flex his fingers with only marginal success, and the effort sent a searing burn the entire length of his arm and through his shoulder. He looked down and saw that one of his fingers was dislocated, compounding his problems – he'd deal with that once he was behind the boulders to his right, which, while not ideal, would have to do.

He staggered the final yards like a sailor on the deck of a ship in a storm and threw himself behind the shelter of the rocks just as the first Raiders entered the narrow gulch. Carl flipped the safety of his AR-15 off and set it to single-fire mode, painfully aware that with his arm and hand in the condition it was in, he might not be able to swap out magazines in a timely manner. He would have to make every shot count.

With only seconds to spare, he popped his dislocated ring finger back into place and then steadied the rifle against the rock and sighted on the lead rider.

Carl squeezed the trigger and the rifle bucked against his shoulder. The Raider pitched forward on his horse, which kept galloping, unaware that his rider had just taken a round through the chest. Carl fired again, drilling the man a second time for good measure. He flew from the saddle and landed headfirst, his foot still caught in the stirrup, and the horse dragged him forward, leaving a bloody streak on the gravel in its wake.

The other Raiders opened fire, and the ravine echoed with detonations as Alan's rifle joined the fray from up the gulch on full auto, striking riders and horses alike. Carl tried to be more surgical in his shots, but it was difficult as the Raiders at the front slowed and the ones in the rear bunched up and pushed past, creating pandemonium in their midst.

Rounds blew chunks of rock in sprays of chips around Carl's position, but he kept firing with the methodical regularity of a clock, choosing his targets. He missed more often than not, but he was determined to make the shots that landed count. Between Alan's shower of lead and his efforts, five of the men met their deaths within the first few volleys, and by the time there was a lull in the shooting as Alan jettisoned an empty thirty-round magazine and slammed another home, the surviving Raiders had gone to ground, taking cover behind whatever they could find – several using boulders like Carl, others the carcasses of their downed horses.

The chatter of Alan's automatic fire resumed, answered by the deeper rattle of the larger caliber AK-47s the Raiders carried, but neither group scored any more hits. Carl waited for a clear shot at the nearest shooter and, when the man's head rose above the rock, loosed three shots in rapid succession.

The top of the Raider's skull vaporized in a spray of bloody emulsion and he fell back, dead before he hit the ground, his

Kalashnikov emptying in a long burst as his trigger finger clutched reflexively. Carl shifted his aim to where another gunman was hiding, and bided his time, waiting patiently for the man to show himself.

Motion from the rocks to his left drew his attention, and he saw too late a Raider, one of the last into the jaws of the trap, drawing a bead on him. Time seemed to slow to nothing, and then he felt two hammer blows to his chest and tumbled backward. The third shot blew most of his larynx away as his head twisted, his rifle sailing from his hands as if of its own volition.

Carl's last thoughts as he lay dying were of himself as a boy, running like a fury through the tall grass in a field adjacent to the trailer where he'd grown up, laughing in delight as he chased his beloved German shepherd, Ringo. The vision dimmed as his brain, starved of oxygen, shut down, replaced by the sun, high in the summer sky, receding into oblivion as everything faded to nothing.

Alan's rifle continued to lay down salvos of fire, but his aim was imprecise at the greater range, and two of the surviving Raiders were able to dart from cover to cover and backtrack to the mouth of the gulch. Another gunman fell to Alan's rounds, and eventually a lucky shot tagged the lone remaining shooter, and the canyon fell silent as the roar of Alan's final shots boomed off the sheer rock walls.

An uneasy silence settled over the area. After five minutes of watching and waiting, Alan cautiously called out from his position.

"Sheriff?"

The absence of a response to two more cries told the deputy everything he needed to know. When he was sure he was alone, he rose and picked his way along the rocks to where his horse was waiting just over the gully crest for his return.

Chapter 19

Lucas belly-crawled forward in an effort to put more distance between himself and the cave mouth, and only once the daylight streaming through the opening had dimmed to nothing did he dare switch on the flashlight again. He had no room to maneuver; if one of the Raiders had caught sight of him as he'd vanished into the hole and decided to lob a grenade after him or loose a few rounds, Lucas would be dead in the water. That left him with only forward as an option, and he inched along, dust blinding him, more than aware that the snake in the other cave wasn't the only menace that awaited the foolhardy.

The passage opened slightly, and he found more room as he slid further into the cave. After an eternity he found himself in a rough chamber carved from the earth by groundwater that still collected in rivulets along the base. Slowly he played the flashlight beam along the length of the natural vault. At the other end he spotted another opening, and he considered his options. There had been only two riders, judging by the hoofbeats. He could either hide in the cave in the hopes that they eventually left when their companions failed to return, or he could crawl back, this time facing the opening, and catch them unawares before they had a chance to react.

Given that they hadn't pursued him, he concluded that they had no idea he was there, which was all the advantage he would need. He freed the M4 and retraced his route, crawling the last ten yards.

At the opening, the sunlight so bright it took his breath away, he peeked out and saw the pair arguing near the fire. Their voices were indistinct but obviously agitated. Both gripped their assault rifles, which was the only bit of bad luck – his ideal situation being one where they'd left them with their horses, which stood patiently near the skeletons.

He estimated the distance at a hundred fifty to two hundred yards, well within the accurate range of his weapon. They were grouped close enough so he could cut them down with a few well-placed bursts, but just in case, he worked a spare magazine free from his flak vest and set it beside him.

The danger of shots drawing more Raiders was now the least of his worries. The girl was in the other cave, and after he took this pair out, he'd retrieve her, make his way to Tango, and ride to where he'd agreed to meet Alan and Carl on the trail by the burned-out ranch house. Any new Raiders would come from their territory to the south, or if the lawmen had failed to neutralize the rest, from the north. Lucas would be heading east and so would have plenty of advance warning if pursued. He knew this stretch of foothills well from chasing mustangs along its crests, and he liked his odds.

Returning his attention to the gunmen, he drew a bead on the closest. He thumbed the fire selector switch from safe to three-round burst mode, the weapon always locked and loaded when in the field, and exhaled slowly while exerting gentle pressure on the trigger.

The rifle barked and shell casings shot to the side as he emptied half the magazine in a deadly hail of bursts. The nearest Raider jerked like a marionette as armor-piercing rounds shredded through him, but the second was too fast and dove for cover as Lucas adjusted his aim.

The Raider was good. He stayed in motion, rolling toward a pair of rocks that would offer protection, and Lucas watched as his advantage slipped away. He fired at the gunman, but his bullets only sent fountains of dirt into the air inches to the man's right.

Lucas fired again, and this time one of the slugs tagged the man's upper arm, wounding him, with the other two ricocheting harmlessly beside him. The gunman was almost behind cover, and Lucas tried again as the shooter paused to raise his AK – his only mistake so far.

But it was sufficient. Two of the next three of Lucas's rounds found their home in the Raider's upper chest, where ruby blossoms appeared as the exit wounds fountained red into the air. Lucas resisted the urge to empty the magazine into the man, and instead waited, his ears ringing so loudly he couldn't hear himself think. The man shuddered and lay still. Lucas watched his chest through the scope, searching for any sign of breathing, but saw none.

After a minute, he emerged from the cave and edged over to the one where he'd heard the little girl crying.

"Eve? We need to get out of here. Can you make it on your own, or do I need to come in and help you? Don't be scared because of the shooting. Everything's okay now."

He didn't hear an answer, but couldn't be sure. He called again, and when he didn't get a response, slid the M4 into the hole and tried crawling through again, this time just barely succeeding. Once inside, the cavity narrowed, and he almost got stuck twice, images of being entombed for eternity due to being unable to wriggle through vivid in his mind.

The passage opened up once past the initial run, and after negotiating the bend he'd seen in the light, he flipped on his flashlight and saw that he was nearing another larger cavern, this one twice the size of the neighboring one. In the center was what appeared to be a pool of still water, but when he emerged from the passage and shined the beam into its depths, he judged it to be a cenote, with no bottom anywhere close. The cave walls were a darker gray than the loose gravel outside, streaked with mineral veins that glittered in the LED light. He swept the chamber slowly, probing the nooks and crannies, but saw no other passage.

She had to be in there.

But where?

"Eve? Come on out. The bad men will be back. We're running short on time. Are you all right? Where are you? Sierra, your aunt, sent me." When he received no response, he tried again. "She told me she hid you in here and left you with some water and food. I couldn't know that if she hadn't sent me, Eve. Please. Call out so I can find you. I know it's scary. So let's get out of here."

A tiny figure in a soiled tunic, her shins skinned, emerged from a depression at the far side of the cave. Eyes the size of saucers stared at Lucas, framed by a mop of unruly black hair. Lucas nodded and did his best to offer a friendly smile. The little girl didn't look convinced, but he was running low on patience.

"Are you okay, Eve?"

A nod.

"My name's Lucas. I'm going to take you to your aunt Sierra."

"I…I'm hungry," she said in a tiny voice he could barely make out, and then Lucas was hurrying over to her as her knees buckled and she sank toward the floor.

Chapter 20

After checking on his horse, Alan worked his way down the slope to where Carl had been, a sinking feeling in the pit of his stomach. He held his AR-15 at present arms, wary of being bushwhacked. When he reached the rocks where he'd last seen the sheriff, his worst expectations were confirmed – Carl lay on his back, his eyes staring into eternity and his mouth open in a permanent O as though startled by death's untimely intrusion.

Alan said a few words, head bowed, and then removed Carl's plate carrier and slung it over his shoulder. He unstrapped the sheriff's web belt, removed his holsters, and finally, retrieved his AR-15. The next sheriff would require weapons, and with a pragmatism born of years of contending with post-collapse reality, Alan knew that despite his despair at having lost a good man, the equipment would still be needed back in town. One quickly learned to waste nothing and to leave nothing behind, and he next moved to one of the dead Raiders and repeated the process of stripping him of guns and ammo.

Two trips to his horse later, he'd stashed away the serviceable weapons in his bags. After a long pause to look around the gulch a final time, he led his horse down the trail to the dry wash, the only sound the moan of the breeze through the canyon and the squawk of buzzards already circling overhead.

Alan felt guilty for not burying Carl, but he was keenly aware of time slipping by, and he didn't want to miss Lucas, who he suspected would wait not a minute longer than he'd agreed to. The man was tough as boot leather and didn't suffer fools, but Alan could think of nobody he'd rather have watching his back in a firefight.

The shoot-out had shaken him, and his hands were still trembling as he passed another dead Raider. He'd had close calls, but had never been in a combat situation before, and even though he'd been shooting from a distance, which made the kills somewhat surreal, the bullets ricocheting around him had been unmistakably deadly. Carl's body drove the point home. Only one of them would be returning to Loving, and he'd be breaking the bad news to Carl's wife.

Alan stopped and leaned to the side. Tears streamed down his face and he vomited, supporting himself by leaning against his horse, heaving until his stomach was empty and all he could do was spasm. He gasped for breath and wiped his nose on the back of his forearm, and then forced himself back under control. He was wasting time he didn't have. There would be plenty of opportunities for remorse on the ride north.

Alan straightened and squared his shoulders, AR-15 in one hand, reins in the other. He was alone and would have to man up. There was no cavalry to come to his rescue if he made a mistake, so he needed to collect himself and push on, saving the emotional storms for when he could afford it.

"Just you and me," he muttered to his steed, who eyed Alan with equine disinterest, waiting for him to indicate what he wanted to do. Alan nodded to himself and climbed up into the saddle, and the horse picked his way gingerly along the gorge, obviously skittish from the shooting and the stink of death around them.

He rounded the bend into the wider canyon and held a hand up to shield his eyes from the sun's glare. It seemed impossible that the day was little more than half over – it felt like he'd been in the ravine for days, not a couple of hours.

A falcon alighted from the far side of the canyon mouth, and suddenly Alan bucked backward in the saddle as pain spread across his chest. The report of the rifle shot arrived a split second later, and then his horse was galloping forward, panic in its terrified eyes. Alan dropped his rifle and felt the front of his flak vest. His hand came away dry.

The ceramic body armor had stopped the bullet.

But he knew that would only happen once.

He hunched down, ignoring the ache from his sternum, and held on for dear life as his horse tore for the open plain. The steep walls of the canyon flashed by, and pain tore through his ribs with each jarring bounce. Another shot echoed from his left, but it must have missed, because he felt nothing.

"Come on, boy, come on. You can do it," he screamed as the flatland neared.

The horse stumbled but didn't go down, and then it slowed as another blast sounded. Alan drove his heels into the animal's sides, but it was no good, and Alan realized too late that the gunman had aimed for the horse instead of the rider, the target far easier to hit and no ceramic armor to contend with.

Alan's heart was in his throat as he leapt off the beast as it crumpled with a heartrending scream. It kicked its death throes, now on its side, and then three more rounds slapped into it as Alan used it for cover.

He felt for the saddlebag and got the flap open, and his fingers latched onto one of the AK-47s. He withdrew it and fumbled with the safety as bullets thwacked around him. His teeth were chattering like he'd been submerged in an icy stream, and he fought for calm even as his body rebelled.

He peered around the horse's shoulder, spotted the shooter seventy-five yards away, and squeezed off several rounds, unaccustomed to the kick of the larger caliber gun. The rounds did no damage – the Raider had selected his spot wisely, and now the tables were turned, with Alan stranded in the open and the gunman occupying the high ground, shielded by rocks.

More slugs struck the now-dead horse, and Alan closed his eyes for a brief moment. The face of his daughter swam into focus, joyful as only three-year-olds can be, laughing at some secret joke only she was privy to. His stomach twisted and sour bile rose in his throat at the thought that he'd never see her again – wouldn't be around to protect her or her mother, to fend for them or watch her grow up.

He opened his eyes, grinding his teeth. If he gave up, he was already dead. That wasn't an option. He would fight until his dying breath. The alternative was unacceptable.

If he was able to hold out until dark, the playing field would be even, or at least more so. Five or so hours seemed like an eternity, but he had plenty of ammo and wasn't going anywhere. The gunman couldn't hit him if he kept his head down and his wits about him, so it was a standoff of sorts.

Alan fired another burst so the Raider wouldn't feel confident in a victory, and thought it through. It was doable. With all of the magazines he'd collected, he could hold off an army, and eventually the Raider would have to show himself – his own supply of ammunition wasn't unlimited.

That would be Alan's edge.

He reached to the saddlebag and removed another rifle and then three more magazines. He could do this. He might have to walk out of the desert under his own steam, but he could make it. No – he *would* make it.

The crunch of gravel from behind surprised him, and he twisted too late. The second Raider who'd escaped Alan's ambush grinned like a demon, his AK leveled at Alan's head from twenty yards away – an impossible shot to miss. Alan swallowed hard.

The Raider snarled at him. "Put it down or I flip your switch."

Alan slowly lowered the Kalashnikov and tossed it to the side. The Raider gestured at his pistol, and Alan removed it with two fingers and set it beside him. The Raider waved at the other gunman, eyes locked on the lawman, and footsteps hurried across the loose rocks toward them. When the second man arrived, he had murder in his eyes, and when he spoke, his words exuded menace.

"Now we're going to have a little discussion, and you're going to tell us everything we want to know," the Raider hissed. "Everything."

Alan stared into the face of death.

He believed him.

Chapter 21

Lucas's return trip through the narrow passage seemed to take forever, even after breaking one of his cardinal rules and removing his plate carrier so he didn't have to contend with the extra bulk. Instead, he employed the heavy vest as a makeshift sling and used it to drag Eve's unconscious form behind him, pulling her along using a coil of trip wire he kept in one of the pouches.

Once they were at the cave mouth, he paused and examined her – her pulse felt weak, and she was probably in low-level shock from hunger, fear, and the last three days spent alone in the dark. He wasn't sure what to do about it, though, other than get her to the doc, his hope being that the old physician would have a solution.

Eve's unconsciousness worked in his favor as he donned the flak vest once again, slung the M4 strap over his shoulder, and then carried her in his arms. At least she didn't have to see the freshly killed Raiders or the pile of skeletons covered with flies. He walked with deliberate care, the girl practically weightless, and was passing the two sprawled gunmen when a scrape sent him into a ducking spin. He freed the Kimber from his holster in a fluid motion with his right hand as he maintained his hold on the girl with his left. The second Raider was struggling to level his AK at Lucas, his eyes burning with hate.

Lucas didn't hesitate. The .45 barked twice, and the man's head slammed sideways as the jacketed hollow points liquefied his brain.

Lucas stood staring at him for an instant before holstering the handgun and cradling Eve again in both arms.

Her eyelids had opened partially at the sound of the gunfire, and she looked up at him with eyes so blue they seemed to be reflections of the sky. His heart skipped a beat and a chill ran up his spine like an electric shock. He looked away, perplexed by the uneasy sensation. His mind was playing tricks on him from the combination of fatigue and adrenaline. That had to be it. Because the depth of understanding compassion in the little girl's gaze was vastly beyond her five years. She'd looked into him – no, had looked *through* him – as though reading his entire life in a flash.

When he glanced down at her again, her eyes were closed.

He shook his head to clear it. *I'm losing it. Imagining things.*

He needed to get to Tango and get the hell out of there before he made a mistake that cost them their lives.

Lucas trudged toward the trail he'd taken down the slope. When he reached the crest, he looked around, and seeing nothing but scrub shimmering in the arid wind off the mountains, headed toward the tree where he'd left the big horse tied.

Tango threw his head back when he spotted Lucas jogging to him and whinnied a greeting that Lucas barely heard. When he was abreast of the stallion, Lucas lay Eve gently on the ground and rummaged in his saddlebag for a canteen that he'd filled in case he was successful finding her. He withdrew it and unscrewed the top, and then knelt beside the little girl and raised her head slightly with one hand while holding the canteen to her lips with the other.

"Here. Drink. This will make you feel better," he said.

Eve's eyes fluttered open and she touched it uncertainly. "What...is it?"

"Orange juice. Fresh from our ranch orange trees."

Confusion clouded her expression. "Orange?"

Lucas realized that she'd probably never tasted an orange. Why would she? It wasn't like the Crew was interested in orange groves or sound nutrition when there was blood to be shed and sin to wallow in.

"It's good. Taste it. You don't like it, you don't have to drink it," he assured her.

He tipped the canteen to her lips and she took a swallow. After coughing, she nodded. "More."

Eve finished the entire canteen in a few minutes, and her color began to return. Lucas offered her some dried fruit and jerky, and she took small bites washed down with plentiful water. When she finished with the offerings, Lucas checked his watch and straightened. He gestured toward his mount.

"This is Tango. He's the best horse in the whole world."

Eve didn't say anything, just watched Lucas with those preternaturally large eyes. Lucas had as much experience with small children as he did with space travel and was at a loss as to what to say next. He tried again.

"Have you ever ridden a horse?"

This time he got a nod. "Aunt Sierra. With her."

"Good. Then you know how to ride. I'll help you up. We need to get going."

Another nod, and he scooped her up and set her onto the saddle, and then swung up behind her, shielding the child from harm with his body. He clucked at Tango, who obliged by sauntering slowly forward, speeding up until he was trotting. Eve bounced in the saddle, her eyes closed, leaving Lucas to imagine what her last three days must have been like – alone except for the bloated corpses in the gully being picked apart by vultures by day and coyotes and feral dogs at night.

He didn't pause to think about how the experience might have scarred her – she was alive and she'd deal with it, and unfortunately would probably see far worse in the future. That was just the world they lived in, and the luxury of worrying about how many years of nightmares the trauma would cause had been lost when the country plunged into chaos.

Still, the eerie lucidity that radiated from her eyes had thrown him.

But he had other matters to concern him.

Like rendezvousing with the lawmen.

And ensuring they weren't gunned down on the way back to Loving.

He glanced at the sky, where streaks of high clouds were drifting slowly south, and reminded himself that they had thirty miles to cover, at least, and less than five hours of daylight left. He didn't want to consider yet another night ride, but given the girl's fragile condition, he could see no other viable option.

Lucas gritted his teeth and nodded to himself. So be it. The hard part was done. Now all that remained was the journey north to reunite Sierra and Eve, and thereby discharge any obligation he had, imagined or not. Then he could sleep for a week and go in search of the herd of mustangs, leaving the rest of the world to figure things out without his meddling.

He saw nobody else on the ride to the burned-out ranch house, and there were no signs of being followed. When he arrived, it was getting dark, and he made a mental note to wait for no more than an hour and then continue on if nobody showed. Carl and Alan knew the way from there. If they'd been delayed or had fallen in their run-in with the Raiders, there was nothing his waiting would accomplish, and his priority now was the girl.

"We're stopping to let the horse rest some," Lucas announced as they paused near the gutted ranch house.

Eve didn't protest or comment, and merely sat in place until Lucas could lift her from the saddle and help her down.

"You feeling any better?" he asked, reluctant to let go of her as she stood unsteadily.

She nodded and tottered back to Tango. She patted his head, and when she smiled, she was momentarily radiant. "I like horses."

"Better than most people," Lucas agreed. "Want some more water?"

She nodded again and continued to stroke Tango, who seemed enamored with the tiny human whose miniature hand was offering appreciation. Lucas removed another of the five-gallon water jugs from a saddlebag and poured a measure into his smaller plastic bottle before giving the rest to Tango. He took a swig, swished the mouthful around, and offered her the remainder.

"Do what I did. It'll make you less thirsty," he said. She mimicked him, and he ferreted around in his bag and withdrew more rations. "Here's some salt. We collect it from a salt lake to the east of our ranch. Put a pinch in your mouth and swallow it – or you can drop it in the water, let it dissolve, and drink it that way."

"Why?"

"You're losing plenty of salt from the heat. Need to replace it. You'll thank me."

She dissolved the granules in the water, drank several gulps, and made a face. "Ew."

"It's good for you. Drink it all."

Eve did, and Lucas tried to focus on busywork. He cleaned the Kimber and M4 with his field kit and mounted the night vision scope to the rail of the assault rifle while Eve watched without comment. When he was done, he switched the scope on and let her look through it.

"See? It makes it look like daytime, but at night when it's dark out," he said.

She cocked her head. "Why not use a light?"

"Takes more power. And sometimes you don't want the other guy to see you."

"Thank you."

He frowned. "For what?"

She looked away, and for a split second he was reminded of Sierra. Then she turned back to him, her expression placid as a mountain lake at dawn.

"Everything."

It was his turn to look away, the air suddenly leaden as the light went out of the sky, the temperature dropping as the sun vanished behind the hills. What had she been through already? He didn't want to imagine.

"Rest for a while. We'll be riding all night, so this is your big chance," he said.

"Can I have some more food?"

"Tango likes the dried fruit, if you want to give him a little too."

Her shy demeanor brightened. "Okay."

"Just watch his chompers. He's a hog."

Chapter 22

Lucas was beyond tired as the hours wore on. Tango's sedulous plodding reminded him not to give in to the temptation to close his eyes, but it was growing increasingly difficult to resist the urge. Eve's head rested against his plate carrier, and the little girl snuffled softly as she slept sitting upright, Lucas's arms framing her to prevent her from falling to either side.

When Carl and Alan had failed to show at the prearranged time, he'd set off, resigned to making the trek on his own. A gibbous moon had risen in the night sky, illuminating the trail sufficiently for him to make his way, and when they'd finally hit the secondary road after crossing the highway with its rusting carcasses ghostly in the moonlight, he'd exhaled a long sigh of relief. The way from here was familiar and relatively safe; the area wasn't claimed by either the Raiders or the Loco Cartel, there being nothing of real value other than Loving and Carlsbad, both of which were fortified and guarded by a citizenry that knew how to use its weapons.

As dawn approached, he heard the thunder of hooves from the west – a large party of riders traveling south on the highway half a mile away. He slowed, and Tango eyed the horizon with him as he swung his M4 up and looked through the night vision scope. The riders were too far off to make out any detail, but he guessed there must be about a hundred.

He'd never seen such numbers, and a coil of anxiety twisted tight in his gut. Why would a group that size be on the highway at night?

The only things that occurred to him were bad and worse, and he clicked at Tango, who resumed his march, showing no indication of fatigue even after a brutal three days.

Lucas's worst fears were realized as he approached Loving an hour and a half later as the sun rose through a line of clouds over the eastern plains. Columns of inky smoke were curling into the peach sky from the town, and as he neared the fortifications, he could see the gate blown off its hinges, scorch marks from grenades blackening the walls on either side. No guards were standing watch, and Eve squirmed against him at the sight of the smoldering buildings.

"What...?" she asked quietly.

"I don't know," he answered, but flipped the safety off his M4. He raised his binoculars and took in the devastation, and then guided Tango to a tree and dismounted.

Lucas's face was all angular planes, his eyes narrowed to slits as he tied the reins to a low branch and helped Eve down. "Stay here with Tango. I'll be back soon," he said, his voice low.

"Where are you going? Where's Aunt Sierra? Is she here?"

"That's what I'm going to see." He unpacked the last of the dried fruit and handed it to Eve along with another bottle of water. "Don't give Tango all of it. You'll spoil him."

She nodded mutely, eyes even larger than usual, and Lucas knelt down so his head was even with hers. "Don't follow me in. I promise I'll come back, but you have to promise to stay put. Even Steven. Deal?"

"What if someone comes?"

"Hide. I won't be long."

"What about Tango?"

"He'll be fine."

"I mean if someone comes?"

"Don't worry about it," Lucas said, eyes on the town. "He can take care of himself."

That ended the exchange, and Lucas set off toward the gate, the M4 cool in his hands. When he reached the barrier, he studied the craters and the damage to the area around it and spat. Probably grenades, he guessed, which meant that the attackers had come loaded for bear.

The wall by the guard outpost was riddled with bullet scars, telling the entire story of the attack at a glance. He passed through the gate and spotted a body face down in the dirt in a black pool of congealed blood. He continued past more corpses, their weapons gone, no doubt taken by their killers. Ahead he saw a flash of color, and he swallowed back the acid that rose in his mouth. It was a little girl's dress, the toddler bloating in the sun, a bullet wound in her temple offering mute testimony to the ruthlessness of the attackers.

Everywhere he looked, the dead lay sprawled, most of them townspeople he recognized, and some the attackers, he presumed by their dress. He slowly took in the ruined homes, many burned to the ground, only their chimneys still standing, and he spied someone he didn't know. The man was clad in a black leather vest, his arms covered with full-sleeve tattoos and his head shaved, and was obviously dead, given the cloud of bluebottle flies clustered on his face. As Lucas approached the figure, he spotted the prison ink – a crude trident that represented Satan's pitchfork and which established him as a member of the Loco Cartel.

"Damn," Lucas whispered.

One of the eventualities the town had discussed was a coordinated move by the Locos, but it had always been dismissed over time as unrealistic – the cartel needed the goods Loving produced, and trade was the best way to get them. A raid would be a onetime event, and then the supply would end. The town leadership had gambled that the cartel wouldn't cut off its nose to spite its face, and years of no belligerence had lulled everyone into the belief that the savages would stay in Pecos and not spread their evil contagion.

The destruction of the town proved that to have been a fatal bet.

But why attack now? What had triggered it?

Nearby, another stranger was curled in a fetal position, a small river of blood running from his torso. Lucas studied the man, who was dressed differently than the cartel killer, his head also shaved except for a long black braided patch at the crown of his head.

Lucas toed the man's head to get a better look and recoiled with a sharp intake of breath at the tattoos that covered his face, lending him the appearance of a demon – which, based on the massacre, wasn't far from the truth. As far as he knew, the Locos didn't ink their faces, so who was he? And what, if anything, did it mean? Another killer, perhaps a former inmate of the Pecos prison, who'd been affiliated with a different gang? That was what it looked like, but Lucas was speculating – and in the end it hardly mattered. The damage was done.

He continued past the carnage to the doctor's house, not a creature stirring in the rubble. Inside, the doctor lay facedown with two bullet wounds in his back. His medicine cabinet and drug refrigerator had been raided, his radio smashed to bits, his beloved piano lay in pieces, the cat lay near the window with its head canted at an impossible angle. Lucas drew a long breath, the air heavy with the peculiar copper stench of blood, and then shouldered through the closed patient room door, already resigned to what he would find.

He drew up short when the wooden slab swung wide.

The room was empty.

That there had been a struggle was clear – the wooden chair was knocked over and the furniture in disarray – but Sierra was gone.

Maybe she'd heard the shooting and bolted, managed to escape the senseless slaughter? She was a survivor from Dallas, a city that was actively dangerous under the Crew's rule, so perhaps her instincts were more finely tuned than the townspeople's had been?

He had no explanation, and it wasn't like him to jump to conclusions. He did a quick search of the room and found the antibiotics Sierra had been taking, the plastic bottle tossed in a corner. Lucas pocketed them and then backed away and returned to the living room to stand over the doctor.

"I'm truly sorry, my friend. You deserved better," he whispered, and then offered an all-too-familiar prayer for the dead, ending with a soft "Amen."

Lucas retraced his steps back outside, noting that the doctor's house was one of the few that hadn't been burned, and then realized that it had more to do with the materials it had been built with than with anything significant in the cartel's approach. His was one of the oldest homes in town, constructed from cinder block in the 1930s, before sheetrock and studs had come into fashion after WWII. The house had been designed to withstand anything nature threw at it, and it had, although now there would be nobody to appreciate it.

Twenty minutes later Lucas returned to where Tango and Eve were waiting, his expression guarded under the brim of his hat.

"Where's Aunt Sierra?" Eve asked.

"Not here."

Eve edged closer. "I heard something over there," she said, pointing into the brush.

Lucas pushed her aside, placing himself between her and any threat, and raised the M4, the fire selector switch clicking to sustained fire with an audible click.

A female voice called from the dense vegetation growing along the top of the riverbank. "Don't shoot."

"Come out with your hands up," Lucas growled. "No second chances."

The bushes rustled and a woman with flowing gray hair, a faded T-shirt, and loose-fitting woven cloth pants stepped out. "Lucas! I didn't see you clearly. These old eyes…"

"Ruby!"

"Isn't it awful?" she whispered, glancing at Eve, who was peeking from around one of Lucas's legs.

"That's not the word for it."

"I know. I heard the shooting all the way out at my place. When it stopped, I came to investigate." She paused, words inadequate. "The devil walked the earth today."

"No argument."

"God rest their souls." Ruby lived three miles from town, an eccentric nature woman who subsisted by trading the specialized herbs she grew. Hal had known her for years, and the pair got along well, his dry delivery and deadpan sense of humor perfectly matched by Ruby's rapier wit and keen intellect.

Lucas nodded. "I heard their horses headed south."

"Yes. They came last night, late, and spent all night..." Ruby swallowed the lump in her throat. "They rode away about two hours ago."

"Nobody left to abuse." Lucas stopped. "Wait. Did you see them?"

She nodded. "I was hiding over here. I thought it was over, so I came to check, and then there were more shots, so I hunkered down here."

"Tell me what you saw, Ruby."

"They were...animals. No. Worse than that. Animals don't inflict cruelty for fun." She paused. "Everyone's...everyone's gone, aren't they?"

Lucas's expression told her everything she wanted to know, and more.

"I saw them ride off. Too many to count."

"Did you go into town?"

Ruby shook her head. "No. I...I can guess. I heard the screams. Mothers begging for mercy for their children, kids crying..." Her voice was barely audible. "It was...it will stay with me forever, Lucas. I've never seen anything like it."

"Did they take any prisoners?"

"No, they just..." Her brow furrowed, and then her eyes widened. "Wait. That's not right. They did leave with a woman. I didn't recognize her, though. I thought I knew all the townspeople, but..."

"What was she wearing?"

"Some kind of man's coat, I think. Maybe some kind of shorts? Why? Is it important?"

Lucas's breathing was ragged. Had he inflicted this abomination on the town by bringing Sierra to Loving? It didn't make any sense. She had nothing to do with the cartel.

Assuming she'd told him the complete truth.

Ruby's face changed as she looked over Lucas's shoulder, past the town, toward the horizon. Lucas slowly turned and followed her gaze.

Another spire of smoke was rising into the sky in the near distance. From the east.

Ruby took a step closer and pointed a shaking finger. When she spoke, her voice was tight. "Is that...?"

Lucas's expression darkened and his hand whitened on the M4 stock. "Looks like it's coming from..."

Ruby's hand flew to her mouth. "Oh no."

Lucas nodded.

"The ranch."

Chapter 23

Lucas pushed Tango as hard as he dared while Ruby followed behind him a fair distance on her mule, Jax, with Eve seated in front of her. Lucas had asked Ruby to mind the child, unsure what he would find when he arrived, but wanting to be prepared for anything – including full-scale war.

He gasped when he arrived at the gate, which, like that guarding the town, had also been blown apart, and jumped down from Tango, M4 at the ready. The barn was nothing more than a charred husk, its frame blackened and the planks burned away. Nine bodies littered the perimeter – cartel, by their appearance. The air was heavy with the odor of ash, and Lucas's heart trip-hammered in his chest as he surveyed the grounds before heading into the house.

The heavy front door was ajar, and when he stepped inside, a low moan escaped from his lips. His grandfather was lying by the gun safe, his lever-action Winchester and one of the shotguns beside him, half the rounds gone from an ammo box by the window. He'd been shot a half dozen times, and had gone hard, by the look of him, dealing out more than the attackers had bargained for right to the end.

Lucas knelt beside him, tears streaming down his face, and closed his eyes. "I'm sorry, Hal. I should have been here. I…" His voice trailed off, ending in a strangled sob, and he sat back, shoulders sagging, grieving for the man who'd made him what he was, who'd taught him right from wrong, who had counseled him and reproached him and celebrated his successes like Lucas was his own son.

That these monsters had seen fit to attack an eighty-three-year-old man and destroy his life's work, after he'd survived everything the planet could throw at him…

"They'll pay," Lucas promised, his voice a hoarse whisper. "I'll send them to hell. Every one of them."

Lucas shuddered again at the sight of Hal's body, and then he drew a long breath. That wasn't his grandfather. That was just the shell he'd occupied, the container that had housed his spirit, nothing more. Hal was not that bit of carbon and water, that jumble of genes and synapses. That was merely the vehicle Hal had used, and now he was done with it, its purpose served.

Lucas slowly rose to his feet and moved to the photos scattered across the floor. He leaned over and lifted the one of his father in his Ranger garb and slid it inside his flak vest, the pain in his heart a ragged wound.

Why had they done this? They'd had to go out of their way and had paid a heavy toll to take the ranch. What possible purpose had it served?

Realization dawned on him. They hadn't come for Hal or the ranch.

"They came for me," he whispered. The words were an indictment. Everyone in town had believed that he'd refused to go look for the girl. That he'd gone back to the ranch and was sleeping off his adventure. He hadn't even told the doctor he was going to meet Carl and Alan, only asked whether they'd left.

But why come for him? The question had only one answer: because he, and he alone, knew where he'd rescued Sierra. Even she didn't. She'd been unconscious.

That stopped him. How had they known he'd been the one to bring her to Loving?

"Clem," Lucas muttered. Of course. They'd tortured him not because they'd wanted to know about Duke's defenses – because they'd wanted to know where he was going.

And when they'd learned that the woman wasn't at Duke's, they'd figured out that he'd taken her to the town the courier had been heading for, in search of the medicine she needed. The smaller search party had returned to Pecos for reinforcements – enough to raze the town and kill everyone in it.

Lucas's despair deepened. The odds that Duke had been attacked again, this time successfully, were high. Unless… There was a chance that they'd taken a stealth approach, having tried a frontal assault before and failed, and instead sent a confederate into the outpost to trade. A seemingly innocent question or two would have quickly confirmed that the woman wasn't there, and the cartel would still have their outlet for weapon and supply trading.

That was how Lucas would have done it.

He nodded, his face impassive. It made sense.

Lucas looked over at the shortwave radio transmitter in the corner and shook his head – like the doc's, smashed. Ruined rather than taken, even though it was worth its weight in gold.

A sound deep in the house froze him in his tracks.

A red streak led to his bedroom, and he swallowed the bile that threatened to flood his mouth. Lucas walked slowly toward the room, and when he heard the sound again, a spike of anguish shot straight through his heart.

Bear lay bleeding at the foot of his bed where he'd dragged himself, shot three times in his massive chest but too stubborn to die. He looked up at Lucas with chocolate eyes filled with pain, as though apologizing for failing to protect the ranch, for not doing better, for failing Lucas, and tried to lift his head.

Lucas's eyes brimmed and he collapsed beside Bear with a strangled cry.

Ruby stood with Eve by the front gate, the little girl taking in the destruction, neither of them speaking. Ruby spotted the corpse of one of the attackers and turned Eve away, but she shrugged loose and continued staring at the house.

"Don't worry," she said, her voice small. "I've seen worse."

A shot rang out from within the house, and Ruby gripped her shotgun tight to her chest. She was preparing to order Eve back to Jax when Lucas appeared at the front door, carrying Hal.

They moved slowly toward Lucas as he walked down the steps and made for the vegetable garden beside the well. When he reached it, he set his grandfather down and turned to Ruby.

"Got a shovel in my kit. I'll bury him and Bear, here, on the land they loved, and then go into Loving and deal with the townsfolk."

"I'll help," Ruby said quietly.

"You don't have to."

"Yes, I do." She hesitated and then put her hand on Lucas's shoulder. "I'm so sorry, Lucas."

He nodded curtly. "There's work to be done."

She watched as he marched to where Tango was drinking from the water trough and retrieved his camp shovel from his saddlebags, his expression hard, steel gray eyes unreadable. When he returned, he removed his plate carrier, strapped his M4 across his back, and began digging in the red dirt. Nothing could be heard other than the abrasive sound of the steel slicing into the earth.

"See if there's any white lightning over in the root cellar," he said. "Should be. Be obliged if you'd put as much as you can carry in your mule's bags and top mine up. We're going to need it."

"Okay, Lucas." She hesitated. "Let me know if there's anything else I can do."

He scooped out another shovelful of dirt and tossed it aside. "There's a gun safe in the house. See if there's anything useable left."

She nodded. "I know where it is."

"Could use as much .45 and 5.56mm as you can find."

"Will do."

"I can help," Eve said.

Ruby patted her head. "Good. I could use some."

Lucas watched them go, wondering at the little girl's poise in the presence of so much death.

An hour later, Hal and Bear were buried. Lucas had wrestled a heavy stone to mark Hal's grave, and they'd said a funeral prayer, commending his grandfather's soul to God's safekeeping. The cartel had raided the gun safe, and there was nothing to be scrounged, but they'd missed the door to the root cellar, where two dozen jars were filled with Hal's potion, stored in the cool soil. Lucas went to his bedroom and packed what clothes he could fit in his saddlebags. Once Jax was loaded to the brim, they took a long final look at the ranch, and then Lucas sat Eve in front of him on Tango and they made their way back to town.

The afternoon was fading by the time he and Ruby had dragged all the corpses into the wood-frame town hall, where they'd hauled as much lumber and cloth as they could find. The cartel had apparently been uninterested in taking the time to destroy the empty structure, preferring to concentrate on murder and desecrating the homes of the innocent, but Lucas intended to put the building to fitting use. Both Lucas and Ruby had done their grim work with bandannas over their noses and mouths. After grouping the dead as best they could, they emptied the contents of Hal's jars on the wood they'd collected, also soaking as many of the bodies as possible.

Lucas stood with head bowed and said words while Ruby and Eve looked on, and then he lit a rag he'd stuffed into the top of one of the remaining jars, tossed the flaming container through the door, and turned to face the setting sun as flame licked from the building before consuming it.

Ruby took Lucas's hand as they walked back to where they'd left the animals by the gate, and gave it a concerned squeeze. "You look like you could use some rest, Lucas."

"Don't think I'll be able to sleep ever again, Ruby."

"Come back to my place. It's safe, and we can figure out what to do next."

"I know what I plan to do."

"Your horse is beat. So are you. And Eve here needs a bath and some food and drink." Ruby studied Lucas's profile. "When was the last time you ate?"

"Doesn't matter."

"That's what I thought. Come on, Lucas. You've got no place else to go. Do it as a favor to me. To Hal, God rest his soul."

Lucas sighed and nodded agreement. "Always a bad idea to ride at night," he conceded.

"I've got plenty of hay and apples for your horse. He looks like he's had a rough go of it, too." Ruby looked down at Eve. "You like apples?"

Eve looked confused. "I…I don't know."

Ruby smiled and patted her head. "Only one way to find out."

Chapter 24

Orange flames shot into the air from bonfires around what had once been Lakewood Church, a mammoth auditorium that could seat almost seventeen thousand of the faithful in the days before the collapse. Now it served as the headquarters for the Crew, which had commandeered the facility several months after the city's infrastructure had failed, with more than ninety-five percent of the population dead from disease and unrest. The Crew leader, Magnus, had been one of the hardest cases serving life in Beaumont, a United States penitentiary, when the grid had failed. Three days after the prison had been deserted by the staff, his gang had broken it open, just as they had prisons all over the state, and embarked on a terror spree that had become the stuff of whispered infamy.

By the time the dust had settled, Magnus had effective control over much of Texas, including Houston and the seaport, as well as Louisiana, Oklahoma, and Arkansas; his men's rapacious violence and cold-blooded willingness to kill had overcome all resistance. When the state apparatus had crumbled as the monetary system failed, Magnus had seized the opportunity to become a regional warlord and ruled with impunity, there being no organization capable of opposing him. He'd earned the instant loyalty of the state's surviving prison population when his gang had freed them, and with the help of this swarm of miscreants, his group's influence had spread like wildfire.

As his crowning achievement in his old hometown, he'd taken over Ellington Field, the military base in Houston, and with the cache of weapons retrieved there, had systematically butchered anyone who might have posed a challenge to his reign – not that there were many after the flu had ravaged the nation and the government imploded. With no police or military to stop the spread of his gang, he'd offered the surviving residents a choice: obey him, or die.

Most chose life, and with the cooperation of the remnants of the urban drug gangs, as well as the Mexican cartels which had crossed the unguarded border in search of easy prey, he'd built a criminal network that reveled in atrocity, no act too disgraceful or foul, no deed too despicable to celebrate.

Tonight, Magnus was overseeing a regular feature of his reign – a public execution of rivals, rule-breakers, resisters, and critics. Early into the collapse he'd discovered the old ways were best, and that it was prudent to demonstrate an absolute willingness to punish in the harshest possible manner even the smallest of violations. Beheadings, drawing and quartering, burning alive, hanging, bayonetting – all were favorites and ensured that the surviving population understood well the penalty for resistance.

Around him at an oversized conference table sat his advisors, a rogue's gallery of felons and quislings, who despite their predilections for chaos and abomination, had achieved some remarkable innovations. One man, Sax Whitely, had been an engineer before being convicted of the double murder of his ex-wife and her new husband, and he'd single-handedly brought limited power back to Dallas using a steam turbine he'd built, as well as to parts of Houston, using geothermal technology and equipment looted from throughout the state.

Whitely was the head of Magnus's research group, which the warlord hoped he could parlay into greater influence when civilization inevitably reestablished itself. His current efforts included attempting to get one of the big Houston refineries operating again, but so far he hadn't been able to, there being insufficient skilled

RUSSELL BLAKE

labor, replacement parts, or power to drive it. Whitely was also searching for a way to revive the rail system using an ancient coal-burning locomotive in Dallas, in the hopes of spreading the Crew's power even further.

Magnus held his empty cup aloft. "More rum!" he called, and one of his minions ran to fetch a bottle.

Magnus had taken his moniker while serving multiple life sentences in supermax prison for homicide and torture connected with his drug-trafficking, extortion, and racketeering ventures. While incarcerated he'd studied the history of the world's great fortunes and had concluded that in times of extremes, wealth was more easily created. From the European banking dynasties, which had funded both sides of every armed conflict for at least two centuries, to American icons like the Rockefellers, whose riches were created in the opium trade before diversifying into oil and banking, to the Kennedy clan, whose patriarch had parlayed stock manipulations and bootlegging operations into the equivalent of an American royal family, cunning, treachery, amorality, and utter ruthlessness had played a large role in their fortunes. Magnus saw himself as a kindred spirit who simply hadn't had the right opportunity. Until now.

When the power had gone out all over the country, and it had become obvious that society was in flux, he'd acted decisively when most others were either cowering in fear or bickering over peanuts. He was utterly fearless and was possessed of a powerful prison-yard physique from countless hours of weightlifting, which along with his above-average intelligence had made him a natural leader in a time of upheaval. Modeling his approach after his idol Genghis Khan, he'd struck hard, eliminated threats to his power, absorbed possible allies and rewarded them for their allegiance, and consolidated territory under his flag.

The servant returned with a fresh bottle of the añejo rum Magnus reserved for his own consumption and poured several inches into his goblet before slinking away to await his master's next order. Magnus took a long, appreciative sip and smacked his lips.

Magnus had chosen the Eye of Providence for his signature,

largely due to its occult legacy and its symbolic importance to the Illuminati, which he'd studied with fascination while behind bars, and which he was convinced was the shadow organization that ran the world, pulling the strings of puppet governments and front groups while always remaining in the background. Magnus had grown obsessed with them, convinced that the trick to claiming a seat at the table of power once a national government was formed was to prove his worth and loyalty to the group, whom he believed responsible for the super flu and resultant economic Armageddon. He had secured forbidden tomes that purported to explain the true significance of the Georgia Guide Stones, the Jesuit "black pope" and the Vatican, Satanic secret societies that operated in plain sight, modern neo-Nazism and global fascist totalitarianism, and a plethora of other arcane and occult interests he believed influenced all events of note.

His men were swigging moonshine and rum, finishing up their daily status reports, anticipating the executions and the debauchery that would follow with the female slaves, many of them barely teenagers, hand-selected for defilement. The current topic was the Lubbock laboratory – one of Whitely's projects that had gone unexpectedly bad, setting him on edge for two weeks as his future with Magnus, and his life, hung in the balance.

"Security should have been tighter," spat Lorne, one of Whitely's rivals. "If I'd been running things there, this would never have happened."

"If you'd been running things there, you'd still have been trying to figure out how to boil water," Whitely countered.

The gathering laughed at the barbs being exchanged, in much the same way Romans might have chuckled as gladiators battled to the death in the coliseum. Magnus took a deep draught of his rum and touched the tattooed eye in the center of his forehead, the pyramid below it extending to his jawline on either side of his face. "I'm tiring of excuses," he said in a low rumble, and the men nodded as though he'd dispensed profound wisdom.

And aide, also covered with prison ink, entered and approached Magnus. The man whispered in his ear and the warlord's face twisted with rage. He rose from his throne, as he referred to the symbolic seat of power he'd set up on the church's altar platform, and stormed after the aide, signaling with a curt gesture that the meeting was over.

In one of the rooms below, a nervous man waited, his body language apprehensive, his clothes covered with road dust. Magnus entered and plopped down on a divan. "What happened?"

"I wanted to tell you in person. We spoke with Garret on the radio. It was too sensitive to transmit to you on open air, so I've ridden all day to report his progress. He has the woman – but not the child."

"What good is that?" Magnus thundered. "That's not a result! That's a failure!"

"He says he's close. He hopes to have a resolution shortly."

Magnus eyed the messenger with an evil glare. "Perhaps I sent the wrong man to coordinate things with the Locos."

The messenger gave a dispassionate report of everything he'd been told. When he was finished, the warlord nodded. "My patience is running thin. Tell Garret that. Use those exact words. If I cannot rely on him to produce a success, he will be responsible for a failure. Tell him."

The man nodded. "I will."

"Fill your belly and drink till you drop. You can return to your duties tomorrow."

"Thank you, Magnus."

The warlord waved him away. "Leave me. I need to think."

The messenger hurried away. Magnus stared at the religious icons that decorated the walls, considering the new information he'd received, and then abruptly rose and moved to the door. His bodyguards framed the entryway, Uzis in hand, and he grinned, gold incisors glittering fangs in the dim light.

"Time for the execution, boys. Let's go watch justice be done!" he bellowed, and the men smiled – their boss was a man of extreme moods, and better a joyous Magnus preparing for the slaughter than an angry one, who could lash out violently at the slightest real or imagined slight. They followed the big man down the hall, overhead lights flickering from the uneven geothermal power, and up onto the roof, where an exhibition stage stood, surrounded by flaring torches. The condemned men, women, and children waited by its side in shackles.

A cheer went up from the assembled throng at the appearance of their leader, and Magnus raised a megaphone to his lips.

"What is the penalty for disobedience?" he cried.

"Death!" the crowd roared.

"What do we do to those who oppose us?"

"Kill them!" the assembly chanted.

"The time is now. The all-seeing eye has spoken, and the bringer of light will be appeased!"

An enthusiastic cry rose from the group as drummers pounded on their instruments in tight cadence. A prodigiously muscled man, naked except for a studded leather codpiece and a black hood, stepped onto the stage with a gleaming machete and held it overhead. The first victim, a young woman, screamed in terror as a pair of bare-chested guards dragged her onto the stage.

Magnus smiled inwardly at the spectacle and took his seat to watch the fun. The herd was easy to control, he thought. Bread and circuses, same as it had been for thousands of years. Nothing had changed – the masses still cried for slaughter, their history as hunters quickening the murderous blood in their veins now that the veneer of civility had been stripped away.

He, Magnus, was their new messiah, their maker of dreams, their Caesar.

And it was time to render unto him and pay tribute.

Chapter 25

Jax knew the way home, and he ambled along a trail until they arrived at a dilapidated industrial building no more than five hundred square feet, part of its front façade caved in and the grounds around it desiccated. Ruby hopped from the saddle and removed the bridle and saddle from the mule while Lucas helped Eve down and surveyed their surroundings, which were barely visible now that it was dark.

"Go ahead and unstrap your gear, Lucas," Ruby said. "You won't need your saddle tonight."

"Where do I put it?" he asked, eyeing the building doubtfully.

"Just do it, and then I'll lead you to my own personal piece of paradise." She paused and patted Jax. "If your horse will come when you call him, we can just let them graze in this field. There's a water trough over by that fencepost for them. Fed by a well."

"That'll work." Lucas unbuckled Tango's tack, and once freed from his trappings, the big horse followed Jax over to the water and drank. Lucas shouldered the saddle and saddlebags, and trailed Ruby and Eve into the building.

Inside, he could see that most of the windows had been broken out, and the cement floor was littered with glass shards, dusty debris, dead birds, and refuse.

"Uh, Ruby…" he started.

She shushed him. "Don't worry. I'm only half mad."

Ruby reached below one of the piles of trash and pulled. The floor rose, and Lucas could see that the mound of garbage was actually attached to the top of a wide hatch. An industrial white light blinked on below. She turned to him and smiled. "Welcome to Casa Ruby."

Lucas neared the opening and saw five-foot-wide metal stairs descending into the earth. With another doubtful glance at Ruby, he descended the steps, which were painted a faded gray and worn from decades of foot traffic. He continued down three stories, where he encountered a steel blast door. He waited there as Ruby resealed the hatch above and escorted Eve to where Lucas waited, and then pushed past him and unlocked the door with a key hanging from a chain around her neck.

"What is this place?" Lucas asked, his voice echoing in the concrete passageway.

"Old AT&T communications bunker. They built them during the Cold War. This is a relatively small one – only fifteen thousand square feet. They ranged all the way up to sixty. Hardened to withstand a nuclear strike and equipped with everything you can imagine, although I don't use most of the gear because of power concerns."

"Solar?" Lucas asked.

"Of course. I've got a decent array up on the roof, but you can't see the panels because of the rim of the building, which is just as well. Nobody has any idea I live here. Which is exactly how I like it."

Ruby pulled the thick steel door wide and motioned for him to enter. Lucas took a cautious step inside the dark expanse, and Ruby reached around him and flipped a switch. Fluorescent lights illuminated along another, wider corridor.

"Cool," Eve said.

Ruby shut the door and locked it, and then led them down the hall to another door. She repeated the unlocking ritual using the same key and stepped over the threshold, an impish smile on her wizened face. "Come on in and set your stuff down."

She flicked on the lights in the room, and Lucas found himself looking at a large rectangular hall, easily forty by eighty, outfitted with throw rugs on the cement floor, overstuffed couches and easy chairs, an elaborate computer workstation midway along one wall, and colorful oil paintings on all the walls, along with stuffed birds whose eyes seemed to follow them as they entered.

"Wow," Eve exclaimed, looking up at Lucas.

He nodded in agreement. "Yeah. Wow."

Ruby switched the hall lights off and closed the door. "Only thing that drives me batty are the fluorescent main lights. I was getting ready to replace those when it all went paws up. I usually work with just the LED area lamps. The overheads are annoying. You mind if I shut them off?" She paused. "Lucas, you can put your gear over there." She pointed at a spot near the door.

Lucas shook his head in wonder. "This is amazing. You own it?"

"Wasn't all that expensive, believe it or not. But outfitting it sure was. Got five acres of surrounding land, no good for much but my herb gardens and for Jax to roam. Surrounded by chain-link fence that came with the deal. So did a generator, sewage pump, ten-thousand-gallon stainless steel water tank – the whole nine yards. But by the time I gutted it, fixed it up so it's livable, furnished it, and got all the solar ironed out, I was into it another six figures, easy." She shrugged. "If I'd known it was going to turn end times, I would have invested even more."

"Ain't that the truth."

Ruby switched on two upright lamps and turned the overheads off. The room darkened considerably, and Eve looked up at the stuffed birds with a worried expression.

Ruby extended her hand to Eve. "Come on. Let me show you two around."

The little girl took her hand with a shy smile, and Ruby led her to an open doorway. "This is the kitchen area. Mostly what I grow up top, but also some stews and curries, plus whatever I can trade for in town." She stopped at the final word, a frown in place. "Those poor, poor people…"

Lucas lightly touched her shoulder to pull her out of it. She sighed in resignation and offered a pained smile.

"Anyhow, we have food," she finished.

Lucas eyed the workstation. "And a radio?"

"Yep. Antenna looks like junk rebar up top – half finished. But it works like a champ."

"No problems running the ventilation and refrigeration off solar?"

"No. I had the vent system modified so it's a low-power-draw unit, and it only cycles three times – twice during the day, when it runs off the panels, and once at night. With just me here, it's not like I use up all that much oxygen, but I figure it doesn't hurt to keep the batteries and the pumps working out. I draw less than a quarter kilowatt per hour, averaged out, during the day, and even less at night. Of course, that spikes when the fans activate or a compressor kicks in, but I have the systems set so there's no big jolt when they come on. More of a slow start."

"What happens when the solar batteries finally go?" Lucas asked. "Nothing lasts forever."

"Won't be doing much at night," Ruby answered with a small shrug. "That's fine. I can charge smaller batteries during the day and read at night. I'm not up that late, so it shouldn't change my busy lifestyle."

Lucas had to chuckle at the older woman's pluck. "As long as you keep the parties to a minimum."

"Bathrooms and sleeping areas are over here," Ruby said, leading them to the far end of the main room. "Four bedrooms, four baths. All big, too."

When the tour was over, they sat on two of the sofas, Eve next to Ruby, and sipped lemonade made from one of the lemon trees on the property. Lucas was again struck by the little girl's composure – a maturity far beyond her years. He leaned forward, set his drink on the coffee table, and eyed the older woman.

"Ruby, why buy this place? Don't take that the wrong way. But it's…unusual, isn't it?"

"I worked on the West Coast most of my life, Lucas, writing software and, later, running coding teams. I made enough money from a startup I was involved with to where I didn't really have to worry about much, but I never liked being around people a whole bunch." She gestured at the art on the walls. "Never saw much reason to interact, you know? I'm happy painting or writing code or reading or working with my herbs. Anyway, one day, I was coming back from the market at night, and I got mugged getting out of my car. I wasn't too badly hurt, but something snapped inside me, and I decided to get out of the city – get back to my roots, if you want to think about it like that."

"I can see the appeal."

"I grew up on a farm in South Dakota, so it wasn't like I didn't know how to plow or tend to animals or ride. So I rooted around for some properties and came across this on an auction site." She took a sip and shrugged. "Flew out, looked it over, and to make a long story short, I was the high bid. The only bid, probably. So I made it a project to redo it to my tastes. With international tensions being what they were even before the flu hit, I wasn't all that sure our leaders wouldn't do something catastrophic, so I figured I was killing two birds with one stone: setting up a compound where I wouldn't be bothered, and a fallout shelter in case the zombie apocalypse happened."

Lucas grunted understanding. Ruby smoothed Eve's hair and continued.

"Even before the collapse I didn't trust the government or the media. There were just too many official narratives I didn't buy, scenarios that made no sense. I had a gut feeling it couldn't end well, and when the feds started agitating to take our guns and do away with cash…I saw the writing on the wall. So I read every survival site out there, bought the equipment I'd need, and hunkered down – my motto has always been to plan for the worst and hope for the best." She took another swig of lemonade and placed her glass on the table near Lucas's. "I still had more I wanted to do when the flu hit, but you probably remember how those days were. I count myself lucky that I got the propane filled before people stopped going to work. Even before the grid went down and they filtered the Internet, I could see it coming, like a slow-motion train wreck. I was lucky I'm a paranoid old fool, I guess."

"Not so paranoid," Lucas corrected.

She sighed. "No, apparently not. I always suspected something big would happen to reset the system. I mean, if you know how money works, you know as it was set up, it was unsustainable. It was already coming apart at the edges, just waiting for a catalyst."

"What?" Eve asked, brow crinkling at the word.

"Something that would push the whole house of cards over," Ruby replied.

Lucas nodded approval. "Pretty smart lady, I'd say. No wonder Hal liked you."

Ruby stared off at one of her paintings. "He was a remarkable man. He's one of the only people I ever showed around here."

Lucas looked surprised. "He never told me."

"No. That wasn't his way. He was a man of honor, and he kept confidences." Ruby's eyes locked on Lucas's. "You are too, Lucas. I see much of him in you."

Lucas stood, suddenly uncomfortable sitting. "Not feeling very honorable right about now."

"What do you plan to do, Lucas?" Ruby asked, her tone quiet.

"They're not going to get away with it."

She considered him. "No. I don't expect they will."

Ruby rose and held her hand out to Eve. "Ready for a bath, young lady?"

Eve nodded. "Okay."

"Water's a little cold, but not too bad."

"I'm used to cold."

Ruby led Eve to her bedroom, leaving Lucas to his demons. He walked around the big vault, eyeing the paintings and stuffed birds. The art was abstract and colorful, and the birds so realistic they seemed alive. He was beyond tired, the fatigue so profound his bones ached. The day's events had commanded all his reserves, leaving him emotionally and physically bankrupt. He wanted more than anything to ride off, find those responsible for his grandfather's death and the massacre at the town, and give them a strong dose of their own medicine – no more mercy offered than they'd shown their victims.

But doing so now would be stupid, and he knew it. He needed sleep. Tango did, too.

There was always tomorrow to smite the wicked, and he would be more than happy to act as the instrument of their destruction.

His thoughts turned to Sierra. He needed to find her and, if possible, rescue her – although for all he knew, she was already dead. Either way, the cartel would be a bloody smudge in the dirt by the time he was done with them. He'd see to that.

Which reminded him – he needed to reach Duke and warn him.

Assuming he was alive.

"Ruby?" he called as he walked toward her bedroom.

"Just a second, Lucas. We're almost done."

Several minutes later they emerged, Eve swaddled in a too-large robe, her hair glistening with moisture and her enormous blue eyes sleepy. Ruby's expression was troubled.

"What?" Lucas asked.

Ruby raised Eve's left arm and pointed to it with her free hand. "Her bracelet. There's no obvious way to get it off, and when I took a harder look at it, I don't think it's just jewelry."

"I'm not supposed to take it off," Eve said with a shake of her curly locks.

"She kind of freaked out when I tried," Ruby said.

Lucas knelt until he was eye level with Eve. "What do you mean? Who told you not to take it off?"

Fear flashed across her face. "Them."

"Well, they're not here, so you don't have to follow any stupid rules," Ruby declared, and practically dragged the little girl to her workstation. The older woman sat down, slid a drawer open, and removed a pair of Fiskars scissors.

Eve shook her head mutely, but Ruby ignored her and sliced through the hard black plastic. When the bracelet came off, Eve practically burst into tears.

Ruby shook her head. "None of that. See? Nothing happened. No reason to cry." She studied the bracelet closely and then set it down on the tabletop. "You ever taste dried apricots?"

Eve shook her head, unconvinced.

"They're like candy," Lucas said.

"Candy?" Eve tried.

"Like the best thing you ever tasted," Ruby assured her, completely serious.

Eve's curiosity surfaced. "Really?"

"Yes. And I have some." Ruby gave Lucas a sidelong glance and bent down to give Eve a hug. "And you can have a few, since you've been so brave today."

Lucas turned the bracelet over in his hand as Ruby and Eve padded to the kitchen, and held it up to the light, close to his face. He could see that there was a thin copper core in the center of the rubberized plastic, and was considering cutting it apart when Ruby returned with a munching Eve. Ruby saw his intent clearly and gave him a single shake of her head.

"Let's get Eve to bed."

"Sounds like a plan."

Eve looked up at him. "Are you going to be right next door?"

"Of course, and Ruby will be in the room beside you. You won't be alone."

She stared at the nearest bird, an owl with wings spread and its claws extended, simulating a landing. "Are there any of those?"

Ruby laughed. "No. Never got around to decorating it. Why, you want one to keep you company?"

Eve shook her head so hard beads of water flew from her hair, and spoke in a small voice. "No, thank you."

When Ruby returned, any trace of good humor was gone from her eyes. "You take a hard look at it?"

Lucas nodded. "Yes. Looks like a wire inside."

"I've seen those before. They were using them on prisoners before the collapse."

"What is it?"

"Tracking device. Probably emits a signal on a radio frequency that can be pinpointed within a mile or so."

"Tracking…" Lucas repeated, and scowled at the bauble. "We need to destroy it."

Ruby slid another drawer open. "No. It could also contain information. Some of them did. All the soldier's vital stats. Blood type, allergies, service history."

"They were ambushed in the middle of nowhere by Raiders. Those idiots don't have the capability to track their own behinds, much less a bracelet." He stared at the black vinyl envelope in her hand. "What's that?"

"An RFID-blocking wallet. It's a kind of Faraday cage. I used to use it for my passport and credit cards, to prevent anyone from reading the RFID chips, but it will stop a transmitter, assuming this has one, which I'm betting is the case."

"Faraday cage?"

"Like in a microwave, to prevent the radiation from escaping. Same thing."

"Oh."

"Of course, being three stories below ground and surrounded by high-density concrete and steel will also work."

Lucas nodded. "How about a cave?"

"Same principle."

"Doesn't the bracelet require a power source? And how would it work? I mean, I understand that there are still satellites working, but don't the signals have to be calibrated or something by a ground station?"

"I read about them. They have tiny batteries that will go for a decade." Ruby paused. "And like I said, this wouldn't require a satellite – just a receiver that was tuned to the same frequency. You're thinking of something different."

Lucas's face hardened. "We should destroy it."

"There's been enough destruction for one day." Ruby slid the bracelet into the wallet and pocketed it.

Lucas didn't protest. He looked to Eve's partially open door. "Does she have a tattoo? On her upper arm?"

Ruby nodded slowly. "An eye. How did you know?"

Lucas's eyes narrowed and he retrieved his lemonade glass. He drained it and handed it to Ruby.

"I just did."

Chapter 26

The muffled creak of his door opening woke Lucas from his deep sleep, and light streamed through the doorway. He groggily checked his watch – it was three a.m., and he'd been asleep for six hours. Ruby's halo of wild gray hair announced her presence before she spoke in a low voice.

"The motion detector triggered. Someone's here."

Lucas sat up as he came fully awake. "Could it be an animal? The horses?"

"No. I have them set inside the building up top. Someone was in there, and they found the hatch. There's a contact alarm on the rim."

Lucas was already pulling on his shirt. "What do we do?"

"The blast door should hold them off. Unless they've got a plasma torch. Or some pretty serious explosives and can blow the lock."

"We can't just sit around while they figure out how to cut off our air."

"I'm not suggesting that." She looked away. "Finish dressing while I get Eve up."

Lucas was waiting for them when Ruby emerged with the little girl.

"They must have tracked us here with the bracelet," he said.

"Probably," Ruby agreed.

Lucas frowned in thought. "But if it's the same group that razed the town...we passed them last night. Why didn't they know we were there?"

"Depends on how the chip is programmed. Could be intermittent, transmitting only every couple of hours to conserve battery time." Ruby patted her pocket. "If that was the case, you simply got lucky."

"Some luck." Lucas eyed Eve. "Good morning." He turned back to Ruby. "So what's the plan?"

Another alarm chirped from the workstation. Ruby blanched. "That was fast."

"More bad news?"

"That's the motion detector outside the blast door. They're inside now."

"But you said the door would hold."

"I said it *should*. But I've been wrong before." She looked around the big room wistfully and then nodded. "All right. I've got a bug-out bag with some basics in it. Lucas, grab your stuff."

"Why?"

"One of the nice things about these bunkers is they came equipped with an escape tunnel."

Lucas didn't need to be told twice. He strapped on his M4 and went to retrieve the saddle and bags, and was back in moments. Eve watched him wordlessly. Ruby reappeared with her shotgun and an overstuffed backpack, and shrugged it on.

"The tunnel's through the kitchen," she said, and made for the doorway, Lucas and Eve right behind her. She opened the pantry, fumbled with a bolt, and then another heavy blast door materialized behind the wooden panel. Her key opened the industrial lock, and she guided them through before pausing in the doorway.

"What are you waiting for?" Lucas asked.

"I need to arm the security system."

"I thought it was already armed."

"No, these are for motion detectors inside the bunker. Any movement, the system gives you half a minute to enter a code, and if you don't, it activates."

"And then what?"

"Then, hopefully you've made peace with your maker, because you'll be meeting him shortly."

Lucas appeared incredulous. "Really?"

"I told you I was a crazy old lady."

"Crazy like a fox."

Ruby depressed a button, entered a four-digit code, and then pushed the door closed. It sealed with a solid *thunk*. She pulled a foot-long LED flashlight from her bag and twisted it on, and the tunnel flooded with light. "This way," she said.

"Where does this let out?"

"About seventy-five yards from the building. The hatch is disguised as a boulder. Very lifelike."

"What if some of them stayed above ground?"

"We'll cross that bridge when we come to it." Ruby's tone left no room for discussion, so they marched the length of the concrete passage until they reached a spiral staircase that led up into the gloom.

"Can you get your saddle and bags up that without a problem?" she asked.

He considered the steps. "Should be able to."

"Then you go first. There's a small room at the top, with a ladder that leads to the surface."

"Any way to see whether someone's standing near the boulder?"

"At one time there was a camera system, but it's long dead. Prehistoric. Thing was the size of an air compressor. I never got around to changing it out."

"Too bad."

"One problem at a time."

Lucas mounted the stairs. His gear grew heavier with each step, as though the earth was conspiring against him making it to the surface, but he eventually emerged onto a platform and switched on his penlight. Rusted steel rungs continued up the far wall to a hatch above. He set the saddle and saddlebags down and waited.

Ruby's footsteps echoed up the stairway, with Eve's less pronounced sandaled footfalls a fast contretemps behind her. The older woman's unruly silver mane rose through the gap and then she was standing beside him, breathing heavily, Eve on her tail.

"I don't suppose you have night vision goggles?" he whispered to her.

"As I said before, I didn't get a chance to finish outfitting the place."

"Once I'm up by the hatch, I'm going to shut my light off so my eyes can adjust. Stay completely still. Understand, Eve?"

The little girl nodded, and Lucas could see that she was taking the situation seriously – oddly understanding for a child, he thought – although what did he really know of children? He turned to Ruby. "If the coast is clear, I'll let you know, and we'll trade places while I haul my gear up."

"Lead the way," Ruby said.

Lucas hauled himself up the rungs, flakes of rust crumbling in his hands, and then shouldered the hatch up. The hinges groaned, and he winced at the sound. Once it was open, he ascended the rest of the way, ending up in a space six feet square, with no more than four feet of headroom and another hatch above, with four steps leading to it.

He extinguished the flashlight and paused, listening for anything that might signal someone nearby. After a long thirty seconds, he moved to the hatch and felt along the rim for the twist handle he'd seen. He slowly turned the lever, sucking in his breath as the latch scraped. When it was open, he unslung the M4, took a deep breath, and pushed the hatch upward a few inches with his shoulder so he could peek through the gap.

Only to see nothing but high grass.

He stood with the hatch ajar, ears straining, cursing the ringing that was the legacy of all the shooting over the last days, and when he didn't hear anything, pushed the hatch higher and, climbing the steps, higher still until the fiberglass boulder above it was lying on its side, the hatch pointing straight up at the night sky.

Lucas stepped into the open air and peered through the rifle's night vision scope. The field appeared empty, but he could make out at least twenty horses by the shabby decoy building. When he was sure that there were no guards with the animals, he ducked back below and hurried down the rungs.

"It'll take two trips to carry all this. I'll be right back," he murmured, his voice low.

Ruby offered a whispered assent, and he hoisted his saddle and carried it to the antechamber, and then returned for his saddlebags.

He leaned into Ruby. "Follow me up."

The old woman took Eve by the hand and showed her how to climb the ladder, and hauled herself up behind her. The girl scrambled up with the ease of youth, while Ruby's limbs complained with every rung. When they were crowded into the small room, ducked low, Lucas eyed them both in the dim starlight. "Eve, stick with Ruby."

"Okay."

"Ruby, you know this area better than I do. Make for the fastest route away from the bunker, and I'll follow you." He stopped, remembering their earlier conversation. "You said the acreage is surrounded by a chain-link fence?"

"I said it was when I bought it. I tore down most of it. Hated it."

"Not a sound once we're outside – noise travels on a still night," Lucas warned. He took another look outside and then angled his head toward them. "Ready?"

They both nodded, and he took the steps two at a time. Once above ground, he crouched low. Ruby and Eve emerged, and Ruby pointed to her right and said in a soft whisper, "Over there."

She moved surprisingly fast. Lucas remained behind, watching the building in case anyone appeared. When he couldn't see Ruby any longer, he snicked out of the corner of his mouth twice and waited.

Nothing.

"Come on, Tango. Listen up," he muttered, and then snicked again.

When Tango didn't show himself, Lucas abandoned hope that the horse would hear him and dragged his saddle through the tall grass, carrying the saddlebags over one shoulder while carrying the M4 in his free hand. He stopped to snick again every twenty yards, and as he was nearing a clump of tall bushes, a huge dark shape materialized out of the night and neared him with a whinny. Lucas's smile came unbidden to his lips, and he whispered Tango's name as the stallion drew abreast of him.

Lucas had Tango's saddle pad and bridle out of the bags in moments and strapped the gear onto the horse while watching the area by the bunker, his Remington in the scabbard hanging from the horn. After a quick inspection of his work, he took the reins and walked Tango to where Ruby and Eve were crouched in the field.

"You found him!" Eve said.

"He found me. Ruby, where to from here?"

"I've got a storm cellar about a mile from the main building. I use it to store bottling equipment for my herbs and a few odds and ends. It's not much, but it'll do in a fix for up to a week. Two rooms, no frills. But it's invisible unless you know where to look."

"That sounds awfully good right now."

"We keep our heads down, we should be fine."

"You still have that damn bracelet?" Lucas asked.

"In my pocket."

"Are you a hundred percent sure it can't give us away?"

"Absolutely. It's harmless as long as it's in the case. Probably even out of it now that the cable's been cut."

Lucas nodded. "Hope you know what you're doing."

Ruby managed a smile. "Even a broken clock…"

They walked through the darkness, Tango by Lucas's side with Eve in the saddle, and made it to the storm cellar in under an hour. The night was quiet around them as Lucas helped Ruby unlock the cellar door, her energy having faded somewhere back in the field. As promised, the interior of the cellar was stark, and they did a quick inspection to ensure there were no unwanted reptilian visitors with Ruby's flashlight, the bright beam dampened through a sheer cloth once the outer door was closed.

A detonation vibrated the ground, and then two more in rapid succession, and they rushed to the doorway and Lucas eased it open. There was nothing to see, no fireball, but the corners of Ruby's mouth pulled downward.

She looked to Lucas. "Well, that's that. Surprised they got in, but that's why you always have a backup."

"Any chance of survivors?"

"I doubt it."

"What did you rig it with?"

"I had eight portable propane tanks – the five footers. I kept each ten percent full, just in case."

"Nice. And to detonate them?"

"Blasting cap and enough TNT from a miner friend to vaporize the whole shebang. Electronic trigger. A baby could have wired it up."

His eyebrows rose. "Must have been quite a blast."

"In an enclosed space like that, nobody's walking away from it."

Lucas regarded her with newfound respect. "Hope you're right."

Her profile looked sharp in the moonlight, her features hard planes, and he had a sudden flash of Ruby as a younger woman, fiercely smart and independent.

She exhaled audibly and stared into the field.

"I am."

Chapter 27

Paco Espinoza Rivera, also known as Loco, forked more scrambled eggs into his mouth as a tall man with elaborate facial tattoos and a puckered scar running from above his milky left eye to his upper lip approached the circular wooden table at which the cartel kingpin was sitting and pulled up a chair. Loco, who had created the eponymous cartel as a teenager, was thirty-six years old, a sociopath who had killed more men by the time he was seventeen as a gang hit man than he had fingers.

He'd spent time in Chula Vista and East San Diego, building support for his group with the gangs there and, with his contacts on the other side of the border, had established an informal collection of vicious lowlifes who'd claimed El Paso as their turf. He'd been arrested countless times, but no charges had ever stuck, what with witnesses disappearing or refusing to testify.

After the collapse, when El Paso had erupted in an all-out turf war between more powerful interests, he and a group of enterprising gang members had moved east and settled in Pecos, which small enough to control and defend but large enough to support his aspirations. Over time he'd taken over the town, the population a fragment of its earlier size after the flu and starvation had worked their magic, and Pecos was now owned and operated by his group, which numbered several hundred strong – or had, until they'd lost a quarter of their membership in the last two days from disastrous operations to the north.

The tall man was Garret, a representative of the Crew, who'd arrived with a small group of men at the start of the week to work a cooperation deal with the Locos – they would provide the muscle in recovering the woman and girl, and in return would keep the spoils of their raids. They wanted trade assistance from Houston as well as protection from the Crew cartel while retaining their autonomy.

Loco had jumped at the deal, but was now having second thoughts. Some of his best fighters had died taking the town, and he'd gotten word only minutes ago that the entire war party that had gone after the child when Garret's tracking device had pinpointed her location had been vaporized in a powerful explosion.

The report had come in via two-way radio from the site to a waiting messenger with another two-way to the transmitter that the Locos controlled in their headquarters at the Pecos courthouse. The operator had demanded details twice, unable to believe that all but one lookout who'd been posted above ground had been killed.

"Garret, want some huevos?" Loco offered. "Coffee? Freeze-dried instant, but it's not terrible. Never goes bad."

"Don't mind if I do."

Loco snapped his fingers, and a short woman with the face of a prizefighter ducked into the kitchen to prepare breakfast for the newcomer. Garret watched the cartel boss munch his eggs like a farmhand, his smacking as loud as a pig chowing slop, one arm on the table to protect his food – the unconscious posture a giveaway of his time behind bars, where everyone ate that way to avoid another prisoner making a grab for it.

The woman brought a steaming cup of coffee and a plate piled high with scrambled eggs, and Garret picked at them as he waited to hear why the gang leader had summoned him.

"We heard back on your girl," Loco said, as though discussing the weather.

"And?" Garret asked.

"Didn't go so good, man."

Garret stopped eating. "How exactly didn't it go so good?"

"Complications."

"Like what?"

"We lost everyone. Place blew up." Loco dropped his fork onto his plate and clapped his hands together with a manic expression, his eyes huge. "Boom! Like that." Loco laughed.

"And the girl?"

Loco shrugged. "*No sabe, kemosabe.* My boy thinks it was a booby trap, and if he's right, she'll turn up alive sooner or later, right? You got that scanner. We just got to wait."

Garret fought to maintain his composure. "I told you that she was to be taken alive."

Loco sat back, a dangerous expression replacing his grin. "You *asked* she be taken alive, homey. Not dissing you, but nobody tells Loco nothin'. Not on my turf. Don't step to me like that or there gonna be problems, you understand what I'm saying?"

"She's very important to my boss. He would be…disappointed…if she got hurt, or died, while in your territory."

"Yeah, well, I can't do nothin' about all that until we know more. But what I do know is we need to talk about things. I lost fifty men on this goose chase. Didn't sign up for that."

No, Loco had signed up for a walk in the park, Garret thought. It was inconceivable that fifty fighters were dead; but then again, nobody had factored in the mystery man the woman had told them about. He was an unknown variable, but things had gone south since he'd gotten involved, and Garret was unsure how to best proceed. What he did know was that he didn't want to have to report to Magnus that they'd lost the girl again, much less that she'd died. If he did, he might as well slash his own wrists while he made the call, because he'd be a dead man walking.

"I hear you made quite a score on weapons and ammo in Loving. Got yourself a bunch of fine horses, too. Seems to me you've done pretty well," Garret observed, returning to his meal.

Loco's stare was gangsta hard. "We coulda done that anytime. Way I see it, they was just holding all that for us. I was fine with it like that."

Garret resisted the urge to mad dog Loco. The little puke had no idea who he was dealing with. But Garret had other fish to fry, so he held back, absently tracing the scar on his face, a souvenir from an attempted shanking by a rival. The man had blinded him and stabbed him six times, but that hadn't stopped Garret from beating him to death, using his head as a hammer against a cell-block wall. If Garret had been so disposed, he could have reached across the table and offed the punk with no more effort than snapping a chicken's neck, but he wasn't there to stir up trouble.

He needed the girl.

"Sounds like you have some ideas about how to even things out, huh?" Garret said, choosing diplomacy over brute force.

"That's right. What can you do for me, man?"

Garret made an offer: homemade methamphetamines Magnus cooked up to keep his troops alert. More advanced weaponry. Training in explosives for ten men Loco could hand select and send to Houston.

They eventually arrived at a deal. Garret's relief was hollow, though, and the eggs tasted like cardboard in his mouth as he finished his food. A straightforward exercise had turned into a major problem for him, and if he didn't stop the bleeding soon, Magnus would express his displeasure in an unmistakable way – and then Garret would be replaced by one of the warlord's other lieutenants.

Garret couldn't let that happen.

He would return to interrogating the woman to see what else she knew. He believed she'd told him the truth, but with women you could never be sure. He didn't trust the female of the species, likely a byproduct of his mother abandoning him when he was three, and he'd had considerable difficulty controlling the black cloud of rage that had threatened to overcome him as he was questioning her. He'd wanted to hurt her in ways she couldn't even imagine when she eyed him with her superior glare, but that wasn't his mission.

At least, not yet.

Magnus might decide to reward him when he was successful.

Garret knew exactly what he would ask for.

Chapter 28

Ruby hummed as she brewed herbal tea over a butane stove while Lucas and Eve slumbered. She'd awakened with first light and hadn't been able to get back to sleep. The prior day's events had so disturbed her psyche that her rest had been filled with horrifying nightmares, each more awful than the last, and she wondered if that was how she'd spend the remainder of her sleeping hours on earth. So many innocents, many of them her friends…

She was as realistic as anyone, but she'd been sure that this many years after the worst of it, things were improving. She had to believe that, or what was the point of going on? If humanity was nothing more than evil running roughshod over good, what hope did anyone have? But the town's sacking had been worse than anything she could have imagined, and when she closed her eyes, her thoughts were filled with the screams of children, the dying moans of the old, the desperate entreaties of the panicked.

No stranger to history, she knew that what had happened barely registered on the human scale of suffering. The same had happened to the Native Americans, with villages eradicated right down to the chickens. And the Mexicans had done that much, and worse, to the white settlers in Texas, who'd returned the favor by embarking on campaigns on the other side of the Rio Grande and slaughtering anything that moved. Misery was the fuel that powered the engine of humanity, and she couldn't think of a time when one group wasn't butchering another over political or nationalistic differences, religious disagreements, or when all else failed, the color of their skin. No, this was nothing new; but knowledge wasn't the same as experience, and after seeing her fellow travelers claw their way back from the abyss and build a tiny slice of civilization from the ashes, she'd had hope. Foolishly, she now knew.

Lucas stirred and groaned in his sleep, and Ruby shook her head. That poor man had lost everything. As had she, but he was haunted by ghosts she couldn't fathom, whereas she was already thinking about how to start over – and where. Her optimism was completely unwarranted, but her faith in God and in her own abilities was strong, and even if she didn't understand everything about what transpired on this earth, she was confident she would persevere.

She looked over at the girl, and her heart melted. So young, so pure, Eve radiated goodness and possibility and hope. If there was evil so dark it blotted out the sun, then it was surely countered by good so obvious and promising.

But Lucas? He was an enigma. The one thing she was certain of was that he wanted revenge – thirsted for it – and would exact it in a terrible manner. He was only one man, but he had an energy, an inner fire that burned white hot, and she didn't envy those who'd incurred his wrath.

He shifted on the old horse blanket he was using as a mattress as she poured her first cup of tea of the morning, and then sat up as she stirred the mixture.

"Good morning," she said.

"Morning." He checked his watch and yawned. "I needed that."

"I figured you did."

He stood and stretched his arms over his head. "Any sign of the bad guys?"

"Fortunately not."

Lucas regarded Eve's sleeping form. "I'm thinking I'll head out this morning. Can I ask you to watch her while I'm gone?"

"Of course. Where are you going?"

"Stop by the ranch and see if I can salvage anything, and then…south."

"Can I talk you out of it?"

"Not hardly."

"Didn't think so." She sighed. "I've got some honey you can put in the tea if you want. And later I'm planning to do some work with my garden. I have a feeling I'll want as much to barter with as I can carry."

"Nobody to trade with here anymore," Lucas observed.

"No. And now that I don't have a home…"

He moved to the door and stepped outside. "Nice day for a ride."

"I knew you'd say that. You really think you can take on the entire Pecos cartel by yourself?"

"Doesn't seem like a fair fight, does it? Maybe I should wait till they can get reinforcements."

Ruby smiled in spite of herself. "Do you have a plan?"

"I've avoided the place since the collapse, but I still remember the layout. Figure I'll stop in at Duke's and see what I can learn, and then make it up as I go along."

She frowned. "Not much of a plan, Lucas. No offense, but you can't just ride in with guns a-blazing."

"I've got the broad strokes. Just need to finesse the details."

Half an hour later, Lucas was packed and mounted up. He said his goodbyes and rode off, Tango refreshed after his night's rest and full of energy. Ruby and Eve watched him go, and when he was out of sight, the little girl tilted her face up toward the older woman.

"Is he coming back?"

Ruby thought about all the possible answers and settled on one a five-year-old would accept without questioning.

"I hope so."

Chapter 29

The ranch was as deserted as a graveyard at midnight, and Lucas wasted no time on sentimental strolls down memory lane, sticking to his agenda, painfully aware of minutes ticking by. Pecos was a good thirty-five miles from Duke's, and he was many hours away from the trading post, so he was already racing the clock and losing.

He first scrounged the last of his grandfather's white lightning and packed six jars wrapped in cloth into his saddlebags. He next did a hasty search of the house and was relieved that the floor compartment beneath his bed hadn't been discovered. In it was a Walther PPK in an ankle holster and a spare magazine, as well as a hundred-round box of ammo for the M4. Finally, he withdrew a portable solar panel with a battery charger and three spares for the night vision scope. Those would be priceless if he was forced to stay on the road for an extended period.

Reality slammed into him with the force of a blow. Of course he'd be traveling for the foreseeable future. He couldn't return to the ranch and live as he had – without anyone to trade with, he'd eventually run out of staples, and he couldn't very well stay awake around the clock to stave off any assault attempts. So what would he do?

Lucas concentrated on filling a sack with the remaining dry fruit and jerky in the back of the pantry, packed two bags of white rice into his saddlebags, filled his empty water bottles from the well, and was in and out in little more than ten minutes. He stopped at Hal's grave and offered a silent prayer, and then made for Tango, who seemed as anxious to be clear of the ranch as he was.

He rode all day and was relieved when he arrived at the trading post by dusk and saw Aaron minding the gate. Lucas waved to him, and he opened the barrier to allow him to pass. The cavity from the grenade blast had been filled in with fresh dirt, and if Lucas hadn't been there during the attack, other than the bullet pocks peppering the wall, he'd never have known anything had happened.

Duke called out to him from the main building as he tied Tango to a hitching post by the water trough. "Look what the cat dragged in," he said with a grin.

"You don't know the half of it. Got a few minutes?"

"For you? Always."

Duke led him into the house, where a swarthy man Lucas had never met was sharpening a bowie knife on a whetstone. The man looked up at him and Lucas took his measure – late twenties, already whip-hardened by life, probably ex-military.

"Lucas, this here's Slim," Duke said. "He's the new man."

Lucas touched the brim of his hat. Slim nodded wordlessly and continued sharpening the knife, the scrape of steel against the stone as rhythmic as a clock.

"You eaten?" Duke asked.

"Not for a spell."

"Well, come help me in the kitchen and we can talk. What's on your mind?"

Lucas waited until they were out of earshot to recount the story of the ranch and town. When he was done, Duke's ruddy complexion was gray.

"You sure it was cartel?" he asked softly.

"Oh, yeah. Tattoos made that pretty obvious."

Duke stirred a pot of fish stew with a wooden spoon, the only light now the lamp in the living room. "What are you going to do?"

"I need intel. Anything you can give me on Pecos. Where the cartel's holed up, what their numbers are, any habits."

"I'll tell you everything I know, but it's precious little." Duke didn't have to ask Lucas what he intended to do – the look in his eyes made that obvious.

"I'd appreciate it. I'll also need a fresh horse I can push hard. I'll leave Tango as collateral. And as many rounds of 5.56mm as you can spare."

"I've got some 5.56mm M855A1 ball that fell off a truck. About three hundred rounds. Might want to use that until you run out – more stopping power with that popgun you carry around than civilian ammo."

"I've used it before. I'll take it all."

Duke nodded and considered his face. "Stretch between here and Pecos isn't safe at night. Stay, and hit it at dawn."

"I expect you're right." Lucas paused. "Still got that night vision monocle?"

"I might. Why? You want to borrow it?"

"If it works and has a decent battery, I'll buy it. I've got six jars of lightning for your trouble."

Duke shook his head. "Which will all be here when you get back. Just take the NV gear and return it in good shape."

"Don't want charity, Duke."

"It isn't. I never properly repaid you for saving our bacon."

"I did no such thing."

"One of the guys you shot had four more grenades. That would have been it, Lucas, if you hadn't bagged him."

"Did he have cartel tats?"

"Oh, plenty of ink, but didn't see any of the Loco's markings. Then again, that doesn't mean much. Only the original members have 'em."

"You'd think they'd have known better than to try to take you."

"Yet they almost did. Which is why I'm feeling all generous. Enjoy it while it lasts."

Lucas looked over his shoulder. "Where'd you find the new guy?"

"Doug's buddy. Lives west of here a day's ride. Big family, meaner than pit vipers. He wanted more stimulation than home offers. So now he's in the big leagues."

"You tell him what happened to Clem?"

Duke's eyes hardened. "All he cared about was there was a vacancy."

Dinner was quiet. Lucas wasn't predisposed to talk, and the others showed no interest in listening. The men limited their interactions to requests for more stew and to pass the salt, which Lucas was fine with. When they'd cleared their plates, Duke showed him to a guest room, and after tending to Tango and loading a dozen magazines with the military-spec ammo and stowing them in his saddlebags, he lay down in the dark, plate holder still cinched tight, M4 with night vision scope beside him like a lover, safety off, and the Kimber on the nightstand within easy reach.

His rest was uneasy, filled with gruesome imagery, and he woke multiple times with a cry on his lips and bathed in sweat. The final time, an hour before dawn, it had been Sierra's face he'd awakened to, her eyes accusatory, as though castigating him for letting her down.

He hadn't been able to sleep from that point on, and instead busied himself preparing for his journey. Duke had offered a capable steed, a three-year-old stallion he'd assured Lucas could make the trip to Pecos in a single long day, though the ride would be a stretch for even the fittest of his species. Lucas carried his tack to the barn, where the horse allowed Lucas to outfit him without protest, and Lucas was finishing up when he spun, Kimber in hand, at a sound behind him.

Duke was watching him from the barn entry, his hair askew. "Got ants in your pants, huh?"

Lucas nodded. "No point in wearing out my welcome."

Duke held up the night vision monocle. "Figured you could use this."

Lucas approached him and took it. "I'll bring it back."

"I hope so. Got kind of attached to it."

Duke had filled Lucas in on the cartel's strength, and Lucas was under no illusions about what he was facing. Duke had suggested posing as a trader when he arrived. Pecos, for all its criminality, served as an important hub for those in the area. Lucas could blend in with the rough crowd as well as any, and his weapons wouldn't draw a second glance from the cartel enforcers; the traders who chose to brave the city's perils were normally armed and extremely dangerous, and military weapons were a common sight on the streets.

Duke had told him that the cartel was headquartered in the courthouse, across the street from the US Marshals' former headquarters, which Lucas was familiar with from trips there with prisoners in his past life. The courthouse was a formidable brick edifice in the original downtown area and would be hell to infiltrate, he knew.

"There's a bar where many of the traders hang a few blocks away. Think the one from *Star Wars*, only worse," Duke said. "That's where I'd start." He mentioned the name of the watering hole.

Lucas nodded. "Appreciate the ammo and the rest. Especially the hospitality."

Duke hesitated. "Sorry about Hal. He'll be missed."

"Me too." Lucas eyed his watch and walked over to where Tango was housed. "Be good, old friend. I'll be back. Catch up on your beauty rest, eat too much, maybe make friends with some of Duke's mares." Lucas turned to Duke. "Take care of him."

"Like my own child."

Lucas hesitated. "If I don't make it back…"

"You will."

"Yeah, but if not…hold this for me. Seeing what a gold bug you are." Lucas handed the trader a small suede bag cinched tight with a drawstring. "Twenty ounces. Use it to take care of my friend Ruby if she comes looking for me, which she will if I don't show up within a week or so."

Duke's eyes widened. "Twenty! I'll kill you myself for that kind of loot."

Lucas managed a sad smile. "Got to stand in line." He led his new horse from the stall. "What's his name?"

"Gunner."

"Fitting."

An uncomfortable silence settled over the barn. Duke offered his hand, and Lucas shook it.

"Give 'em hell, Lucas."

Lucas's eyes were cold anthracite in the predawn glow as he escorted Gunner from the barn and mounted. "Count on it."

Damp earth scented the breeze on the trail south as the trading post receded into the distance. Lucas calculated that with rest stops he would be in Pecos after nightfall, assuming that Duke's assurances about Gunner were accurate. The chestnut stallion covered ground at a reasonable clip, and the day passed without event, no one else on the trail that paralleled the highway. In the distance, the occasional ruins of a ranch house or farm stood in dry fields turned a fallow beige, sacrificed to looters or Raiders.

He could make out Pecos two hours before he arrived, the distant city's bonfires lighting the horizon with bright tongues of yellow and orange. As he drew near, he was forced to navigate the main highway for the final two miles. At an overpass above the train tracks that marked the boundary of the city, a cartel gunman greeted him from a fortified guard post with the barrel of an AK.

"Where do you think you're going?" the man growled.

"Got some trading to do, and need a place to bunk for the night."

"What you got to swap?"

"Ammo."

"Yeah? How much?"

"Plenty. You going to let me through, or do I head elsewhere?"

The gunman considered Lucas carefully and then motioned with his rifle. "Let's see what you have."

Lucas sighed and reached behind him for one of his saddlebags.

"Easy," the Loco cautioned.

"I've got ten STANAG thirty-round mags of 5.56mm to trade. Like new. Only used by Grandma on Sundays."

That drew a laugh. "I'll bet."

"Want to see them, or are we done?"

The thug lowered his weapon. "There's a place down that road that rents out rooms. Cost you five rounds per night. Used to be a motel."

"Safe?"

Another laugh. "Assuming you know how to use your gun, it should be."

Lucas nodded. "I do. Where can I get some grub and a drink?"

"Couple joints downtown. You'll see 'em. Only places that are open."

Lucas rode on into Pecos. As he approached the courthouse, he heard music blaring from its grounds, which answered any questions about whether the cartel had figured out solar power. Shouts and whoops drifted down the boulevard, and as he drew closer, he could see a pair of gunmen camped in the parking lot. The interior ground floor of the building was illuminated, and he could make out a large foyer that had been converted into a bar, from which rap boomed with bombastic insistence, at least fifty men inside yelling at one another over the music.

He continued past without slowing, the guards' eyes burning into his back as he guided his horse down the street, and two blocks further along he spied one of the restaurants, a half dozen empty plastic tables outside on the sidewalk indicating business wasn't good. He stopped at a storefront next door, whose picture window and door had been destroyed, and tied Gunner to a wrecked pickup truck's door handle before moving to one of the tables.

The meal was tasteless gruel served in tortillas, and he wolfed down four of them, opting for his own water rather than what was offered, and paid with ammunition. After eating, he watered Gunner and then walked the horse down a dark street that ran parallel to the courthouse, where one of the bars Duke had told him about was located. The shabby watering hole, whose façade was pocked with bullet holes, was identified by a sign over the door boasting a cigar-smoking rooster with a ten-gallon hat and six guns. He'd reached the Half-Cocked Saloon, which looked even worse than Duke had described.

Lucas tied Gunner off beside eight other horses and nodded to an old man sitting on a milk carton in the shadows, pistol in hand. "Watch my ride?"

"On the house, Señor," he said. "Although tips appreciated."

"What do you drink?"

The old Mexican gave him a toothless grin. "Anything."

Inside, the scene was as dangerous as any he'd ventured into since the collapse: a smattering of marauders, traders, and murderous-looking locals – but to Lucas's surprise, no obvious cartel members. He approached the bar and nodded to a rail-thin bald man who was staring at him like he planned to rob the place.

"What are you serving?" Lucas asked.

"Moonshine, tequila, home-brew beer."

"How cold's the beer?"

"Room temperature." The man named a price: three bottles for one round of ammo.

Lucas tossed one of the 9mm rounds he'd brought for barter on the bar. "Perfect."

He spent the next half hour nursing a beer that tasted like sweat socks, commiserating with a trader from San Antonio way who'd gotten a lousy deal on a pair of horses from a cartel buyer, milking him for information on the group's habits.

"They stick to their joint at the courthouse. Locos only. Keeps the murder rate down to something tolerable, according to the locals."

"Yeah? What do most of the locals do for a living?"

"Whatever the cartel tells them to."

"What about the people who don't go along?"

"They're all dead. Cartel made a point of exterminating them, going block by block. Of course, weren't many left after the bug got done with 'em. Hit hard here. But nothing like as bad as in the bigger towns."

"Yeah?" Lucas said, pretending interest.

"El Paso, Austin, San Antonio…you wouldn't recognize 'em. Tell you what, buddy, you ain't a believer in God, you'll believe in hell once you seen what I have."

"That bad, huh? I was in El Paso for a couple weeks after the flu hit. Got out when the power died."

"Just in time. Turned into a free-for-all. No border patrol to stop the beaners from crossing and killing anything that moved. Local gangs going nuts. No law, no army, nothing. A friend said that for a solid month, all you heard from sundown to sunup was shooting. Looters picked the place clean, raped anyone with a pulse, you name it. Once the food ran out, they turned on each other. Good riddance."

"What's it like now?"

"Divided between two Mexican cartels. Gun battles every day. Meth labs all over town. Still a trade for that. Some things never change."

"No sign of the government getting its act together?"

The trader's laugh was a dry hack. "What government? Ain't none. Although I heard rumors about D.C. having power. Probably, knowing how things work. They probably got champagne and hookers and AC while the country's starving. Ain't that how it always is?"

"Anywhere else?"

"Parts of Houston and Dallas, but only gang areas."

"You'd think people would have organized and taken their cities back by now."

The trader checked furtively around and lowered his voice. "That's dangerous talk there. The gangs are organized. They kill if you look at 'em wrong. Try to set up resistance, your kids get burned alive in front of you, and then your wife gets gang-raped, and then they skin you alive and drag you down the street until you're hamburger." The trader shook his head. "One thing to talk about standing up, another to do it. See that a few times, trust me, bruthah, you're not steppin' outta line."

"Just hard to believe."

The man smiled sadly. *"And it was granted to the one who sat on it to take peace from the earth, and that people should kill one another."* He took a sip from a shot glass half full of tequila. "That's the Good Book.

Revelation 6:3-4. Tells it all right there in black and white. This here's the end times. Just got to keep our heads down and wait for it all to play out."

The trader didn't know where the cartel kept its prisoners, and as he grew drunker and more morose, he gradually lost interest in any further discussion. Lucas detached and, sickened by the aroma of unwashed bodies and rancid sweat in the bar, carried his remaining two beers out to the old man and handed them to him.

"Where would be a good place to camp in town?" Lucas asked.

The old man studied him and shook his head. "I wouldn't."

"Anyplace safe to leave my horse?"

"All dangerous." The man looked to his left. "There's a lot down by the courthouse, maybe two blocks away, has some grass growing. Horse might like it. But I'd sleep with your eyes open."

Lucas nodded and, after checking his saddlebags to verify nothing had been filched, led Gunner toward the courthouse, a plan taking shape with every heavy step.

Chapter 30

After tying Gunner to a tree in the vacant lot, Lucas filled every available compartment of his plate holder with magazines and made for the cartel's clubhouse. He darted from building to building toward the rear of the courthouse, having verified that the disinterested sentries were only guarding the front on his ride by. He paused on the corner and noted through his binoculars that they were bored, playing cards and not paying attention to their surroundings, secure in the knowledge that they owned the town and that nobody posed any danger to them.

He hoped to leverage that complacency and make it work against them. His only advantage was surprise, and once he lost it, he would be a dead man unless he could force the cartel to play the game he had in mind. His chances weren't stellar, but he didn't care – he wanted blood for blood, and by his reckoning, a hundred of the cartel needed killing if it was to be an even score. Although preferably he could exterminate them all.

The only way he could see of inflicting maximum casualties was to blow up the building, but that wouldn't be easy. He had no explosives, there was no gas to ignite, and it was just him and a few guns.

But he would find a way.

He edged along an abandoned hulk on the final block, and when he was across the street from his target, he stood motionless in the shadows and studied the building through the NV monocle. Nothing moved, and from what he could tell, there was nobody minding the back side.

Lucas glanced at his watch. Closing in on midnight, and no lights were on except in the front area. The music from the festivities carried, reverberating off the brick buildings that surrounded him, which would further mask the sound of his entry – at least, that was his hope.

He lowered the NV scope, darted across the street, and moments later was at one of the ground-floor windows. Most had been broken out and were now boarded up, but several still held their glass, and it was one of these that he selected for his entry. He tried the frame, but it was locked. After scanning the area a final time, he withdrew his hunting knife from its sheath and slammed the metal handle base against the glass.

The pane shattered and collapsed into the building, and Lucas cringed at the sound. Not waiting to see whether he had attracted unwanted attention, he knocked out the fragments along the bottom that thrust upward like broken teeth and pulled himself through.

His boots crunched the glass on the floor as he made for the door. The room he found himself in was an administrative office that had obviously been sacked. At the door, he listened with his ear against the wood panel – hearing nothing, he pulled it open.

The hall was pitch black, and Lucas took cautious steps toward the stairs that led to the second floor, using the monocle to guide him. At the stairway, he paused at a noise from the far end of the corridor and ducked into the stairwell at the sound of a door opening. Pounding music from the foyer momentarily flooded the hall, accompanied by men's raucous laughter and yells, and then faded as the door closed.

A flashlight beam played along the floor and footsteps approached. Lucas gripped his knife and set the NV monocle on a step behind him as he waited for whoever was nearing to reach him. The hallway brightened as the flashlight drew even with the stairwell, and a wiry man with tattoos ringing his neck stepped into view, a pistol in hand, unaware of Lucas only a few feet away.

Lucas kicked the man's pistol hand hard enough to send the weapon clattering down the hall, and then clocked him in the temple with the heavy knife handle. The flashlight tumbled from the man's hand as his eyes rolled into his head, and Lucas dropped him with a left hook that nearly broke his jaw.

The gunman slumped to the floor, stunned, and Lucas sheathed the knife and scooped up the flashlight and pistol. He turned to where the thug lay on the floor and trained the man's Glock on his head.

"Get up. Nice and slow. Now," Lucas said menacingly.

The man struggled to rise, and Lucas motioned to the stairwell.

"Up the stairs. Come on," Lucas instructed.

The thug looked confused, but not alarmed, and Lucas wanted to keep him off balance until he could have a discussion in a more private area. He shined the light into the man's eyes, causing him to wince and twist away.

"Start walking or I pop a cap in your skull," Lucas warned.

"You a dead man," the man managed.

"We all go sometime," Lucas agreed. "Move."

The thug staggered up the steps, and Lucas snagged the monocle on the way up with his flashlight hand, his right steady as a rock holding the pistol. At the second floor, Lucas glanced down the hall and directed the man to one of the doors. "Inside," he said.

The man twisted the handle and sneered at Lucas. "Locked, homeboy."

"Try the next one."

He did, and the door opened. Lucas motioned with the flashlight. "Inside."

The man stepped into the dark room, and Lucas followed six feet behind him. As the man was turning around, Lucas clobbered him again, this time with the base of the aluminum flashlight, and then closed the door behind him.

Four minutes later Lucas exited the room. The man had told him what he needed to know before Lucas dispatched him, the sharp crack of the Walther PPK muffled by a seat cushion. Lucas made his way down the hall to the last door, which he kicked open.

Inside he used the monocle, the flashlight now a liability, and surveyed the room's contents. After a scan of the items on the floor he moved to a crate of grenades and inspected one, and then slipped three into an empty pocket of his plate carrier. Smiling, he opened a green ammo box of 7.62mm M13 link belt rounds, and then reclosed and latched it. He shouldered an FN Mag M240B medium machine gun before hefting the ammo box, the glow from the bonfires providing just enough light through the window for him to make his way back to the stairwell.

Lucas felt his way down the steps and retraced his route along the hall to the back room through which he'd entered. Once inside, he moved to the window, set down the ammunition case, and freed the NV monocle to survey the street. Satisfied it was empty, he slipped the monocle back into his plate carrier and lowered the machine gun to the ground outside, leaning its barrel against the brick exterior. He set the ammo box on the windowsill for easy recovery and then dropped from the window, landing in a crouch.

He was back across the street in moments, with the gun shouldered and the ammunition case in his left hand, and he inched along the street until he was near the jail across the plaza from the courthouse. The façade was scorched from where the cartel had torched the building; the windows were missing and the interior black as death. Lucas made his way to the rear of the jail on the side hidden from the guards and entered through the back exit, whose heavy steel door stood ajar.

A maintenance ladder led to the roof, and five minutes later he'd prepared his spot: the M240B waited on its bipod, barrel angled toward the stars, and the belt of ammunition was locked and loaded into place. He checked the time and returned to the ladder, his pulse pounding in his ears, and descended to the ground floor.

If he was successful, they'd never know what hit them. After some persuasion, the thug had told him that at least half the cartel's foot soldiers were partying in the courthouse, enjoying the free alcohol and drugs that were their reward for their raid on the town. The celebrants numbered over a hundred, and Lucas's mouth twisted into an ugly grin. He would bring the hurt to them in a way they'd never imagined, and would either succeed or die trying.

And he didn't plan on dying tonight.

Not when there was work to do.

Chapter 31

Eddie, one of the pair of guards chartered with staying sober and keeping the fiesta at the courthouse safe – from what, he didn't know, since nobody in their right mind would have tried anything in the heart of the cartel's stronghold – looked up from his cards as a tall figure in a cowboy hat materialized out of the darkness to his right.

He dropped the straight he was trying for and reached for his AK. "What the hell you think you—"

Lucas's Kimber roared. The first hollow point caught Eddie in the base of the throat, expanded as it passed through his body, and took his life with it when it exited the back of his neck, leaving a wound the size of an orange. His partner was raising his gun when Lucas's second round punched through his nose and blew the rear of his skull across the pavement.

Lucas accelerated to a flat-out run and covered the twenty yards to the front entrance of the courthouse in Olympic speed. His bet that with the music blaring, the cartel vermin wouldn't hear his shots paid off, and he pulled one of the tall wooden front doors open and tossed in two of the grenades, one after the other. He didn't pause to view the reaction of the drunken crowd, instead pouring on the steam and making for the jail as the cartel members registered the armed grenades and fought to make it through the exit before they blew.

He was rounding the front of the jail when the grenades

detonated, and picked up his pace. In twenty more seconds Lucas was on the roof, and at the M240B moments later, sighting down at the courthouse as the surviving cartel killers stumbled from the building, some with weapons in hand sweeping the plaza for a target, others wounded and streaming blood, several missing limbs.

The gun's percussive blasts lit the night, and Lucas cut down the survivors without mercy. Rounds from the gunmen below blew chunks of mortar from the roof lip around him, but backlit by the blaze from the courthouse and mostly blind in the darkness, they had no chance of hitting him.

When he'd slain the first group, he waited for more to tumble from the building, and mowed them down with the systematic precision of a machine, in his imagination seeing his friends in Loving meeting their fate at these animals' hands. His jaw set, he fired in economic bursts, wasting no ammunition, wanting every shot to count.

The flow of cartel members slowed after the first minute, but Lucas remained until the last shell casing flew in an arc and joined its fellows on the roof. He rose and, with a final glance at the bodies littering the plaza, ran for the roof exit, the revenge part of his plan having played out better than he'd thought possible.

He made it to the ground floor and out the back door, and jogged through an access way before hanging a left at the old water department building. By the time any of the rest of the cartel scum had a chance to arrive at the courthouse, he would be blocks away, riding Gunner toward his second objective of the night – the hospital on the other side of town, where according to the thug's final words, the cartel kept its captives.

The explosions and shooting would attract most of the remaining Locos, who would be trying to assess the threat while he was heading to the last place they would expect. He tried to imagine the thinking of the surviving scum. Most of their criminal clique had just been annihilated in minutes by faceless enemies of unknown strength and origin, who'd then vanished like ghosts; that it was only one man would never occur to them. Like most cowards and bullies, they would seek solace in their numbers, which would draw most of them away from the hospital, making his job easier and his getaway more likely. They'd be panicked, many of them high, drunk, or both, groggy from sleep, and limited in their response because of the dark. It would take them time to rally, to get organized, and even assuming they eventually did, they'd have no idea how to direct their response.

The taking of life was nothing to delight in, but in spite of himself, Lucas felt righteous. The Locos were hardened killers who would have cut out his heart and eaten it in front of him without hesitation. Ridding this small patch of the planet of their kind was justified, and the population would be the better for it. Perhaps they'd see just how pathetic these thugs were and finish the job. Either way, the cartel's power had been gutted, and they would now be fair game for stronger predators, the smoldering crater that had been their headquarters proof of their inability to defend themselves.

His thoughts shifted to the coming hurdle – getting in and out of the hospital with Sierra, assuming she was there. The man he'd questioned had said that much of the facility was in ruins, and that it would be obvious which section was in use. It was possible he'd lied, but Lucas didn't think so. Either way, he'd find out soon enough.

He pushed Gunner hard, galloping through the dark streets, and saw no one during the mile and a half ride. As he neared the facility, he spotted the glow of a torch in one of the windows and slowed, Gunner's labored breathing from the exertion clearly conveying that he couldn't keep up the pace.

Lucas dismounted and tied Gunner to a tree. The horse gulped from one of the five-gallon containers, and Lucas thought about how best to gain entry to the hospital. A frontal assault would be suicide now that the cartel knew it was under attack, so stealth was the best option. But how to manage it? If he had been guarding the place, he would have been on the roof with his rifle, waiting to tag anything that moved toward the hospital. That was the natural reaction, even for dullards like the Locos. So how to get inside without being cut down?

An idea occurred to him, and he nodded in the gloom. It might work. Worst case, he'd waste some time. After all, if his guess about how the cartel was reacting was correct, he had some to spare.

Lucas removed his compass and eyed the luminescent hands. He adjusted the strap of his M4 and set off to see if he could locate a manhole cover – the way in would be through the sewer, assuming the pipes were large enough to fit through, which he thought likely given the size of the facility.

Two blocks away he found what he was looking for and used a piece of rebar he'd scrounged as he'd passed an empty lot to lift the heavy iron disk. He slid the cover to the side and lowered himself down the rungs built into the side of the shaft until he was standing in the storm drain. The odor was musty and dank, any sewage stink long since washed away by five seasons of rain.

He powered the monocle on and studied the compass. The passage ran beneath the street, and he set off toward the large intersection that connected to the hospital's approach. A block later he arrived at a junction and veered left, which if he'd reckoned correctly, would lead to the outlets for the hospital – and his way in.

Rats scuttled away as he walked, his footsteps spongy in the layer of muck collected in the base of the tunnel, and he calculated the distance he had traveled since turning, counting each step under his breath. He reached where he believed the hospital grounds began, but saw nothing but dark passage stretching ahead. Maybe he'd gotten it wrong, and the hospital dumped out into a different artery?

He continued, his breathing as measured as his strides, and fifty yards further spotted a shaft leading up. Lucas peered upward and saw a series of openings – smaller pipes that would spill downward if there were any fluid in them. He climbed a corroded metal ladder until he reached another manhole cover, and using all his muscle, managed to raise it enough to inch it aside. Once a gap had opened, he gripped the rim with both hands and pushed as hard as he could. The disk scraped across cement, leaving open air above.

Lucas heaved himself out of the shaft and found himself in a large pump room. He scanned the walls with the monocle and spied a door, and then paused to unstrap the M4. The handle offered no resistance, and he stepped into a wide hall whose walls were moldy from disuse.

At the end of the corridor he reached a stairway that led up, and he took the steps cautiously, wary of making a slip that would alert any guards to his presence. At the first floor he paused, looking around for stairs leading to a second floor, and realized that the hospital was only a single level there, making his search both harder and easier.

Lucas eased the door open and regarded his surroundings through the scope, crouched low in case anyone fired at him. He was rewarded by an empty hall, patient room doors stretching along either side. Seeing nobody, he moved down the corridor, peering through the doorways at empty rooms. As he neared the lobby area, he came to a closed door – one with a bolt mounted crookedly on the outside. His pulse quickened and he continued to the lobby. Outside, two gunmen were talking in hushed tones. A radio clipped to one of their belts occasionally squawked with static, followed by alarmed shouting.

He debated gunning them down where they stood with one sustained burst, but thought better of it. Best would be to slip out undetected. The goons would think she was still there until they checked on her, at which point he'd have a head start – since they wouldn't know where she was or which route she had taken.

Lucas slowly backtracked until he reached the door and, shouldering his M4, slid the bolt to the side. When he stepped inside, he heard a gasp from the far side of the room.

Sierra was staring in his direction, her eyes searching for the intruder. He realized that she couldn't see him, and took a few steps forward before whispering to her.

"Sierra, it's Lucas. Can you walk?"

"Lucas?" she whispered back.

"I saved you. And I found Eve."

"You what—"

He moved closer and shushed her. "Can you walk?"

"Barely."

He looked her over. She'd been given some cargo shorts and a T-shirt that were both too large. "Do you have any shoes?"

"Over in the corner. My boots."

He retrieved them and handed them to her. "Put them on. You can tie the laces later."

"How did you find me?"

"Later."

She nodded and slipped on her boots, her face pained as she struggled with the right one a bit. Lucas helped her and then leaned into her. "Take my arm. We need to go. Stay on my left side – I need my right hand for my rifle."

"Okay. I can't see anything."

"I know. Just grab my arm. I'll do the rest."

She did as instructed and he led her to the door. Once through, he closed it softly and slid the bolt back into place. "What now?" she asked.

"This way," he said, leading her down the hall.

Static sounded from inside the hospital and a light bounced off the wall behind them. Lucas pushed her toward one of the empty rooms and murmured, "Stay here. Don't make a sound."

"Wait. Don't go," she said, panicked.

The light bobbed as someone approached, and he squeezed her hand to reassure her before pulling away.

He moved across the hall to another open doorway and waited, hunting knife clutched in his free hand. He set the NV monocle down and held his breath as someone rounded the corner and stopped at the locked door. Nothing happened for a long beat, and then a radio crackled. Lucas's grip tightened on the knife as the footsteps continued toward him, and then they stopped no more than three feet from where he stood.

The radio screeched and a disembodied voice called some names, advising them to seal off the two roads out of town. A bead of sweat trickled from Lucas's hairline, down over his eyebrow, and into his eye. He blinked the sting away, and a rustle emanated from the room where Sierra was hiding.

The man moved toward Sierra's room and Lucas lunged out of his doorway, closing the distance between them in two strides. The guard spun, but not fast enough, and Lucas sank his knife into the man's neck and sliced up with a brutal thrust. The guard's scream was a muted burble as his hands flew to the wound and he twisted away. His AK hit the linoleum floor with a crash, and then Lucas was on him, reaching for the knife to finish the job. But the man evaded him and struggled to break free, knocking them both backward against the wall. Lucas grabbed the man's head and twisted with everything he had; the guard's neck snapped and he went limp, limbs twitching as he dropped.

"Lucas?" Sierra whispered, terrified.

"Hang on," he said, and went to retrieve the monocle. When he returned, more lights were approaching from outside. He unclipped the radio from the dead guard's belt, twisted the volume down, and slipped it into his plate holder pouch with the last grenade, and then unstrapped his M4, flipped the selector switch from safe to three-round burst, and stepped to where the Kalashnikov lay. "You know how to use an AK?" he hissed.

"I can figure it out."

He scooped up the rifle. "Come on. They'll be here any second. We need to get to the end of the hall."

She emerged from the room and bent to pick up the flashlight. Lucas shook his head.

"Switch it off."

She did as asked, and then running boots approached from the lobby. Lucas pointed at the stairwell door. "It's steel. Wait for me there." He handed her the NV monocle and the rifle. "Safety's on the side. Look through that end of the goggles. Now run."

Sierra didn't have to be told twice and made for the door as Lucas steadied his M4, gazing through its night vision scope as the gunmen neared.

Chapter 32

The guards must have sensed danger because they stopped short of the hallway, their light beams bouncing like oversized fireflies against the wall. Lucas waited, finger on the trigger guard, aware that every passing second increased the likelihood of reinforcements arriving. The beams grew stronger and his finger eased over the trigger. With the dead shooter on the floor, there was no hoping that the guards wouldn't be ready for a fight, so there was no reason to hold his fire.

A figure stepped into the corridor and Lucas loosed a burst. The cartel gunman was wearing a plate carrier, but Lucas was crouched and had deliberately aimed low in case the shooter had body armor. His rounds slammed into the man's pelvis, and the guard screamed in agony as he fell backward. Lucas fired again, finishing the gunman, and waited for the second to show himself.

He didn't have long to wait. An AK reached around the corner and opened fire on full auto, showering the hall with bullets – a classic amateur move known as "spray and pray." Lucas ducked back, but not before a ricochet grazed his right shoulder, burning like a hot brand. He sucked breath through his teeth with a hiss but kept his focus – he could tend to the wound later, assuming he was alive.

The shooter exhausted his magazine and ejected it with a snap, and Lucas made his move. He charged down the hall and threw himself onto the ground, rolling as he cleared the wall, and fired at the gunman, who was fumbling another magazine into place. Lucas's M4 barked death, burst after burst. Three rounds caught the man in the thighs and he pitched forward, dropping his gun as he tried to stop his fall with his hands. Lucas fired again and liquefied his face, killing the gunman before he hit the ground.

More flashlights bounced toward the lobby from outside, and Lucas drove himself to his feet and sprinted back down the hall, hurtling over the nearest corpse without hesitation. He was at the steel door in seconds, where Sierra greeted him with the barrel of the AK.

"Lower that before you blow my head off," he said.

Lucas ejected his spent magazine, tucked it into a pocket of his plate carrier, and slapped a fresh one home. He chambered a round and held out his hand to her. "Give me the NV scope."

Sierra handed the monocle to him, and he shouldered his M4, wincing at the pain radiating from his wound. Ignoring the burn, he grabbed her hand and led her down the stairs, aware that he only had moments before the gunmen were on top of them.

They ran down the basement hall and he swung open the pump room door. Footsteps pounded from the stairwell – at least three pursuers, judging by the sound. He slammed the door and twisted the lock, but didn't kid himself that it would buy him much time. They would just shoot it off. But seconds counted, and it was worth a try.

"What now?" Sierra whispered.

He slid the monocle into his belly pouch beside the radio, freed his penlight and switched it on, and directed the beam at the open manhole. "We go down."

She eyed the opening and nodded.

"Can you make it with your leg?" Lucas asked.

"What choice do I have?"

He shook his head. "Can you hold onto me while I climb down? That'll be easier on it than the ladder."

"I think so."

"Sling the AK over your good shoulder and give it a try."

She did and wrapped her arms around his neck with a small cry of pain.

"You okay?" he asked.

"You're bleeding," she said, registering the slick blood on his shoulder and arm.

"Don't worry about me. Ready?"

A slam from down the hall echoed through the room. The gunmen were trying the doors, which apparently were open.

He was out of time.

Lucas lowered himself down the shaft, the pair of them barely fitting through the opening, and when they were in the tunnel, squinted up at the hole.

"Are you going to pull the cover closed?" she asked.

"No time. Can you run some more?"

"Yes."

"Then come on."

Lucas set the pace and she managed to keep up. He heard voices from the shaft and gave her the flashlight. "Make a right at the junction, and keep going a hundred yards. You'll see another shaft leading up. It's open. Wait for me there."

"What are you going to do?"

His face darkened. "Welcoming committee."

Her footsteps receded as she moved deeper into the tunnel, and Lucas waited for his eyes to adjust before unslinging his M4 and sighting it on the area by the hospital's chute. Light flooded the tunnel from above, announcing the arrival of the cartel gunmen. He didn't wait for them all to make it down, opting to shoot the first Loco and then pirouetting to follow Sierra, using the M4 night scope to see.

That would give them something to think about before another shooter dared to drop into a kill zone. His hope was that they would find reasons not to pursue him any further, at least until it was too late.

He was at the junction when boots in the tunnel behind him announced that they hadn't delayed long.

Lucas made for where Sierra was waiting, closing the distance quickly, and hissed at her as he arrived. "Arms around my neck," he ordered.

He was halfway up the rungs when gunfire exploded through the tunnel. He forced himself upward, ignoring the shooting, and cleared the passage in seconds. Lucas climbed with all his might, muscles burning from the strain of both their weight, and was almost to the open manhole when Sierra whispered to him, desperate.

"I can't hold on."

He raised his right foot another rung and growled at her. "You have to."

"I…can't."

Lucas let go of the rungs with his right hand and locked his fingers around her forearm. "Just another couple of seconds."

She didn't say anything, her breath hot against his neck, and he pushed himself higher. Sierra let out a small cry from the strain of maintaining her hold, and then they were through the hole and he was scrabbling onto the dusty pavement with her. She released him and he rolled toward the manhole cover, reaching into his flak vest as he did. His hand emerged with the last grenade. He pulled the pin with his teeth, counted a few seconds, and dropped it into the tunnel before rolling away.

The blast shook the ground, and then he was on his feet, helping Sierra up. "I have a horse a block away. Can you make it?" he asked.

She looked up at him in the faint moonlight and nodded. "I'll try."

They ran together, Sierra clinging to Lucas's left arm for support. The two of them were the only ones on the desolate street, the surrounding buildings little more than ruins. When they rounded the corner and she caught sight of Gunner, Sierra exhaled in relief. "Thank God."

Lucas scanned the vacant lot to verify they were alone before shouldering his rifle strap and retrieving the radio from the pouch. He twisted the volume knob louder and listened to the chatter for several moments before turning to her, his expression glum.

"Wouldn't start celebrating. We're not out of the woods yet."

She eyed him in the moonlight. "Your arm…"

"It's clotting. Flesh wound. I'll deal with it once we're clear."

"Where are we going?"

Lucas glanced at her and then up at the stars.

"To see Eve."

188

Chapter 33

Garret slammed his fist against the table as Paco paced by a broken window, two-way radio in hand.

"What do you mean, she's gone? How the hell can she be gone?" Garret roared.

"I had six men guarding her. Someone must have broken her out."

"Six?" Garret considered the implications. "Damn it. We need to find her. Whatever it takes."

"After the attack on the courthouse, we're thin, man. Got to regroup."

"How many do you have left?"

Paco looked away. "Maybe…fifty? Sixty? I don't know. Not that many."

Garret glared at him. "Get your best ten saddled up. Now."

Paco shook his head. "We don't know what we're up against. I'm not going to lose any more men tonight."

Garret was up in a flash and launched himself at the cartel leader. Paco wasn't prepared for the move and stiffened as Garret's fingers locked around his throat, pressing him against the wall. Garret's knife flashed in the starlight from the window and the blade pressed against Paco's neck.

"Now listen, you little prick. You've screwed up every bit of this you've touched. You want to live to see morning, you do exactly as I say, or I'll rip your throat out and feed it to the rats. Do you hear me – *homey?*" Garret growled, mouth close to Paco's ear.

"You crossing lines, man," Paco warned.

"You don't get it, do you? I say the word, five hundred of my boys will drop on you like a building. They'll erase you so fast you'll think the earth opened up and swallowed you whole. So figure it out, *ese*. You want to live and play ball, or do I shut you down right now?"

Paco tried to stare him down, but Garret was through with the punk's swagger. His blade drew blood and he squeezed harder. Paco's eyes bugged out and the veins in his temples popped so close to the surface the older man could see them pulse.

"That's your carotid artery, *vato*," Garret whispered into Paco's ear. "I cut you, game over. You should know that. You want to mad dog me, throw shade? Last thing you'll ever do. Now you going to get real, or is it lights out for you?"

Paco nodded slowly and looked away. "I hear you. Don't need to get all up in my face, dude. Back off."

"You try to take me down, I'll wipe the floor with you," Garret warned, not releasing the cartel leader yet.

"Yeah. I got it."

Garret loosened his grip and stepped back. He wiped his blade on Paco's shirt front and sheathed the knife. "Call your men. We're wasting time we don't have."

Paco stood staring at him, unmoving.

Garret eyed him. "We cool?"

"This ain't finished."

Garret nodded. "Fine by me. But we need to get the woman back, or there's no place you'll be able to hide from Magnus. You know his reputation. You really want to step to that?"

"Don't have to dis me like you did."

Garret decided to extend an olive branch. Anything that might help get the job done. "I needed to get your attention. I figured you want to live. No way you do if we don't get her back." He paused. "Nobody has to know what happened here. It's between us. I'm sorry I had to do it."

"I know."

"Then we settle it later. But for now, call your men."

Garret turned from Paco and walked toward the door. He stopped and twisted in a crouch, his Sig Sauer P226 in his hand, so fast it was like a cobra strike. Paco's sneer froze on his face, his gun only halfway clear of his holster.

The two men stared at each other. Garret motioned with his weapon. "Drop it."

Paco's eyes darted left, and then the fight went out of him. His pistol, a chromed Desert Eagle .45, clattered on the floor. Garret closed on him in three steps and slammed the butt of his pistol against the thug's skull. Paco bucked like a fighter taking a knockout punch, and Garret hit him again. Paco stumbled backward against the wall, and Garret continued pummeling him with his gun butt until Paco's face was mush.

The dead gang leader slid to the floor, and Garret wiped blood spray from his cheek with his forearm. He kicked Paco hard in the ribs and shook his head. "Stupid bastard. Got that trophy gun, size of a cannon. Takes way too long to get it clear." Garret spit on the ruins of Paco's face and kicked him again, and then lost interest in the dead man and moved to the two-way. He keyed the transmit button and spoke softly.

"This is Garret. Paco wants ten of his best to meet us in front of the jail in ten minutes, mounted up, with NV scopes, and ready to rumble. And I need a horse for myself."

After several seconds, the radio crackled and the voice of Paco's second-in-command, Luis, came over the channel. "Got it. See you there in ten."

Garret sat back at the table and poured himself a shot of tequila. He tossed it back without expression and swallowed, enjoying the burn. The Mexicans were still making it in small batches, using the same primitive techniques they had for hundreds of years; tequila and meth were two of their most sought-after products. He made a mental note to search some out when he got back to Houston, and poured another shot as he wiped the rest of the blood and bone fragments from his face.

After they found the woman, he'd break the news to Luis in person: he'd just been promoted. Garret was certain he wouldn't have a problem with the man. A violent repeat offender, prison-hardened and mean as a fighting dog, Luis would immediately grasp that it was his lucky night. He would cooperate, Garret was sure, or he'd wind up like Paco.

No, Luis would understand who was in charge.

Garret dropped his eyes to Paco's still form and grinned.

He was confident in his powers of persuasion.

Chapter 34

Lucas and Sierra bounced against the saddle as Gunner trotted along a bleak road. Sierra sat behind Lucas, her arms around his waist. He held the reins in his left hand as he stared intently through the monocle, watching for any hint of the cartel, the radio turned low, but audible. His ears perked up at the broadcast for a search party, and he nodded slowly as he backed off the volume.

"Only one way north, and we've got to get past a guarded outpost."

"We can't sneak across the tracks somewhere else?" Sierra asked.

"No. They built a barrier along the railway. Closed off all the other approaches. And this horse is too tired to haul two of us at anything more than a crawl."

"You weren't kidding about still being in the swamp."

"I don't kid."

"I read between the lines." She paused. "So what do we do?"

"The guard will be on alert, so there's zero chance we can take him. Only thing I can think of is try to find a weak spot in the barrier to slip through."

"That sounds better than shooting it out with a guard."

"Possibly more than one," Lucas corrected.

Sierra hesitated. "How's your arm?"

"When we stop to rest, I'll bandage it and put some ointment on. Didn't hit anything vital. Only a scratch."

Sierra fell quiet as they made their way toward the barrier wall. When they reached it, Lucas nodded as he inspected it. "Sloppy. We might just be able to do this."

"Really?"

"Yes. See that?" he asked, pointing. "Those are just pallets they hooked together. I can probably pull them loose. They must have degraded some from the weather."

He dismounted, walked to the area he'd indicated, and heaved on the nearest pallet. It didn't budge. Lucas unsheathed his knife and wedged it where the pallet was nailed to a post, and worked the wood free. He repeated the maneuver at the bottom, the post half rotten from the elements, and then pulled it loose. The pallet crashed aside, and he went to work on the upper one. Three minutes later he'd created a gap large enough for Gunner to get through, and they picked their way along the railroad tracks, looking for a promising part of the steep slope the horse could easily negotiate.

Garret stalked to the waiting cartel gunmen, Kalashnikov in hand. He regarded the men and nodded to Luis.

"All right. Whoever broke the woman out is probably taking her north. We need to spread out and cover all the possible trails. If you spot anything that looks like fresh tracks, holler, and we'll follow them." Garret eyed the riders. "What kind of night vision gear do we have?"

"Three rifle scopes and two goggles."

Garret nodded. "That should do the trick."

"How do we know they're headed north?" Luis asked.

"That's where the girl was last seen and where we found the woman originally. And it's where your other men were killed. All roads lead north." Garret paused. "Besides, there isn't anything south for two days' ride."

"Paco agreed with this?"

"Yes."

Luis's expression was guarded. "Good enough for me." He hesitated. "Only one problem, though. They'd have to get past our guards watching the road north, and they've been radioing in regularly. Nobody's passed their position."

Garret grunted. "That's the only way?"

"Yes. We built a wall to protect the perimeter."

"What about south?"

"Same deal. Only one road out. Nobody's left the city."

Garret thought a moment. "Let's do a run around this wall of yours, see if it's been breached. If not, then they're still here." Garret paused. "I don't think that's likely."

Luis led the procession to the guard outpost and the group split up, half riding east with Luis, the other west with Garret. Ten minutes into their inspection, Luis's radio beeped and one of his men called in. "We've got a hole."

Luis swore. "Where?"

"Twelve blocks from the road."

"We're on our way."

Luis spun his horse around, put the spurs to it, and led his men at a gallop to where Garret was waiting.

Garret pointed to the gap in the barrier wall. "There's your escape route."

"Right. Lead the way."

The riders filed through the opening, Garret at the head of the line, and picked their way down the slope toward the railway. Once on the tracks, he and Luis stopped again to confer. Garret motioned to his left. "We'll do this the same way. Split up, you go east. Holler if you find anything. They have to have left a trail of some kind."

Luis nodded. "Keep your radio on. They can't have gotten far."

Half an hour later, Luis received a hail on his two-way. Garret's rasp emanated from the speaker.

"We found fresh tracks."

"How big a party?"

When Garret spoke after a long pause, his voice was soft. "Looks like one horse."

"One! The rest must still be back in town. I'll warn the others. This may not be over."

"Maybe. But time's running out."

"We're already riding toward you. Keep your eyes peeled."

Chapter 35

Gunner rested, grazing in the moonlight, as Sierra sat on a nearby rock with Lucas's first aid kit, eyeing her handiwork. He flexed his arm to test the wrap around his bicep and nodded. Sierra had cleaned the wound with alcohol before applying a bandage and swathing the dressing with gauze. The white lightning had hurt like an unanesthetized root canal, but Lucas had suffered in silence, and the pain was already fading.

He'd been keenly aware of Sierra's proximity as she'd worked on him, and had done his best to mask his interest, but a part of him had to admit that it had been a long time since he'd felt the touch of a woman. Too long, he thought, and then banished the errant idea – this was neither the time nor the place.

They'd both heard the exchange on the radio, and Lucas's face was drawn in the gloom. He stood and eyed Gunner. "No way can this horse outrun the cartel's fresh ones after an all-day ride. He's beat."

"So what are we going to do?"

Lucas looked off into the darkness and then indicated the ruins of a roadside café in the near distance. "You hide out in there, and I'll continue northwest until I get to some terrain where they won't be able to follow the trail. Then I'll circle back to the south. They'll waste hours trying to pick up my tracks, by which time we'll have enough of a lead so they'll never find us."

"What makes you think they won't find your tracks sooner?"

"They know we're headed north, so they won't be looking south. Plus, it's dark out, so they'll be hard-pressed to find anything."

"You think that will work?" she asked skeptically.

"Got any better ideas?"

"We could send Gunner on his way, park in the building, and gun them down as they ride by."

"Right. Except we don't know whether they've got night vision gear. If they do, that could be our death sentence." Lucas paused. "Rule number one of successful engagement: always avoid a fair fight."

She nodded slowly. "How long will you be gone?"

He looked off at the night sky. "Long as it takes."

Sierra frowned. "I can't shoot them as they pass by? Not even a little?"

Lucas studied her and turned without comment. She followed him to Gunner and repacked the kit in his saddlebag.

"Don't make a sound," Lucas warned. "Or all of this will have been for nothing."

"What if something happens to you, and you don't come back?"

"I'll come back."

"But what if you don't?" she pressed.

"Start walking at sunup."

Sierra looked like she was going to argue, but instead nodded wordlessly. Lucas climbed into the saddle and watched her with more concern than he showed as she limped to the building. The riders were an hour behind them, but would be closing fast, and he couldn't waste any more time holding her hand. He gathered the reins and directed Gunner west in the hopes that the terrain turned rockier as he neared the foothills.

The young horse had performed admirably, but he was losing steam, and Lucas felt sorry for him having to haul two riders, even at a slow walk. Still, Lucas was keenly aware of the search party on his tail, and so drove the beast to a trot, hating that he had to do so.

Twenty minutes later the texture underfoot transitioned from the alluvial soil created by runoff from the foothills to hard-packed dirt.

Another quarter mile and it changed again, from dirt to gravel and then to rock. He craned around to study his tracks and saw that they ended ten yards behind him, and he nodded to himself as he continued due west for another five minutes before slowing Gunner and whispering to him.

"Good boy, partner. Now I just need you to turn in one more burst, and we're home free."

The horse plodded south with the monotonous resignation of a prisoner to the gallows, and when Lucas judged that they'd traveled far enough that the tracking party wouldn't be able to easily pick up the trail, he circled back toward the east and coaxed the horse to greater speed. By his reckoning he was on a bearing that would take him across the path of his pursuers a good mile behind them, assuming they were moving at a fair clip.

He stopped to listen every few minutes, but heard nothing. Eventually, he crossed his own tracks headed north, and noted with satisfaction that they were obscured by multiple hoofprints.

When he arrived at the ruins, Sierra gimped from the interior of the building, gun in hand, and gazed up at him. "It worked," she said simply.

"So far. Come on. Let's walk Gunner some, and I'll use a branch to erase his hoofprints. We only have to do it for a few hundred yards."

"I didn't shoot them," she said with a small smile.

"Good work."

~ ~ ~

Garret's hopes evaporated as the hunt for the rider's tracks entered its third hour. They'd lost sight of the trail earlier, and Garret had directed the men to scour the northern edge of the rocky area. After two sweeps, Luis had complained that there was nothing to find, and warned that they needed to wait until daylight to have a better chance – the night vision goggles were only so good, and they couldn't display the sort of nuance that a trained eye in sunlight would detect.

Garret had refused, and the search had shifted to the west. He had no idea why the rider had tacked in that direction, but he suspected a rendezvous of some sort – perhaps to pick up a security detail or meet with the other members of the party that had attacked the courthouse and the hospital? Whatever it was, he couldn't give up until he'd exhausted all other options.

Another hour passed, and when they hadn't met with any success to the west, where the soil transitioned to hard rock as the hills rose from the plain, he'd ordered the men to stand down. They would wait until morning, which would be there soon enough.

Luis busied himself with the two-way radio as casualty reports continued to come in from Pecos, and by the time the first faint tendrils of dawn were glowing in the east, it had become obvious that the Locos' strength had been reduced by three quarters, if not more. When an anxious broadcast informed Luis that Paco had been found murdered, Luis looked like he'd been gut shot. He seemed numb from shock and sleep deprivation when he broke the news to Garret, who pretended surprise.

"Beaten to death? Then the attack must have been a rival gang, don't you think?" Garret asked.

"We don't have any enemies. We cooperate with El Paso, and we do deals with everyone else."

Garret resisted the urge to smile. "Well, you apparently have some now. Good thing we did a deal before this happened, or Magnus might not have been interested. He only approached you because of the size of your force." He paused. "Guess that makes you the new head honcho, right?"

Luis grunted. "Yeah. I expect it does."

"Well, don't worry. A deal's a deal. We'll honor it. You just need to do whatever it takes to get the woman back – and find the girl."

Luis nodded mutely, digesting the news that he'd just been catapulted to the head of the cartel – and that he was fronting a group that might not be able to defend itself any longer, whose ranks were in disarray and its power center eroded to a sliver of what it had been just yesterday.

Garret watched him walk away and then leaned back against his saddlebags and closed his eyes. It would be daybreak soon, and he'd need his energy.

The woman was out there somewhere. He could feel it.

And she wouldn't escape him again.

Chapter 36

Gunner was on his last legs as the trading post came into view, the afternoon sun baking the fields of tall grass surrounding it. Lucas had chosen a trail well to the east of the ones he would normally have used, figuring that on the offhand chance the cartel got lucky, they'd never be able to track him through scrub and grass – or if they did, it would take days to ferret out the evidence of his passing. It wasn't like he was leaking yellow paint for them to follow, and he doubted that anyone in the criminal gang possessed the outdoor skills necessary to run them to ground.

Earlier, he'd probed Sierra for more detail on her story, but sensed that she was holding out on him by the time she was through.

"Tell me again how you wound up in the gulch, and who the men were, Sierra," he'd asked.

"I told you. We were headed away from Dallas. They helped me escape."

"Right, I remember. But why? Out of the goodness of their hearts?"

"Of course not. They were friends with one of the guys who took pity on me. On us."

Lucas had shaken his head. "What's the story on Eve, Sierra? Seems like some pretty dangerous people are pulling out all the stops to find you two."

"They can't allow anyone to rebel or escape. It's a challenge to their dominance. They have a zero tolerance policy. You try to break away, you're dead. Simple."

"I hear you, but the lengths they're going to don't make sense."

"None of this does. Look around you. We're living in a waking nightmare."

"Back to your escorts. They looked like they were paramilitary. Militia."

"They sort of were."

"Sort of?"

"Look, Lucas, I don't know everything about them. An opportunity to get away from miserable conditions presented itself. We had almost no notice, and on the spur of the moment, we took it. We almost got away with it, and then we got blindsided by – what was it you called them? Raiders? We got hit by killers out in the middle of nowhere, after surviving all the way across the state. What makes sense about that? That we would get taken down by pure chance, with the Crew on our tail?" She'd laughed bitterly. "Don't tell me about things not making sense. Nothing has for five years."

Lucas had shifted gears. "How old are you, Sierra?"

"Twenty-two. Almost twenty-three."

"It can't have been easy. I can understand why you'd risk everything to get away."

"I don't want to talk about it."

"So what's your theory as to why the Locos are after you?"

"Houston probably put them up to it. That's my guess. Birds of a feather, isn't that right?"

"Maybe. I'm just surprised they didn't kill you." He'd told her about the town and his grandfather, and she'd gone quiet. The miles had dragged by, but she hadn't volunteered anything more, and as they neared Duke's, Lucas knew about as much as he had when he'd started the discussion.

Sierra's long sigh of relief at the sight of the outpost pulled him back to the present. "Is that it?"

"It is. But don't get too comfortable. We're just going to switch horses. I want to get back to Ruby's by tonight."

She groaned. "The idea of rest sounded too good to be true."

"At least you'll have your own horse. You can sleep in the saddle."

"My luck, I'll fall off and break my neck."

Lucas smiled at that. "Tell me more about this Magnus who runs the operation in Houston."

Her face clouded. "He's the devil."

"Pretty crowded field these days."

"No, I mean it. He's a monster. You name a depravity, he's behind it. Bestiality, pedophilia, gang rape, torture, slavery, satanic rituals. And he delights in killing. He's probably responsible for at least half the surviving populations of Dallas, Houston, San Antonio, and Lubbock dying. Makes Hitler seem like Mother Teresa."

"Where did he come from?"

"Out of nowhere. He just…appeared, and suddenly his men were everywhere. The guy who helped us escape said Magnus had been on death row. I don't know if that's true, but he should have been. The world would be a better place with him six feet under."

"This place you broke out of in Dallas. What was it?"

"One of their facilities. They have a bunch."

"What do they do there?"

"You don't want to know."

He bit back his impatience at her deflections. "Try me."

"Use your imagination."

Lucas twisted to look at her. "You're not telling me anything, Sierra. You're saying words, but there's no information."

"Maybe that's because I don't know much. Or I'm just stupid. Or I'm injured, I've been up for days, and I'm barely breathing. You think that could have something to do with me not being chatty?"

He resisted the urge to apologize. He knew BS when he heard it, and for whatever reason, she was playing him for a fool.

But he'd get to the bottom of it. In the meantime, he needed to do a trade with Duke for a fresh horse for her, a shower, and a couple of meals. The white lightning would cover that tab, along with some of the ammo he'd conserved. Not that he could ever adequately repay Duke for his generosity – the night vision monocle and Gunner had saved their bacon.

Fatigued as Lucas was, the feel of Sierra's arms around his waist was distracting him in a pleasant way. He had mixed emotions about their ride together as the trading post swam into view. He knew nothing about this woman; he simultaneously distrusted her and was drawn to her, and wondered that two conflicting emotions could occupy so much of his rusty emotional bandwidth, especially with so much else going on.

Aaron was on guard duty again and waved as they drew near. Lucas tipped his hat in return, and the gate opened.

"Any more trouble?" Lucas asked as he rode through.

"Nope. Quiet as a cemetery."

"No traders?"

"Not today."

Had it really only been twenty-four hours since he'd ridden south in search of vengeance? It seemed like a week. Lucas shook his head to clear the cobwebs.

At the sound of their arrival, Duke stepped out onto the porch, followed by Doug and Slim.

"How'd it go?" Duke asked.

"Eventful," Lucas said.

"I picked up some reports. Doesn't sound like you left many of 'em."

"I was pressed for time, or they'd all have bitten it."

Duke studied his face. "I reckon they would."

"Probably cut down your trading some."

Duke shrugged. "I can use the rest."

Lucas dismounted and helped Sierra down. Duke eyed his bandaged arm. "How bad?"

"Graze."

"You bring my monocle back?"

"Of course." Lucas removed the scope from his pouch and handed it to Duke. "Need to do some trading with you."

"Gunner behave himself?"

"Horse has the heart of a superhero."

"Yeah, he's a good one. Lot of stamina," Duke agreed. "Whaddaya need?"

"Shower, food, and a horse and saddle for the lady. And some clothes, if you've got any that'll fit her."

Duke nodded slowly. "I can probably find something. We can dicker after you get cleaned up. Looks like you could use a clean bandage."

"Add it to the bill."

"Oh, I will."

Lucas gave him a tired grin. "I know."

Sierra bathed first, and Duke returned from his stores with a smaller pair of shorts and three T-shirts, all faded, one with several small holes. "These work?" he asked, handing them to Lucas.

Lucas inspected them and nodded. "Assuming they fit."

"You fixin' to spend the night?"

"No. Got to keep riding." Lucas glanced over his shoulder at Doug and Slim. "You may get some company. They sent a war party after us."

Duke's face was a blank. "I know nothing."

"It's your new boys I'm worried about."

Duke chewed on his lower lip. "I'll keep 'em on guard duty. Aaron's about ready to rest anyway."

"These are some bad dudes, Duke. If they show up, just tell them the truth – I rode off with Sierra and didn't say where we were going."

"Can I at least tell 'em you went west?"

"Long as your boys don't contradict you."

Duke grinned. "They may not even show up. Or we may be closed for repairs. Been thinking about a little fishing trip. All work and no play…"

"Don't underestimate these scum, Duke."

"Yes, Mom." Duke cleared his throat. "Didn't you say you wanted to trade something?"

"Got the six bottles of white lightning. I can let eighty rounds of .32 go. And I only used up a few mags of the 5.56mm, so I can part with, say, three of those, too. The civilian ball, if that's okay."

Duke sighed. "That's mighty light for a horse and saddle." He sat back and regarded the ceiling. "Look, we can go round and round on this all day, but you're in a hurry and I'm a busy man, so let's just cut to the chase." Duke named a price.

Lucas closed his eyes and took a calming breath. "I want a crossbow, too."

"I expect I can find one of those."

"And lunch."

"I'll let you keep two bottles of your grandpa's poison, for old times. I'm a fair man. Hang on to the 5.56mm ball as well. You might wind up needing it."

Lucas shook the trader's hand and stood. "Highway robbery, you know."

Duke nodded. "Have to support my lavish lifestyle somehow, partner. You want a drink?"

"Nah. I'd collapse. I'm going to wash up, clean my guns, and then we'll hit it. Got anything cooked up?"

"Leftover stew from yesterday. Dove. Over white rice. The rice'll keep for thirty years."

"I know."

"I'll warm some up."

Lucas smiled. "Thanks, bud."

"For my new favorite customer? Nothing's too good."

Chapter 37

It was well after dark by the time Lucas and Sierra made it to Ruby's. Lucas was one gold coin lighter, but both of them were fully outfitted, complete with the NV monocle a magnanimous Duke had thrown in as a bonus. The crusty trader had also restocked and expanded Lucas's first aid kit and supplied Sierra with a sidearm: a battered Colt 1911 that was well used, but would do in a pinch. Lucas had wanted something that was interchangeable with his weapons for ammo reasons and had finally talked Duke into a swap of Sierra's AK-47 for one of the AR-15s he'd recovered when rescuing her, even though they commanded a higher trade price. Four of Hal's white lightnings had lubricated the transaction, along with a gold one-ounce maple leaf that Lucas had hated to part with, but had seen no alternative to trading if he wanted a horse and reasonable weapons.

Sierra's palomino mare was young, well behaved, and powerfully built for her gender, easily capable of carrying both Sierra and her niece. Tango at first seemed distracted by her presence, but quickly lost interest as Lucas pushed him harder, wanting to minimize trail time after dark. He had a bad feeling about the cartel – he didn't think they were just going to give up, and every mile he could put between Pecos and himself seemed like a worthwhile investment in life insurance.

When they reached the storm cellar, Lucas noted a few solar panels strategically located in one of the surrounding trees, where a black cable twisted around the trunk before disappearing into the earth. He smiled at Ruby's ingenuity. Despite her age, she was sprightly and had the fighting spirit of a thoroughbred, which had served her well after the collapse.

He tied off the horses and Sierra helped him water them, and then he removed the saddles and bags and turned them loose to graze. Duke had told him that the mare, named Nugget, had been trained not to wander far. Lucas hoped he hadn't been exaggerating, or his gold coin had just trotted off with Tango, never to return. Lucas saw the familiar shape of Jax by a grove of skinny trees, and Tango led Nugget to the mule for an introduction.

Sierra touched his arm, a wan smile on her face. "Thank you for everything, Lucas. I can never repay you, but I'll try."

Lucas turned to her, and forced himself to ignore the look in her eyes – an expression that hinted at the possibility behind her words. She rose on her tiptoes and was leaning into him when he stopped her and held her at arm's length. "You can start by leveling with me, Sierra. I can't ride with someone I can't trust. You haven't told me everything, and it's sticking in my craw."

The storm shelter door opening interrupted Sierra's response, and Ruby emerged, shotgun in hand, with Eve, who ran to Sierra when she saw her in the moonlight.

"Auntie!" Eve exclaimed joyfully, and Sierra knelt to hug her. Sierra held her for a long time, tears rolling down her cheeks.

"Eve," Sierra murmured, rocking her slightly and smoothing her hair, "I'm so glad to see you. I'm sorry I had to leave you."

"It's okay."

"I'll never do that again. I promise."

Lucas stepped away to give them a little privacy and nodded at Ruby, who took in his bandaged arm. "Souvenir?" she asked.

"You should have seen the other guy."

She nodded. "Nice to see you back in one piece."

"Likewise."

"Any trouble?"

"No more than expected."

"You eaten? Got some leftovers. Eve helped me make vegetable curry."

"Sounds great."

Sierra stood, Eve's hand in hers, and joined them. "Thank God, Lucas. And thank you."

"More the former, I think," he said. "Let's eat."

He carried his tack into the cellar and then reemerged to cart Sierra's in. Once the cellar door was closed, Ruby switched on a tiny LED lamp. "I took the liberty of going to the ranch and getting a few panels, the inverter, and a couple of batteries. Hope you don't mind," she said.

"Not at all. Find anything else they missed?"

"A few odds and ends."

"You're welcome to them."

"This pot and the plates and silverware might look familiar."

"Not doing anything sitting in a cabinet."

They ate in near silence, and then Ruby put Eve to bed in the other room, which she'd tidied up and converted into passable sleeping quarters. Lucas laid a pair of bedrolls inside, said good night to Eve, and then returned to the outer room, where Sierra was helping Ruby.

"You take your antibiotics?" he asked Sierra as he sat on one of Ruby's collapsible camp chairs.

Sierra nodded. "Of course."

"Good." Lucas hesitated. "We got interrupted earlier. But we still need to talk."

Sierra uttered an exasperated sigh, but Lucas was having none of it. He fixed her with a hard stare. "You need to come clean, Sierra, or this is where we part ways. And frankly, I don't much like your chances on your own. So you're going to tell me everything, and I mean everything, or this party's over. Clear?"

Sierra looked over to Ruby, as though for support, but the older woman's face could have been cast from iron. Sierra finished her task and then sat in one of the chairs facing Lucas.

"What do you want to know?"

Ruby looked over at them. "You can start with why Eve was equipped with a tracking device."

"She was?" Sierra exclaimed, her surprise appearing genuine.

Lucas nodded. "Her bracelet."

Sierra's hand flew to her mouth. "Oh, my–"

Lucas cut her off. "Ruby disarmed it, but you have some explaining to do."

Sierra closed her eyes, and when she opened them, there was no fight left in her. When she began speaking, her voice was tentative.

"Eve's a very special child."

Ruby smiled. "We know that."

"No. No, you don't." Her eyes searched Lucas's face. "She's one in a million. Maybe in hundreds of millions. They weren't sure, or they never said."

"Who?"

"The doctors working for Magnus."

"He has doctors?" Lucas asked.

"He has everything. Engineers, doctors, scientists, you name it. Like I said, if you want to live, you work for him. If not, you're just another body for the cremation pits."

"What were they doing, Sierra? These doctors?" Ruby asked, moving her chair next to Lucas and sitting down.

"First off, you need to know about Eve's background. Magnus found her in Vicksburg. He'd sent a trading party there, and when they arrived, the city was a mausoleum. Everyone was dead, except for Eve."

"Everyone dead? How?"

"The doctors believe it's a new, mutated variant of the flu. Far more lethal, if that's even imaginable. Same basic mechanism as the original, only more contagious and with a much higher mortality rate."

Ruby's face was white. "The original was like the Spanish flu. It triggered a cytokine storm in the body. That's why the Spanish flu was so devastating to the general population and hit healthy people the hardest – the old and very young had weaker immune systems, but the healthy…they were the perfect hosts."

"Cytokine?" Lucas asked.

Ruby nodded. "Turns the immune system against itself. It sends so many immune cells to fight infection in the lungs and airway that they swell to the point where they can't function. We all saw it – people suffocating and drowning with no way to stop it. The stronger the immune system, the more lethal a cytokine storm is."

Sierra nodded. "That's it exactly. Anyway, Eve was wandering the streets, crying, looking for her mother in a city of the dead."

"But I thought you said that the very young weren't as affected by the virus," Lucas countered. "So how was Eve unusual?"

"In the Spanish flu and the last generation of this flu, that was true. But not the new one. It kills everybody just the same – at least, from what the doctors could tell. Only not Eve." Sierra allowed that to sink in.

Ruby held Sierra's eyes. "I've heard rumors of a new virus. But I thought that's all they were. You know how that goes; every day there's a new one. Dime a dozen."

"This one's true," Sierra said. "The only reason it hasn't killed everyone is that people aren't traveling much anymore, and the ones who have it die before they can get very far. So it's limited, for now. If there were still airplanes, we wouldn't be having this discussion."

Ruby frowned. "Just when you think it can't get any worse…"

Lucas interrupted. "So they were trying to figure out how Eve survived. Why?"

"To develop a vaccine."

"They have the ability to do that?" Lucas asked, surprised.

"Vaccines have been around for centuries, Lucas," Ruby said. "First one was smallpox – back, I think, around 1800. It's not that technically sophisticated. You don't need electron microscopes or anything. Properly educated scientists could do it, even under the present circumstances." She paused. "But why would they need Eve after they've drawn her blood and gotten their samples? Wouldn't that be enough?"

Sierra shrugged. "I'm no scientist, but the way I understand it, there's something about this virus and the way it mutates that makes Eve necessary for every step of the process. They weren't able to develop it on their own, even with Eve's blood, and they were still working on why. But they won't give up until they figure it out and create the vaccine. That much I do know."

"Why is Magnus trying to create one?" Lucas asked. "He doesn't strike me as the Good Samaritan type, from what you've been saying."

Sierra frowned. "Power. Wealth. Think about it. Whoever has a vaccine could dictate terms to everyone. They'd have the power to decide who lives and who dies. Theoretically, once a vaccine exists, they could deliberately infect areas that didn't cooperate." Sierra blinked rapidly, her chest rising and falling as she grew visibly agitated. "Magnus wants to run things. With the vaccine, he would have the power of a god."

They sat in silence, absorbing the implications: a madman capable of anything, with the power of life and death over the entire country, if not the world.

"It really is the end of days," Ruby said quietly.

"Wait. How did you find Eve, if your sister died in Vicksburg, Sierra?" Lucas asked.

Another long sigh from Sierra, and then she sat forward and locked eyes with him. "I'm not Eve's real aunt."

Chapter 38

"What?" Ruby cried, rising from her chair.

"It's not like that, Ruby," Sierra insisted. "When they first brought Eve to Dallas, they needed someone to take care of her. That was a year and a half ago. They put me in charge of tending to her, keeping her company, teaching her. I called myself Aunt Sierra, and she just picked it up. But by now, I might as well be. I'm the only family she has. And...and I love her like she was my own." Her eyes glistened with tears. "Isn't that enough? Who cares whether we've got the same blood? She needs someone, and I'm her best hope."

Lucas nodded. "Tell me about the escape. How did that happen?"

"I told you we escaped from Dallas. That's not completely true. I'm sorry I lied, but I...I didn't completely trust you, and I was afraid you might sell us out or something."

Lucas's expression darkened. "Sell you out? I saved you – not once, but twice, and Eve as well. Does that strike you as the kind of thing a sellout would do?"

"I'm sorry. Maybe I wasn't thinking clearly. But after all we'd been through... I mean, I was responsible for Eve. I had to be careful."

Lucas visibly struggled for composure. "Fine. Where did you escape from?"

"Lubbock. We had been in Dallas, at the hospital there, but about eight months ago they moved us to Lubbock – they have a more advanced lab at the university medical center in town. Anyhow, I befriended one of the scientists, and over time, we got...close. He confided that he wasn't working with Magnus voluntarily. His child was being used against him – blackmail. But he wasn't an evil man, and he had contact with a resistance cell in Lubbock that had a link with some people out of the Crew's territory – another group of doctors working toward the same goal, only not to extort power from what's left of the world, but to develop a vaccine and give it to everyone. He contacted them and arranged for us to escape." She exhaled hard. "He's still there. Might be dead by now, for all I know."

"So what happened?"

Sierra held Lucas's stare. "Lucas, I had no idea that stupid bracelet was some kind of tracking device."

"I believe you. It would be counterproductive to escape, only to lead them straight to her."

"That's right. Anyway, one night the scientist slipped me a note. I had ten minutes to make it to a laundry chute with Eve. The hospital is guarded like an army base, Lucas. So I woke her up and we left with just the clothes on our back. The men who died in that gulch, defending us, were from the resistance group."

"Where were they taking you?"

"Shangri-La."

Lucas's eyes narrowed. "You're exhausting my patience, Sierra."

"No, that's what they called it," she insisted.

"Shangri-La," Ruby repeated. "Why?"

"Because nobody knows exactly where it is. I don't."

"But they did."

"Correct. But they never told me where we were going. Just to Shangri-La. Then they'd all laugh."

Lucas's glare bored into her. "But what is it? What did they tell you about it?"

"That it has power. And water. And that everyone there is God fearing and is working against the evil that the criminal gangs were inflicting on the country. They have a militia there – well armed and trained, apparently. And a doctor who's trying to figure out how to save humanity. Eve's the only survivor he's heard of. So the plan was to bring her to him, along with the data the scientists in Lubbock had collected, so he could make a vaccine, assuming that's even possible."

"What did your...*friend*...think?" Ruby asked.

"He thought they were making progress, and that it looked good. Which was one of the reasons for the timing. They needed to get Eve away from Magnus's group before he could finish the process, or...or we'd be living in a world shaped by one of the most sadistic men who's ever lived."

"Where is this data?" Lucas demanded.

"On a USB drive."

"They have operational computers in Lubbock, I take it?" Ruby said.

"They do. They have power from a big wind farm outside of town they were able to connect up to and get operational again. They have everything electric-powered, at least for Magnus's operation. The rest of the city lives without. See, that drives home the point to everyone else that the Crew is in charge and decides who suffers and who doesn't. Same thing in Dallas, Houston, you name it. They're in total control – you take one wrong step and they squash you like a bug."

"Where's the USB drive now?"

"I don't know."

Lucas snorted. "That's where this all leads? To a shoulder shrug and a blank look? Come on, Sierra."

"No, really. The leader of the militia group who was taking us to Shangri-La had it. Kept in in his tactical vest. His job was to defend it, and us, with his life. Which is what happened."

"Why not send a bigger group?"

"We were supposed to meet up with one in another couple of days. They wanted to stay under the radar until they were out of Texas."

"And you have absolutely no idea where they were heading?"

"I wish I did. But no, I don't. The leader referred to a set of directions or something – he kept a note with the USB drive in an inside pocket of his tactical vest – but even with the directions, we'd have a pretty hard time finding the place without the help of someone who knew more."

"Why's that?"

"I got a look at them once when he was cleaning off in the river. They were in some kind of code. Gibberish. I wish I knew how to find Shangri-La, Lucas. I really do. Because that sounds like the only place we'll ever be safe." She swallowed hard. "They're never going to quit, Lucas. Magnus's entire vision of the future depends on that vaccine and the power it will give him. Imagine him with the fate of the world in his hands. Imagine him with the keys to nukes."

"They can't hurt you if they can't find you."

"They'll find us," Sierra stated flatly. "You don't know these people. They have no choice."

"Nothing is inevitable, Sierra."

Her brow furrowed. "I believe in destiny, Lucas."

"Believe in whatever you want, but I've never been good at quitting."

Sierra appraised him. "So I see." She paused for a moment, working something out. "We need to find that USB drive – even if the note's in some kind of code, we might be able to figure it out. That's our only hope. Are the bodies still in the gulch?" she asked.

"They'd been stripped. A tactical vest has value. Someone took their clothes."

"Then we're screwed," Sierra said simply.

Lucas studied his boots. "Let me think on that some."

"What's your background, Sierra?" Ruby asked, changing the subject.

"I was in high school when the flu hit. My mom was a teacher, my dad in construction."

"Brothers and sisters?"

"Nobody alive." She winced as she touched her bandaged shoulder. "So that's my story. Now you know the whole thing. Not that it's going to change anything."

"You leave anything out?" Lucas asked.

"What would be the point?"

"How did they select you to care for Eve, Sierra?" Ruby asked. "In the first place, I mean."

"I'm good with kids. I caught someone's eye. Kismet. Fate. Who knows?"

"That's it?"

"If I sat around trying to figure out why everything's happened to me, I'd drive myself mad. I got picked. Could have been anyone else. I'm not sure I understand – what's the difference?"

Ruby shrugged. "Just a question."

"The important thing is that we need to find the vest and see if we can figure out what the note says. Lucas, what do you think?"

Lucas shook his head. "I think I haven't slept for days, and I'm not going to discuss going back into harm's way half-cocked. That's a good way to get killed."

"But you have to," Sierra protested.

Lucas held her stare. "I don't have to do anything. Let's be real clear on that. I've done what I have because I chose to, but nobody tells me what I do or don't need to do."

"I…I didn't mean to offend you."

"None taken. We're all tired."

Sierra yawned. "Can we continue this tomorrow? I'm falling asleep on my feet, too. I'm really grateful for everything you've both done. Especially you, Lucas." Her blue eyes seemed to look deep inside him. "You're a good man."

Lucas and Ruby watched her make her way to the sleeping room, and when she was gone, exchanged a glance.

"You believe her?" Ruby whispered.

"Mostly."

Ruby sat back and considered Lucas with a knowing expression. "She's an attractive young woman, isn't she?"

"Not hard to look at," Lucas acceded.

"And not the kind of girl who takes no for an answer, Lucas. A woman can sense these things. And the way she looks at you…"

Lucas averted his eyes. "She's grateful I saved her life. Don't make it more than it is."

Ruby smiled. "Be careful what you wish for."

"Gave up wishing a while ago."

Her smile faded into a serious expression. "What are you going to do?"

Lucas studied his dusty boots with a weary sigh.

"Beats me."

Chapter 39

Garret sat hunched in front of a shortwave radio, waiting for Magnus. He was dreading the discussion, which might easily conclude with Magnus ordering his execution. It wouldn't be the first time the Crew leader had eliminated a subordinate who'd disappointed him. Garret would have to read between the lines, gauge what was said and what wasn't, to understand whether he was a dead man already or might live. Magnus wouldn't tell him, of course, and part of the complication of the exchange would be that Magnus was a master at masking his true intentions.

Garret had ordered everyone from the room in anticipation of the unpleasantness to come. He couldn't afford to lose perceived authority in front of the Locos. They were already reeling from the effective destruction of their cartel, and the last thing he needed was for one of them to overhear his rendition of the true nature of what had occurred – and to blame him.

He blinked away fatigue and stared through the window at the stars. They'd searched for tracks half the day, but had come up empty. Garret's return to Pecos had been a somber one, with dread in every step, the men exhausted and their horses spent.

The radio hissed and crackled like a living thing, and then the Houston operator's voice emanated from the speakers.

"Magnus is here. Stand by. Over."

Magnus's baritone voice was unmistakable when it barked at Garret. "It better be good news."

Garret opted for the direct approach. "I'm afraid not. The woman escaped, aided by a force of unknown strength. All told, the Loco cartel lost a hundred and fifty men."

"What?" Magnus demanded in disbelief.

"I've already taken steps to retrieve her. I'm headed back out after my report."

"How can this have happened?"

"The Locos had her in a tightly guarded facility that I was assured was impenetrable. It obviously wasn't."

"How did they gain access?"

"Through the sewer."

Magnus went silent for several seconds. "They must have had an accomplice on the inside."

"I doubt it. Everyone at the facility was killed."

"This is a complete disaster," Magnus said, and then his voice dropped to a menacing whisper. "On your watch."

"I agree. But as I said, there's a trail to follow. We'll find her." Garret paused. "We'll need reinforcements, though. There are only a handful of Locos left. Which gives us an opportunity to move in, of course. We already have Odessa and Lubbock, and I know you've been wanting to expand."

Going after Pecos hadn't seemed worth the fight if Magnus's men were going to try to take over the trading town. The paltry spoils would be almost inconsequential; but now, if it could be used as a final staging area before moving into El Paso, it could be worth it since there would be no resistance.

Magnus's tone changed to thoughtfulness. "That's an interesting idea. I'll think about it." He paused. "Did the woman's information prove helpful?"

"She told us that she left the girl in a cave to the west, but couldn't be more specific. She was wounded in the battle that killed the rest of her group, so she was unconscious when the girl was rescued."

"Who were these men in her group?"

"She said that they were helping because the leader wanted her."

"I remember her well. She could have that effect."

Garret went in for the kill. "Send more men, Magnus. We can turn this around."

"So far your assurances have proven to be empty."

"I'm working with idiots and amateurs. Doing the best I can. But a group capable of killing three quarters of them must be met with equal force. We can't rely on these fools. It's up to us. I can get the woman and child back, but I need competent men I can rely on."

Magnus's voice quieted. "I shouldn't have to remind you of the stakes, Garret. You're my most valued lieutenant, but there are limits to my patience."

"I understand what's in the balance. I will succeed. This is a temporary setback I'm in the process of fixing."

The next pause lasted longer. When Magnus spoke, his tone was businesslike. "Very well. I'll send fifty men. Will that do?"

"It should. You have no idea how disorganized this group is. I had to terminate the leader yesterday."

"Were there any repercussions?"

"No. They believe rivals carried out the execution."

"Find the woman and child. I don't want any more reports like this," Magnus growled.

"I will."

The operator came back on the airwaves. "Magnus has left. Over."

Garret pushed back from the console and brushed away sweat that had beaded on his forehead. The report had gone as well as he could have hoped, but he was still uneasy. There was a fifty-fifty chance that one or more of the men Magnus sent would have instructions to kill him – an icepick to the spine, a bullet to the back of the head, poison in his food, the method didn't matter – Magnus had scores of skilled assassins who could carry out the execution without fail.

Which left Garret with two choices: either he could go after the woman and hope that he could pick up the trail again, or he could keep riding and pray Magnus never found him. The second option wasn't practical because Magnus would scorch the earth to locate him, and also because without Magnus's organization, the truth was that Garret was nothing.

His decision made, he moved to the door and pushed through it. He would sleep and then lead a larger team back into the wilderness. If they couldn't find tracks, they would continue moving north, toward the remains of Loving, and interrogate anyone in their path. Someone would know where their quarry was. Nobody could simply vanish without a trace, at least not a party capable of the attack on the courthouse. That had required organization and timing, especially without a single enemy casualty.

No, he would find the woman, one way or another. As Magnus had underscored, he really had no choice. Too much depended on it.

"Luis!" he called.

The Loco boss entered with a wary expression. "Yes?"

"I want every available man mounted up. We're going to head north and spread out in groups of three or four. They must have left a trail."

"What – you mean now?"

"That's what I said, isn't it?"

Luis debated reminding him of the hour, but decided against it when he saw the look in Garret's eyes. "Figure thirty minutes to rouse the men and get them ready."

"Have them pack for a week in the field. We don't give up till we find them. Enough men working the area, eventually we will."

Luis nodded, wondering at the man's tenacity. Like a pit bull, even if the effort was a wasted one. He saw nothing to be accomplished riding all night to chase dreams, but didn't voice his opinion, preferring to remain alive another day.

Garret watched him leave and shook his head in disgust. That he had to work with these cretins was bad enough; that he had to tolerate their thinly disguised insolence was another matter – one that he would resolve later. Garret had planted more than a few men in the ground for less than the expression on Luis's face. Once they found the woman, he'd have a little discussion with the Loco.

Likely the last the man would ever have.

Chapter 40

Ruby turned from the corner where she had been rummaging in a burlap sack, and held up a bottle and two glasses for Lucas to see. She blew dust from the bottle and returned to her seat beside him.

"Glenlivet," she announced. "Eighteen-year-old single malt. Been saving it for a special occasion. Stashed it here, in the cellar, so I wouldn't be tempted late at night. But this seems as good a time as any to open it."

"Not sure I can do it justice," Lucas said. "But I'm willing to try."

"That's all I ask."

Ruby handed him a glass and poured two generous fingers. After a moment's consideration she added another half inch, and then poured an equal measure into her own. She set the bottle beside her and screwed the cap into place, and then clinked her glass against his.

"Tumblers might be a wee bit dusty," she warned.

"Adds character."

They sipped the amber nectar appreciatively, and Lucas reclined in his camp chair, as relaxed as he'd been at any point since the ordeal had begun. After several moments he closed his eyes and allowed the smoky Scotch to trickle down his throat, savoring the warmth spreading through his stomach.

"They won't stop. She's right about that," Ruby said.

He opened his eyes. "I expect so."

"They butchered an entire town, Lucas. They're going to keep coming." She paused. "What are we going to do?"

Lucas's eyebrows rose. "*We?*"

"You can't go back to the ranch. That's one of the first places they'll look."

"Nothing there for me now. The cows will have to figure things out on their own." He took another swallow. "Bastards killed the horses."

"Sending a message."

"I replied in kind."

Ruby scowled. "And my bunker's history."

"Maybe not. It's blast proof. Although the interior's probably going to need some cleanup."

"I don't have it in me."

"I was kidding."

They drank in silence, and when their glasses were empty, Ruby poured a second helping. "Got some tough choices to make, Lucas."

"Seems like they're being made for me by circumstance, Ruby."

"That's not entirely true."

He scowled. "You see me letting them get their hands on Eve again?"

She shook her head. "Not likely."

"Like I said – not a lot of choices to be made."

"So what do we do?"

Lucas rolled some Scotch around in his mouth and then smacked his lips. "You keep saying *we*."

Ruby ran her fingers through her hair. "You going to leave a helpless old woman to be eaten by wolves?"

"Helpless?"

"A euphemism."

"Huh."

She gave him a chiding stare. "I'm serious. They'll be here soon enough. We both know it."

"They won't know where to look."

"True, but eventually we have to leave the cellar."

Lucas grunted. "Eventually we die of old age."

"Some sooner than others. It's the meantime that worries me."

"I know."

Ruby sighed. "What do you make of her Shangri-La story?"

"She knows how to spin a yarn, I'll give her that."

"That she does. Question is whether it's true – and if so, what we can do about it."

Lucas nodded thoughtfully. "Sounded convincing to me. What's your take?"

"I don't think she told us everything."

"Agreed. But have we heard enough?" he asked softly, half to himself.

"Let me put it this way: after hearing about that Magnus character, my nightmares will be having nightmares."

He nodded again, his expression unreadable. "Lot to think on, that's for sure."

She eyed him. "What's going on in that head of yours, Lucas?"

"Nothing. Same as always."

"Lucas…"

He spoke softly, as if to himself. "Not many places that vest could have gone."

"That occurred to me." She paused and regarded him quizzically. "And?"

"And what?" Lucas deflected.

"What about Sierra and Eve?"

Lucas finished his glass, stood, and gave Ruby a grim frown as he handed it to her. He removed his hat and placed it on the back of the chair, smoothed his hair carefully, and inclined his head toward her.

"Be sunup before we know it," he said.

She stared at him for several long moments and then offered a resigned smile. "That it will."

"Good night, Ruby. Thanks for the drink and the company."

She watched him walk to the sleeping quarters, his steps heavy. When he disappeared inside, she drained the last drops of her drink, tapped the side of the bottle wistfully, and shook her head.

"Good night, Lucas. Sleep well."

Chapter 41

Lucas rolled over with a groan to avoid the sunlight shining through a crack in the door. He shifted on the uncomfortable cement floor and tried to continue sleeping, but it was no use. He checked the time and sat up.

Ruby was snoring softly a few feet away, her head resting on a rolled-up towel doing service as a pillow. Lucas peered into the gloom at the far side of the room and was instantly alert.

He rose, grabbed his M4 and Kimber, strapped on the pistol, and moved to the outer chamber, leaving Ruby to rest. He paused at the cellar door and froze when he saw that Sierra's rifle and saddle were gone.

Lucas pushed the door open and squinted in the bright morning light. All around him the tall grass shimmered in serpentine waves, undulating in the light breeze. He spied Tango and Jax near the trees, but no Nugget.

"Damn," he muttered, turning toward the cellar as Ruby shuffled out of the sleeping chamber. "They're gone."

"What!"

Lucas nodded, his expression sour. "I know."

Ruby didn't have to ask him what he planned to do. He went for his saddle and had Tango ready to ride within a few minutes. She looked up at him with a worried frown as he swung onto the horse's back. "You think you can track them?"

"Shouldn't be too hard. Not too many ways out of this area, and she wouldn't go back toward the bunker, I don't think."

"That leaves west."

"Exactly. Doubt they left before dawn, so they're only an hour or so out."

Ruby nodded. "Good luck, Lucas."

"I'm half inclined to let them keep riding."

"They'd never make it."

"Not really my problem – unless I make it mine."

Ruby pursed her lips. "Little late for that, I'd say."

Lucas sighed. "I know."

Sierra had left a trail that posed no problem for Lucas, and Tango was full of energy after a long night's rest. Lucas let the big stallion trot along the faint trail, and he seemed to instinctively understand what his master wanted, unwaveringly following Nugget's tracks.

Lucas spotted them half an hour later, Eve on the back of the horse and Sierra in front. He spurred Tango forward and was almost on top of them before Sierra heard him and swung around with her rifle. He continued at speed until he drew alongside her, and then brought Tango to a halt.

"Decide to go for a ride?" he asked, his eyes slits.

Sierra's jaw clenched. "Lucas…"

He tilted his hat brim at the little girl. "Morning, Eve."

"Morning," she replied.

Lucas gave a nod to Sierra. "Nice day for it, huh?"

"We have to try to get the vest. It's our only hope, Lucas. And you said you're not going to help, so we're going to do it alone."

"When did I say that?"

"Last night."

"No, I said I was tired and that nobody tells me what to do."

"I…I can tell you don't want to."

Lucas gritted his teeth, trying to bite back his exasperation. "You can tell I don't want to risk my life trying to find some note that we may not be able to decode, hidden in a vest whose whereabouts are unknown, to guide us to a place that might not exist? Why do you think that could be?"

"It's our only chance, Lucas."

"So you say," Lucas agreed, his expression neutral. "What were you planning on doing? Help me understand your strategy. You're wounded, two to a horse, with a five-year-old everyone in the country's trying to get their hands on, leaving a trail a blind man could follow. What was step one?"

"These Raiders of yours must have it."

Lucas nodded. "Let's say that's right, and that some scavenger didn't come along and grab it before the Raiders returned to collect what they could. How do you proceed from there?"

"I find them and get it."

"How?"

Her expression hardened. "I'll figure it out. I'm not defenseless."

He nodded agreeably. "No, what you are is stubborn and unrealistic. You don't stand a chance in hell." He paused. "Here's how it would actually go down: you're female, so the first thing the Raiders would do when they spotted you is enslave you. They wouldn't ask or care what your views on the subject were; they'd just do it. Then they'll rent you by the half hour to whoever wants you, and probably do the same with Eve, assuming they don't sell her to Magnus's people. And that's the best case."

"Without that note, we have nothing."

"That's not true. You have your lives. Courtesy of me. Which means I have some say in the matter."

Sierra bristled. "You don't own me."

"No. But I have a responsibility, and you now have one to me, whether you acknowledge it or not. You owe it to me to stay alive and to keep Eve safe. That's your obligation." He drew a calming breath. "Riding into the badlands throwing a dust cloud the size of a blimp isn't a good way to do either."

"Then what do you suggest?"

"Come back with me to Ruby's. We'll figure it out from there. What we won't do is act impetuously and endanger everyone on a whim."

Sierra's tone hardened. "I won't take no for an answer, Lucas."

"I'm not saying no, Sierra. I'm saying let's do this the right way – not this way." He stopped speaking, and a frown creased his face as he stared past her shoulder.

"What is it?" she asked, and twisted to follow his gaze.

"Not our lucky day." He pointed. "See that?"

She squinted, and then nodded. "Dust."

"Looks like you attracted some attention." Lucas raised his binoculars and swept the horizon. "Three men. Riding hard. Be here soon."

"We have to lose them."

He eyed Nugget and then Eve before turning back to Sierra. "Not a chance. They'll follow our trail. No way we can conceal it. Not enough time."

Her face hardened. "Then we have to ambush them."

"There are two dust clouds. That one's just the nearest. There's another off to the east."

"What are we going to do?"

He nodded to her AR-15. "You know how to use that thing, right?"

"I'm not a sharpshooter, but I do okay."

"Follow me," he said, and spurred Tango forward.

"Where are we going?" she called after him.

"See if we can find some cover. They'll be on us pretty soon. No more questions. Just follow me, and do as I say."

Lucas galloped off and she urged Nugget after him, heart pounding in her chest, her hair streaming behind her as she drove the mare forward for all she was worth.

Chapter 42

Lucas cursed as he pushed Tango to the limit. Sierra's lack of stealth had led the pursuers right to them, leaving him no option but to fight it out. Lucas scoured the terrain and spotted an outcropping of rocks that could serve their purposes. He dared a glance over his shoulder and estimated the approaching dust to be no more than five minutes behind them; whatever they did, it would have to be fast.

He slowed Tango to a walk and guided him past the rocks before circling back higher on the gentle slope, Sierra tailing him at a slower pace. He swung down from the saddle and led the horse to a small grove of saplings well beyond the rocks, where the animals would be out of sight from the trail. He secured Tango to one of the trees as Sierra arrived, and he pointed to a branch.

"Tie your horse up there and follow me to the rocks. Eve, stay here with the horses. If you see anyone but us coming this way, untie Tango, climb into the saddle, and hang on tight. He'll do the rest. Think you can pull that off?"

The little girl nodded.

"Good. Sierra, bring your spare magazines. Got your pistol?"

"Right here," she said, patting the holster on her hip.

"Know how to fire it?"

"I've practiced with a .45 before. Like riding a bicycle, I hope."

Lucas took off at a jog. Sierra kept up in spite of her leg wound, and when they reached the rocks, he spoke in a low voice.

"They'll be expecting a trap – I would. But we don't have a lot of options. If we're lucky, they'll follow the tracks past us. Wait until I start shooting, and then fire at will. Three-round bursts. No point in conserving ammo."

"That's it? That's the plan?"

"Got anything better?" Sierra didn't give an answer, there obviously being none. "Now move over there," he said, pointing to a spot twenty feet away. "We'll get them in a crossfire."

They were soon interrupted by the sound of pounding hooves from the trail. Lucas switched the M4 firing selector to burst, wishing he still had some grenades left. Hitting moving targets would be difficult, even if he allowed the riders to get on top of them, but every yard closer improved their chances.

"Remember, don't fire until I do," he warned. "Keep your finger off the trigger until you want to shoot."

Sierra didn't say anything. A quick glance at her yielded a vision of a determined but frightened woman, who for all her assurances looked uncomfortable with the assault rifle. Lucas refocused his attention on the trail just as the riders came into view. From across the reach, he heard Sierra's sharp intake of breath at the sight of the prison ink that covered their faces and shaved heads.

"Easy," he whispered as they neared, and then the lead rider slowed, Kalashnikov in hand. Lucas ground his teeth as he watched the man size up the rocks, and held his breath as he willed the gunmen forward, into the kill zone.

It wasn't to be. The leader barked an order to his men.

Sierra's rifle stock scraped against the rocks, and then all hell broke loose as the men opened fire with practiced precision. Chips flew as bullets whined off the boulders beside her, and she ducked down. Lucas squeezed off a burst at the nearest man, which missed by a hair but drew their fire as well. More inbound slugs peppered the rocks, and he heard a burst from Sierra's gun.

Lucas fired another burst and hit his target, knocking the gunman off his horse. He fired again to ensure the man was neutralized, and then more incoming rounds drove him behind the safety of the rocks.

"Lucas!" Sierra cried, and he looked over to her. She fired again, ducked back behind the stones and yelled, "They're riding away. I can't hit them."

The last of the gunmen's rounds struck the outcropping, and the chatter of their rifles stopped. Lucas peered at the trail and called to Sierra. "Where did they go?"

"I…I think back down the track."

"You didn't see?"

"They were shooting as they rode. I didn't want to get hit. What about you?"

"Stay put," he said, eyeing the area. He had a bad feeling about the sudden retreat. It had been too easy. Those men had looked as hard as they come, and he couldn't imagine they would turn tail at the first barrage.

His doubts intensified as he listened, ears ringing, for the sound of galloping horses. He heard nothing. And now they knew where he and Sierra were, their element of surprise squandered.

"What now?" she asked.

"Watch and wait."

"How long?"

"Long as it takes."

A minute dragged by, and then another. Sierra called to him again. "Sorry about earlier. I didn't mean–"

"Look out!" Lucas cried, and fired over her shoulder at a gunman who had materialized on foot from the dense brush to her left. Bullets thumped into the dirt around him, and he fired again as she tried to twist to face the threat. Two of Lucas's rounds caught the man in the lower abdomen, doubling him over as he continued to fire. Sierra loosed a burst as well, but her shots went wide. Lucas was calling out to her when a round slammed into his chest with the force of a freight train. The M4 skittered away, and Sierra turned to him, eyes wide in horror.

"Lucas!" she screamed. More rock fragments geysered from the boulder near her head, and a voice rang out from the brush.

"Drop the gun, or I cut you in two."

Sierra hesitated, and then tossed the AR-15 aside. Garret stepped into view, his weapon trained on her. Sierra's face twisted with hate.

"You…"

"Did you really believe I'd give up? You're even stupider than I thought," he said as he approached. He reached Sierra and backhanded her with a smack that echoed through the clearing. Sierra's head jerked like a marionette's and she went down. Garret moved toward where Lucas lay, and was raising his rifle to finish him when Sierra's 1911 barked three times behind him.

Garret jolted forward, and then recovered his footing. He turned slowly, a sneer in place, and shook his head. She glared at him, her pistol hand shaking so badly that she'd missed twice after the plate holder rear panel had stopped her first round. Her face fell at the realization that she'd failed when it had mattered the most. She tried to squeeze the trigger again, but her hand wouldn't obey, the strength in her fingers suddenly gone.

He laughed harshly. "You're going to regret that, you stupid bit—"

A gunshot rang out and Garret's throat exploded. As he staggered to the side, another shot vaporized his skull. He collapsed in a heap in front of Sierra, and she looked past him to where Lucas was struggling to his feet, Kimber in hand, the pistol still leveled at the dead man.

"You're alive!" she cried.

"Evidently."

She ran to Lucas and threw her arms around him.

"Hey, easy there…" he started, and then his words were cut off as her lips crushed against his.

The kiss lasted for a small eternity, until finally Lucas pulled away and looked down at the bullet hole in the upper left quadrant of his flak jacket. Sierra put her index finger through the hole, her eyes searching Lucas's as she felt inside.

"Going to need a new plate," Lucas said, and pulled the shattered one that had saved his life from the front compartment of his flak jacket.

She nodded. "That one did its job."

He cocked his head and looked down the trail, and then stooped to gather the M4 along with his hat. "Come on. We need to get out of here."

"What is it?"

"The second set of riders. I don't want to do this again here. We'll find a better spot." Lucas pushed past her and knelt to inspect Garret's vest. He looked up at Sierra, his face grim. "Go up to the horses. I'll be right there."

"What are you doing?"

"I need a plate. And he's not going to be needing his."

Chapter 43

Three Loco riders drove their horses hard toward the gun battle, drawn at first by the dust and then by the shooting. They'd been communicating with the other search parties by radio, and when the Crew gunmen had radioed in that they were in hot pursuit, they'd given free rein to their horses and let them run themselves out.

Now that the shooting had stopped, they slowed, and the radioman tried to reach Garret's group on his two-way. When he got no response, they slowed further, on alert as they ventured along the trail.

The Locos were far more comfortable in town than in the field, horses a necessary evil since there was no more fuel – but not one they'd grown fond of. The cartel's strength was in their ability to terrorize the Pecos population and defend their stronghold, and its members had spent more time behind bars than around any animals other than their own species.

They rounded a long bend and arrived at a stretch of trail with dense scrub on either side. The lead rider gave a curt hand signal and they spread out, guns at the ready. He pulled up sharply when he spotted a dead man lying face up in the dirt, and eyed the corpse with trepidation.

"One a' the Crew," he said, and the rider behind him nodded.

"Where you think the other two are?"

"Gonna find out."

The lead rider circled his horse around the body and tilted his head at the rifle a few feet away. "Didn't bother to grab his gun."

"Probably in a hurry."

They picked their way along the trail and the lead man indicated the outcropping. "Bet that's where the shooters hid."

"How you know there was more than one?"

"You think only one did this? Those Crew dudes were hard, homey. Ain't no one shooter take them down."

"Where are the others?"

The lead man shrugged. "Let's keep goin'."

They negotiated the area below the outcropping, and then the lead Loco's eyes caught a flit of color by the rocks.

"There," he said, and spurred his horse up the slight incline.

When they reached the outcropping, they stopped and stared at the two dead Crew members for a long beat. The Locos looked at each other and the second man shook his head.

"Lights out for these chumps, huh?"

"Yeah. For real."

The lead rider raised his radio to his lips and gave a brief report. The three men waited for instructions, and when they came, listened to Luis's words with relief.

The radioman slid the two-way into his vest. "All right. Let's get their stuff and head home. Screw this noise."

"That's right. Ain't our fight anyhow. They dead, so game over."

Luis had told them to collect the weapons and ammo and leave the dead men where they lay. He'd sounded as tired as the three gunmen were after riding all night, and with no further incentive to continue trying to pick up the woman's track, they were calling it quits. A good thing, the lead rider thought – they had no idea who'd killed the three Crew badasses, but whoever it was had taken down that group's best, and they had no interest in discovering more the hard way.

Three minutes later, they were retracing their steps, glad to be away from the killing field, the prospect of sleep hurrying them along as they rounded the bend.

Lucas lined up the Remington's crosshairs on the first rider when the trio stopped by the rocks, providing him a decent shot from his position six hundred yards away. He estimated the breeze at five miles per hour, no more, and adjusted the scope settings to compensate before peering through the lens again. Lucas's finger was on the trigger, beginning the gradual squeeze that would snuff out the first man's life, when his target raised a radio and spoke into it.

Lucas held off, watching as the Locos dropped from their horses and scrambled for the dead men's guns. After a quick search of the bodies they remounted their steeds and rode away. He whispered to Sierra, who was lying a few feet away with her rifle, Eve beside her.

"Looks like they're giving up," he said.

"Really?" Sierra asked, her voice skeptical.

Lucas nodded. "Guess they lost the stomach for it."

"That last one you shot with your pistol? That was Garret. One of Magnus's top dogs. Want to bet he was the one in charge of this?"

"Fair guess. Cut off the head, and the body withers."

He kept a bead on the riders until they had vanished around the bank, and then rolled toward Sierra. "That was a little too close," he said.

She eyed his plate carrier. "I'm not arguing. You think we're in the clear?"

Lucas took another look through the scope. "For now."

When they were back on their horses, Lucas set the pace north, keeping Tango to a fast walk to avoid throwing up any dust. Sierra kept Nugget alongside him, Eve in front of her on the saddle, riding in silence.

"I'm sorry I dragged you into this, Lucas. I realize I should have stayed with you and Ruby." Lucas didn't respond, so Sierra tried again. "It's just that, without the flash drive and the note, it's only a matter of time until Magnus sends someone else after us. He's got an endless supply of men." She swallowed and glanced at him. "When you said you wouldn't go after the vest, I…well, I guess I didn't really think."

"I never said I wouldn't go after it. I said I'd think on it."

She studied his profile. "What are you saying? That...that you'll do it?"

"I'll consider it on the way back to the bunker."

Sierra looked as though she was going to speak again, but thought better of it and merely nodded. Eve had watched the exchange in silence; if she had any opinions on the matter, though, she didn't voice them. Lucas continued on wordlessly, worry lines furrowing his brow as he considered his next step.

It was madness. To try to reclaim a vest from murderous cutthroats who would just as soon gut him as give the time of day – and that was assuming they even had it. There was a very real possibility that one of the men Alan and Carl had ambushed and killed, presuming they'd been somewhat successful at it, had been wearing it and was lying face down in the gulch, long since eaten by scavengers.

No matter what plan he came up with, he was sure it would mean danger, slim odds of success, and the very real possibility of being killed.

"Only die once," he muttered. Tango shook his head as though in agreement, and Lucas spit to the side of the trail, cursing at how his heart had skipped when he'd kissed Sierra.

He was in deep water and sinking fast.

And worst of all, it didn't feel altogether bad.

About the Author

Featured in *The Wall Street Journal*, *The Times*, and *The Chicago Tribune*, Russell Blake is *The NY Times* and *USA Today* bestselling author of over forty novels, including *Fatal Exchange*, *Fatal Deception*, *The Geronimo Breach*, *Zero Sum*, *King of Swords*, *Night of the Assassin*, *Revenge of the Assassin*, *Return of the Assassin*, *Blood of the Assassin*, *Requiem for the Assassin*, *Rage of the Assassin* The *Delphi Chronicle* trilogy, *The Voynich Cypher*, *Silver Justice*, *JET*, *JET – Ops Files*, *JET – Ops Files: Terror Alert*, *JET II – Betrayal*, *JET III – Vengeance*, *JET IV – Reckoning*, *JET V – Legacy*, *JET VI – Justice*, *JET VII – Sanctuary*, *JET VIII – Survival*, *JET IX – Escape*, *JET X – Incarceration*, *Upon a Pale Horse*, *BLACK*, *BLACK is Back*, *BLACK is The New Black*, *BLACK to Reality*, *BLACK in the Box*, *Deadly Calm*, *Ramsey's Gold*, *Emerald Buddha*, and *The Day After Never – Blood Honor*.

Non-fiction includes the international bestseller *An Angel With Fur* (animal biography) and *How To Sell A Gazillion eBooks In No Time* (even if drunk, high or incarcerated), a parody of all things writing-related.

Blake is co-author of *The Eye of Heaven* and *The Solomon Curse*, with legendary author Clive Cussler. Blake's novel *King of Swords* has been translated into German by Amazon Crossing, *The Voynich Cypher* into Bulgarian, and his JET novels into Spanish, German, and Czech.

Blake writes under the moniker R.E. Blake in the NA/YA/Contemporary Romance genres. Novels include *Less Than Nothing*, *More Than Anything*, and *Best Of Everything*.

Having resided in Mexico for a dozen years, Blake enjoys his dogs, fishing, boating, tequila and writing, while battling world domination by clowns. His thoughts, such as they are, can be found at his blog: RussellBlake.com

Books by Russell Blake

Co-authored with Clive Cussler

THE EYE OF HEAVEN
THE SOLOMON CURSE

Thrillers

FATAL EXCHANGE
FATAL DECEPTION
THE GERONIMO BREACH
ZERO SUM
THE DELPHI CHRONICLE TRILOGY
THE VOYNICH CYPHER
SILVER JUSTICE
UPON A PALE HORSE
DEADLY CALM
RAMSEY'S GOLD
EMERALD BUDDHA
THE DAY AFTER NEVER – BLOOD HONOR

The Assassin Series

KING OF SWORDS
NIGHT OF THE ASSASSIN
RETURN OF THE ASSASSIN
REVENGE OF THE ASSASSIN
BLOOD OF THE ASSASSIN
REQUIEM FOR THE ASSASSIN
RAGE OF THE ASSASSIN

The JET Series

JET
JET II – BETRAYAL
JET III – VENGEANCE
JET IV – RECKONING
JET V – LEGACY
JET VI – JUSTICE
JET VII – SANCTUARY
JET VIII – SURVIVAL
JET IX – ESCAPE
JET X – INCARCERATION
JET – OPS FILES (prequel)
JET – OPS FILES; TERROR ALERT

The BLACK Series

BLACK
BLACK IS BACK
BLACK IS THE NEW BLACK
BLACK TO REALITY
BLACK IN THE BOX

Non Fiction

AN ANGEL WITH FUR
HOW TO SELL A GAZILLION EBOOKS
(while drunk, high or incarcerated)

Made in United States
Orlando, FL
09 February 2023

29778784R00150